THE HOUSEWIFE ASSASSIN'S GAMBIT

Book 23

The Housewife Assassin Series

JOSIE BROWN

A BOOK BY

SIGNAL
PRESS

Library of Congress Cataloging-in-Publication Data is available upon request

Cover Design/Book Conversion by Austin Brown

Trade Paperback ISBN: 978-1-970093-26-1

Hardcover ISBN: 978-1-970093-22-3

V060723

"This was an addictive read–gritty but funny at the same time. I ended up reading it in just one evening and couldn't go to sleep until I knew what the outcome would be! It was action-packed and humorous from the start, and that continued throughout, I was pleased to discover that this is the first of a series and look forward to getting my hands on Book Two so I can see where life takes Donna and her family next!"

"The two halves of Donna's life make sense. As you follow her story, there's no point where you think of her as "Assassin Donna" vs. "Mummy Donna', her attitude to life is even throughout. I really like how well this is done. And as for Jack. I'll have one of those, please?"

Novels in The Housewife Assassin Series

The Housewife Assassin's Handbook

(Book 1)

The Housewife Assassin's Guide to Gracious Killing

(Book 2)

The Housewife Assassin's Killer Christmas Tips

(Book 3)

The Housewife Assassin's Relationship Survival Guide

(Book 4)

The Housewife Assassin's Vacation to Die For

(Book 5)

The Housewife Assassin's Recipes for Disaster

(Book 6)

The Housewife Assassin's Hollywood Scream Play

(Book 7)

The Housewife Assassin's Killer App

(Book 8)

The Housewife Assassin's Hostage Hosting Tips

(Book 9)

The Housewife Assassin's Garden of Deadly Delights

(Book 10)

The Housewife Assassin's Tips for

Weddings, Weapons, and Warfare

(Book 11)

1

Blunder

In chess, the term "blunder" indicates a very bad move;
for example, one that may take a win and turn it into a loss or a
draw.

Just as bad is a move that turns a draw into a loss.

In either case, you'll experience a setback.

The best way to protect yourself from a blunder:

First, examine possible offensive moves that your opponent
can make. Think like they would.

Next, think through your own subsequent offensive move.
That way, you'll find any weakness in your game play.

Finally, since a blunder can cost you the game, play as if it
can cost you your life.

It's almost two in the morning, and only nine of us are
on Los Angeles Metro's Number Two bus, heading south
on Santa Monica Boulevard from San Vicente to North
Canon. Right now, I couldn't tell you which of the other

passengers is the domestic terrorist here to give a thumb drive containing intelligence vital to our nation's security to a Russian spy.

Acme Industries, my black-ops intelligence organization, doesn't know what it contains. All we've been told by our contact—U.S. Director of National Intelligence, Marcus Branham—is that it's of great national importance. The traitor, who works at the Pentagon, was smart enough to stay anonymous while negotiating the deal on a Signal encrypted messaging account. If the traitor is working with another Pentagon insider who could alert them that the mission is on the FBI's radar, it becomes a job for Acme.

A good thing since our mission isn't just to capture the culprits but exterminate them via an "accident" and then return the stolen intel.

Your guess is as good as mine whether a suspect is one of the two gorgeous drag artists. The tallest sports a strapless body-hugging Alexander McQueen asymmetric leather dress in galactic blue. The redhead is in a hot pink vintage Dior suit to die for.

Frankly, I hope it's neither. It would be a shame to ruin either outfit with a bullet hole.

Maybe our suspect is the drunk snoring in the back of the bus. Then again, it could be the guy in a Brioni suit perusing an issue of *Fortune*.

Or is he one of the three Lakers fans burning off their winning game high by flirting with the blonde decked out in a berry-red belted cashmere coat?

The old bag lady sprawled out on a seat facing the middle passenger exit door of the bus is *moi*. It's a new look for me and, frankly, one I find freeing. Unlike the posh pashmina-draped princess, I don't have to pretend to ignore the rowdy basketball fans' catcalls. And while I'd covet both of the cross-dressers' ensembles, chasing down a suspect is a sure way to ruin their magnificent couture. It's bound to end up drenched in sweat.

Or worse yet, blood.

This isn't a solo mission. Abu Nagashahi, one of the operatives on my team, is driving the bus. Frankly, when he realized the pay for the overnight shift was so generous, he told our boss, Ryan, he may swap professions. (The blood ran out of Ryan's face, and rightly so. Abu is the best getaway driver-slash-wet work handler we've got.)

Another team member, Arnie Locklear, slumps into one of the front seats. He sports saggy jeans, a baseball cap, and a tee shirt that declares:

ASKHOLE:
A person who constantly asks for your advice,
yet always does the opposite of what you've told them.

Possibly a gift from his wife, Emma Honeycutt, our ComInt director.

My mission co-leader, Jack Craig (my husband and the love of my life), is tailing the bus in a panel van. Another member of our team, Dominic Fleming, also follows us in a car.

We wear earbuds and special contact lenses that give feedback on what we see and hear to Emma back at Acme headquarters. Having eyes and ears on us, if she notices obstacles that may trip us up, she'll let us know.

Three stops later, the Lakers fans give up on the woman who's clearly out of their league and jump off the bus. I wince when I see that they're headed for a car and pray that, before they do any real damage, some cop stops them for a DUI. In any case, I can check them off my list.

Brioni Guy pulls the bell to get off at the next stop. He leaves the magazine on the seat and walks toward the front door.

Interesting.

I cough to alert Emma.

"Yep, I see it," she says. "Jack, cover the male suspect who's now getting off the bus."

"On him," Jack assures her.

Just before the next stop, in unison, the drunk and Pashmina Princess pull the bus's departure bell.

Hmmm…

Drunk Dude, seated behind the bench holding the magazine, moves toward the front. At the same time, Pashmina, who sat several rows in front of the magazine, moves toward the exit door in the center of the bus.

As they pass each other—and the magazine—Drunk Dude leans in for a kiss.

Pashmina practically falls into the magazine's bench to avoid him. They both topple onto the floor. Shoving Drunk Dude away, she screeches, "Get off of me, you smelly brute!"

Trying to get his footing, Drunk's hand lands on her breast. Yelping, Pashmina slaps it away, then starts pounding him with her Dolce & Gabbana clutch.

Abu is so busy watching that he has to stop short to avoid rear-ending a car.

Drunk Dude falls backward onto the seat across the aisle. "Admit it!" he whines. "You…you've been making goo-goo eyes at me all night!"

By now, Abu has eased into the next bus stop.

Drunk scrambles to his feet and then careens toward the middle door.

Pashmina also rights herself and huffs off the bus through the front door.

I move toward the bench holding the magazine—

Which is gone.

"Talk about intriguing cosplay," Emma murmurs.

"Arnie, follow the drunk, on foot. Detain him," Ryan orders Emma's husband.

"On it, Boss." With a sigh, Arnie breaks free of the fantasy conjured by his wife's innuendo and scrambles off the bus.

"Dominic, give Arnie backup," Ryan adds.

Our British colleague groans. "The pissed git? I was hoping for the posh bird—"

"Too bad," Ryan growls. "Get on him now. Donna, you–"

"Yep, I'm already on her tail." I leap off the bus from the middle exit.

"And I'm on yours," Abu assures me.

"Woah—wait! *Hellooo*?" Dior yells. "Who's driving us to WeHo?"

Ignoring him, Abu looks left while I look right. Since Pashmina is not in our sight lines, I motion for him to move in his direction, and I move in mine.

I run three blocks. But seeing and hearing nothing, I backtrack—

Until I notice a small alley, the width of a driveway, on my right. I would have missed it, except that the wind is strong enough that the tattered banner hanging off the roof of one of the flanking buildings slaps against its second-story window, catching my attention. The alley is the back end of a gas station and its auto repair garage.

It's so dark that I can barely make out anything except for the rows of open crates, stacked five high, lining both sides of the alley. The crates are filled with metal gas canisters.

The alley is deep and pitch black—

Until Pashmina opens the driver door of a black BMW M4-CSL. Its dim light shows her shrugging off her coat, then flinging it onto the backseat floor, all the while murmuring on her cell phone. A moment later, she strips off her wig, revealing short dark hair.

She's now putting what was in the magazine into her purse.

Only then does she notice me and the gun I've got pointed at her. "Drop it on the ground!" I bark.

Instead, she leaps into the car with her purse, slams the door shut, starts the engine—

And heads right at me.

When I shoot, the bullets ricochet off the glass and metal.

A reinforced car?

Oh, darn.

Since the model is the Competition xDrive Coupe and the alley is narrow, I've got about three seconds to jump out of her way. Otherwise, I'll get laid out flatter than a pancake.

Instead, I do something that is either stupid or genius:

Grabbing the banner, I leap onto one of the stacked crates. Then, holding on tight, I swing over and behind the car—

Only to land on another stack of crates—

Which, like dominoes, slams into another, and another, all the way down the alley.

The canisters hit the ground, spewing liquid —

Yikes…

Gasoline!

As the car speeds through the growing puddle, its undercarriage catches fire.

Pashmina's foot must still be on the gas pedal because she's in the middle of the street—

Until she crashes into a car flying by.

Oh, hell—Jack's van is on its tail—

But he skids to a stop as both cars explode.

Just as he leaps out of the van, I run over. "Was that the traitor?"

Jack nods. "Yep. Brioni Guy. And let me guess. That was his contact?"

"Yes. The blonde on the bus. Really, a brunette."

"Not that either will be recognizable when this fireball is put out." He nods toward the inferno, then sighs. Like me, through his earbuds, he hears Ryan's rantings.

Emma suggests that Abu stick around and give a report to the police and fire units that are careering toward us from both sides of the street.

The rest of us are ordered to go to Acme headquarters and face the wrath of Ryan—like *now.*

Jack mutes the phone so that Ryan can't hear his curses.

He's got a great reason to belly-ache about it. With our eldest, eighteen-year-old Mary, finishing up her summer internship at the U.S. National Security Administration, our sixteen-year-old, Jeff, at a UCLA Summer Coding Camp, and thirteen-year-old Trisha at soccer camp, we were looking forward to having the house to ourselves until this Sunday. This five-day staycation was to be filled with the best sort of "us" time. By that, I mean the next one hundred and twenty hours were earmarked for waking up late, sharing a bubble bath, then wrapping ourselves in warm towels and ending up back in bed for scintillating sex. We'd planned to order take-out to quell our hunger pangs between Kama Sutra positions. Were the delivery guys to come a'knockin' while the house was a'rockin,' generous tips would have alleviated their curiosity.

Alas, at least a couple of hours will be spent hearing Ryan jaw on about how we—okay, how *I*—cocked up the mission.

Hopefully, it won't squelch our desire to make love afterward.

"The clock is ticking. Let's get this over with," I mutter.

2

Initial Set-Up

Before you or your opponent can move on your chess board's thirty-two squares—each designated by a letter and a number—the sixteen game pieces given to each of you must take their places on the two farthest opposing eight rows of squares.

The player who moves first has the light-colored pieces and is called "White." The opposing player who uses the darker pieces is called "Black." The eight shortest pieces, known as pawns, comprise the front row.

The farthest row is where you'll place the larger pieces. Beginning from the outside and working to the center of the row, the pieces mirror each other: rook (the castle) knight, then bishop.

Kings stand on their opposite colors: White king on e1 and Black king on e8. That puts the White queen on the white square to the right of her king (d1) and the Black queen on the black square (d8) to the left of her king.

As in real life, a queen's color palette reflects her unique personality.

~

RYAN GROWLS THE OBVIOUS: "THE PLAN WAS TO TAKE THEM IN —*not incinerate them.*"

"Would you prefer that Donna be dead?" Jack argues.

"No, of course not," Ryan growls. "Though there are days I could strangle her myself."

"Aw, thanks, Chief. I love you, too." I blow him a kiss.

"Quit being impudent," he grumbles. From his blush, I know I'm forgiven.

"At least Arnie and I grabbed their supposed diversion —the drunk," Dominic points out. "We've got him in an isolation tank. He doesn't seem to be a fan of strobe lights or the sound loop I chose for him. It's already driving him barmy. He's squealing for his mum."

I smirk. "Let me guess. Shakespeare soliloquies by the great Patrick Stewart?"

Dominic frowns. "Indeed not! It's *Lord Sutch and Heavy Friends.* Considered a classic for having been disowned by every musician who played on it. I've got it looped so that it plays backward too."

Abu snorts. "I'll bet he wasn't drunk, and his breath doesn't stink."

"I wasn't going to test your theory. But when I finish our captive's interrogation, he'll be pissing his pants," Jack vows.

"Because of the on-bus video footage, we can still identify the others," Emma insists. "My team has put all three suspects through various facial recognition programs. The military personnel database has already identified the guy in the suit, who also went up in flames. He's Ralph Whitlaw, a twenty-year Army veteran working in the Pentagon's Insider Threat Security Management program. He was close to retirement and was supposedly using one of his vacation weeks to meet with a few private sector companies interested in hiring him as a consultant."

Jack gives a low whistle. "That's one way to keep his hand in the pie and double-dip simultaneously."

Emma's secure cell buzzes. She looks down to read a text. "My ComInt team just ID'd the female operative."

"Put her on the monitor," Ryan suggests.

A moment later, the photo of the woman who almost ran me down takes up one of our conference room walls. "She is—*was*—Tina Woodruff, a.k.a. Luda Morozova, a long-embedded FSB cell. Luda passed herself off as a free-lance journalist based in Chicago. Most of her stories were travel features that appeared in numerous international publications, primarily one media outlet the CIA had long suspected was part of Russia's propaganda network. The agency also suspects her articles were SigInt communiques," Ryan explains. "As it turns out, the CIA only learned of her existence a few years back when its video surveillance picked up a brush pass in D.C. between her and a known Russian embassy official. It followed her until she went underground."

"Now we know where she's been hiding," I reply. "Right here in Los Angeles."

"Under another name, assuredly. And since the FSB assumes she's still among the living, DNI Branham has a few thoughts on how that comes in handy for U.S. intelligence—and how this presents Acme with a mea culpa." He nods to Emma to patch in the director of our country's intelligence community.

Marcus's face now appears on our screen. "Good to see you all again. And thank you for your efforts on this mission." He sighs. "Unfortunately, before her untimely death, Luda successfully uploaded the cipher intel she'd received in the brush pass."

So, that's why it took her so long to drive out of the alley.

His shrug indicates his disappointment. "On the plus side, since the app is also how Luda interfaces with her FSB handlers, at my behest Acme ComInt will continue to respond as Luda." Marcus leans forward. "Which brings us to your next mission. Russia's largest arms dealer, Grigori Lenkov—a.k.a. 'the Angel of Death,' is being released in a prisoner swap with a high-profile American."

A photo appears on our conference room screen. Grigori is a hulking giant of a man with dark, deep-set eyes and a nose smashed to one side. His incisors are sharpened into points, making his smile even more menacing.

"Let me guess," Abu declares. "He's being swapped for Mason Ledbetter, America's chess master."

"Correct," Ryan replies.

"Wasn't he the guy fishing in the Gulf of Finland a few years back, and when his boat's engine died, he drifted onto the Russian side?" Arnie asks.

"That's the one. Ledbetter has spent the last four years doing hard labor in a Siberian penal colony." The thought makes me shiver.

"The swap is not only validated because of Mason's high public profile but because he has always been an outspoken advocate against Russia's human rights violations," Markham explains.

"Brilliant!" Dominic exclaims. "Jody will be chuffed! Mason is one of her social media clients. Since his imprisonment, she's kept the home fires burning with photos and video clips from his winning games and his speeches against Putin's atrocities."

Dominic has every right to be proud of his girlfriend, Jody Keleske. Just as bright as she is gorgeous, her independence—and kindness—attracted him to her in the first place. They met when Acme hired her to give our mission team a crash course on social media so that we could infiltrate an event filled with brand influencers to weed out those who were assets sending covert signals online and in plain sight. Not only is she adept at that task, but she also knows to keep her head down when bullets are flying. She didn't hesitate to adopt Genghis and Guang, two children raised by spies embedded stateside and groomed to be assassins. Now they thrive, living the lives of ordinary teens.

Dominic revels in the love of these new relationships.

"However, Luda's death presents us with a new problem," Marcus explains. "She's supposed to escort Lenkov onto the flight and back to Russia."

"Is the FSB calling her home?" I ask.

"Apparently. The exchange is to take place at the Al Bateen Executive Airport in Abu Dhabi," Ryan explains. "Donna, with the right prosthesis, you'll pass as Luda. You'll be there before the Russian jet lands. As airport representatives, Acme's pilot—George Taylor—along with Abu, Arnie, and Jack, will greet the Russian plane's crew and Lenkov's FSB escort. They'll exterminate those onboard and take their places before Lenkov arrives, as will you. At the same time, Dominic will escort Lenkov to Singapore on the plane from the United States Penitentiary in Marion. He'll then accompany Mason back to Los Angeles."

"Excellent! I'll be home in time for dinner." Once a party animal, Jody has turned Dominic into a homebody.

"The plane to be sent by the FSB to retrieve Lenkov is his own tricked-out Dassault Falcon 7X jet. Because his business dealings have him flying in and out of war zones and over territory hostile to Russia, the plane is equipped with stealth technology. Once the Russian plane is airborne, Jack will release a drone created in DARPA's test labs that mirrors the plane's coded tracking signal so that Russian Intelligence assumes it's on its way to Moscow. In reality, the plane will fly in stealth mode on a different course: to a U.S. black site in Morocco."

"If anyone deserves an extraordinary rendition, it's that son of a bitch," Abu declares. "He's sold arms to every rogue nation and terrorist organization in the world."

"When does all of this go down?" Jack's question comes with a wince. Like me, he's hoping we've got at least one night to ourselves.

Ryan stands. "Your flight to Singapore leaves immediately."

In other words, our staycation is over.

3

Exchange

WHEN ONE OF YOUR PIECES REACHES YOUR OPPONENT'S BACK row, you're allowed to trade it for another of greater value that has already been captured. For example, you may exchange a pawn for a rook, or a knight for a bishop.

It's the chess equivalent of the playing gold-digging trophy wife, so enjoy!

AL BATEEN EXECUTIVE AIRPORT LOOKS LIKE A DISNEY fantasy. Its onion-shaped domes—the largest, in the center, is flanked by two smaller ones and circled by a cluster of smaller domes crowned with spikes, as are the four towers behind it—mimic the Saudi royal family's palace.

There are around fifty large-body jets on the tarmac. About half belong to airlines from around the world. The other half are private planes owned by the One-Half of the One Percent.

It'll be several hours before the exchange takes place:

time enough for Lenkov's flight crew to clear its official papers. Grigori's plane has just landed. I listen and watch through my secure lenses as Jack, Abu, and our mission pilot, George Taylor, greet them and board the aircraft armed with clipboards and dressed as members of the airport's official VIP Security Team.

After their inspection, Lenkov's crew must sign affidavits verifying their layover's purpose. My team members wear gloves because the pens to be used are covered in a sedative-hypnotic agent—a "stun drug," if you will. Once touched, the victims are asleep within a few minutes—

Forever.

(Or, as Dawn Mortimer, one of Acme's forensic scientists, explained, "Melatonin is one of its active ingredients. It's also a great moisturizer! Goodness knows we all want skin to die for—*though not literally*. Therefore, I'd suggest avoiding our concoction for that purpose.")

The bodies of the Russian flight crew will be dumped when we're over the ocean.

I now saunter over to the plane and climb its air stairs. Because the FSB has ordered Luda to go home with Lenkov, she'll be officially designated "missing, presumed dead" when the plane disappears.

Jack waits until the door is shut to kiss me.

Sweetness. Calm. Contentment. He is my everything.

I look around. "Where is Mason? He must know the plane landed."

"He's locked in one of the rooms." Jack holds up a key to one of the jet's bedrooms.

I roll my eyes. "Let me guess: the FSB did it to taunt him; you know, wait until the very last minute before allowing him to come out to experience freedom."

"It works in our favor. Ledbetter would have lost his plausible deniability if we exterminated the FSB flight crew in front of him. I'll unlock the door and bring him out when the plane carrying Grigori Lenkov taxis over."

"Good call."

We don't have to wait too long. Emma tells us the plane has just landed and is taxiing our way.

Twenty minutes later, Arnie, now attired as one of the airport's security team, knocks on the plane's door. From a window, I see Abu doing the same on the plane that brought Grigori Lenkov.

Jack unlocks Mason's door. As they walk through the main lounge, I see that the fear has not left Mason's face. He shivers when Jack puts a hand on his elbow to take him down the air stairs. Taking note of me, his eyes narrow. "What is your role in this gambit?"

I don't know what to say. With a smirk, I shrug and turn away as if I'm too bored by the question to answer it.

I follow Jack and Mason down the air stairs but go no further.

Dominic shakes Mason's hand when they reach the halfway mark between both planes. Mason stays mute, but his eyes scan Dominic's face. Our colleague takes this as tacit approval to guide Mason onto the American plane, where his last stop will be the land of the free and the home of the brave.

Mason embodies both adjectives.

As Grigori's American guard releases his hands from his cuffs, Jack greets the freed prisoner with a nod. Jack is fluent in Russian. Something he says has Grigori roaring with laughter. At the same time, Grigori catches sight of me by the air stairs. He shouts, "Luda!" and then throws me a kiss.

So he knew Luda…

Shite.

Jack follows his gaze. Like me, he now knows why Luda's presence was requested.

His scowl lasts only a second, but I read it loud and clear:

Grigori better fasten his seatbelt because it's going to be a bumpy ride.

HE ONLY HAS EYES FOR ME.

Grigori ignores Jack, Abu, and Arnie as his mouth savages mine.

He wastes no time before whispering sweet nothings—or, according to what Emma says through my earbuds, making vulgar vows about what anatomical gymnastics he'll put me through once we're wheels up.

In return, I murmur some of the naughty Russian phrases Emma has taught me—

Not that it's needed. What's the purpose of begging, *"Poceluy menya…"* (kiss me) when his tongue is already down my throat? Or, commanding *"Kosnys' menya"* (touch me here) when he's already fondling my breasts?

And no way in hell will I answer his question, *"Tebe eto nravitsya?"* (Do you like this?), now that his hand is under my skirt and between my legs.

As George starts the plane down the runway, Jack gruffly barks, "Take a seat" in Russian.

Grigori glares at him but obeys, pulling me down onto his lap.

Abu comes over with a tray bearing two crystal lowball glasses and a five-million-dollar bottle of Eye of the Dragon vodka. In truth, the bottle is authentic, but it's filled with a cheap vodka spiked with a sedative.

Grigori shouts with glee. "Another way in which Putin kept his promise!" With me in one hand and the bottle in the other, he stomps to the bedroom, slamming the door behind us.

Then he bolts the lock.

His timing couldn't be worse: we're wheels up.

JUST ONE DRINK.

That's all it will take to have him sleeping like a baby until we land in Morocco.

But Grigori isn't thirsty. He's horny.

I take this hint when he rips off my dress and tosses me down onto the bed.

I feel the plane leveling off—

And pray for turbulence: the kind that will toss a two-hundred-pound behemoth so high that he'll hit the plane's roof hard enough to be knocked out.

Desperately, I beg, "Wait! Shouldn't we toast your release?"

"*Nyet*. We will drink after our first fuck—to celebrate being somewhere other than that shithole conjugal visit trailer." He strips off his belt, unzips his pants, and lets them fall to the floor.

Emma whispers in my ear: "Jeez! How do you say 'humongous shlong' in Russian?"

Those are my thoughts exactly.

The next thing I know, he's on top of me, spreading my legs, positioning himself—

Quick! Think fast…

"But…but we have something of immense importance to toast! It is worth the few seconds of savoring the great news before" — I gulp — "sharing our bliss."

He sighs, then eases beside me. "You've always been ravenous for Satan." He points to his penis. "If you're holding back, it must be important."

"Wait…he's named his salami after Russia's intercontinental-range ballistic missile?" Emma guffaws. "What an ego!"

And, unfortunately for me, apropos.

I slide off the bed. "I've got very important news!" Taking the bottle, I pour it into two glasses and hand one to him. "You see, Grigori… I'm… I'm… pregnant."

Stunned, he sits up.

In a second, he's at my side—

And slaps me so hard that I fall to the floor. "*Suka!*" He kicks me in the stomach. "Who else are you fucking?"

"No one!" I gasp. "Only… only you!"

"*Blyat!* Then you know it isn't my bastard—*because you know I am sterile, whore bitch*!"

"Ah…shit, Donna!… I'm sorry!" Emma cries… It wasn't in his dossier!"

"With me in prison, you decided to fuck your way to the top, eh?" Grigori stares down at me. "Let me guess: the Black King! Am I right?" He stalks the room. "Did you know he sold me out to the Americans? And now that you've helped him retrieve the one thing Putin wants above all else…." He slams my face against the wall.

Twisting my arm behind my back, he hisses, "Where is he now? *Where is the Black King?*"

"I...I don't know!"

He turns me over to study my face. A moment later, he's clawing off my prosthetic nose and throwing it onto the floor. He slams me against the wall again and shouts, "Who are you?"

Grigori ignores the pounding on the bedroom door and Abu and Arnie's shouts. He's too busy dragging me toward the bedroom's emergency exit door. When he gets there, he releases an oxygen mask and places it over his nose and mouth before wrapping his forearm around a safety strap.

With a flick of his wrist, the door's hatch is released.

Knowing what's in store for me, I encircle his waist with my arms and hold on for dear life. If I go out, I'm taking him with me.

When he tries to pry me off with his free arm, I grab him by the wrist with one hand and his nuts with the other, twisting hard and holding on tight.

His pained screams can be heard above the ferocious crosswinds, validating a fundamental rule of combat: never fight naked.

Grigori is so strong that he lifts the arm I hold toward his mouth. His fangs pierce my wrist. I hear my own screams. Still, I hold on for dear life—

And squeeze his nuts again with all my might.

Now he's screaming too.

I laugh at the irony of our standoff—

Until Grigori wrenches free of me. He fights the current to go further into the cabin while I'm pulled away and then straight up, bumping my head on the ceiling—

He rises too—

Before flying out the door and into a clear blue sky.

It's as if the wind wants to strip off my face. I close my eyes, afraid that I, too, am hurdling down to earth and to my death…

"She's finally coming around." Eyes still shut, I hear the concern laced in Jack's murmur. "Donna…darling, you're safe."

I bolt up, eyes opened wide. "But—I went out the door!"

He flew out, but I was tethered and holding onto you," Jack explains.

"And I was tethered and holding on to Jack," Arnie adds.

"Grigori was tethered too!" I scan the room.

"He was in so much pain he tried to reach the champagne's ice bucket just as we hit an air pocket. His head slammed into the ceiling, and he passed out. In those few seconds, he lost his grip on his tether. He got caught in a crosswind and went out the door," Jack replies.

"How did you get into the room?" I ask.

"The bathroom to his suite is shared with the second bedroom," Abu says. "From what we found in security feeds of the plane's hidden cameras, Grigori thought nothing of crashing his guests' trysts. As far as he was concerned, the more the merrier."

I shudder. "Yeah, I'm sure he was the life of the party."

"Not from what I can see on the videos in his private stash." Jack points to an open cabinet filled with DVDs and thumb drives. "If anything, he terrorized the women into having sex with him and his buddies. If they weren't there under their own free will, they were drugged and carried onboard, where they were raped—and sometimes snuffed out. Yours wouldn't have been the first body he'd have dumped over open seas."

"Arnie and I are going to deploy the drone carrying the plane's signal," Abu adds. "Then the plane will go stealth. Since we now have no reason to fly to Morocco, we're heading back to L.A."

"Ah, great," I mutter. "I take it Ryan is already aware of our failed mission."

"Yes, he saw the whole thing," Jack admits. "I'm sure he's figuring out how to break the news to Marcus. In the meantime, Abu is turning this place inside out to see what other goodies Grigori has onboard, and Arnie is trying to hack Grigori's onboard computer. Supposedly, our host wasn't allowed access to it after his arrest. However, he may have bribed a prison guard and accessed it remotely. In any event, I'm sure it's a gold mine of intel on his personal life, arms sales, and deals with Putin, including any kickback."

"Obviously, Grigori had a history with Luda. He said she'd visited him in prison."

"If so, she was acting as Putin's go-between," Jack replies.

"I really think there was more to their relationship than that. Grigori also referred to her presence on the plane as his welcome-home gift from Putin," I insist. "And he was livid when I told him I was pregnant. Knowing her role as a sparrow, how could he have assumed she'd never had other lovers?... Unless..."

I take out my cell and call Emma. "Quick question: was Acme able to triangulate cell communication between

Luda, the fake drunk dude we're now holding in the tank, and the traitor who went up in flames?"

"She communicated with the man wearing the suit—the Pentagon guy we've identified as Ralph Whitlaw. But we still don't know the identity of Drunk Dude…" She pauses. "However, he'd made contact with Whitlaw. Or I should say he went on a phishing expedition."

"What do you mean?"

"He sent Whitlaw a Signal message. Thinking it was from someone he knew, Whitlaw responded. This allowed Drunk Dude to break the security code on Whitlaw's cell and read all his texts and emails—including those with Luda."

"I'll bet that's how Drunk Dude knew to be on the bus for their brush pass," I reason. "And why Luda fought him so hard for it. It wasn't just for show."

"Has Acme been able to break him?" Jack asks.

"No, and we've tried everything," Emma concedes. "Waterboarding, torture, you name it. He's strong-willed."

"Beg Ryan to lay off the guy. I have something in mind to try when I get back."

"Will do." Emma signs off.

As I rise, I put my hand on Jack's shoulder to steady myself. "We should help Abu sweep the plane. Maybe Grigori left a few crumbs to appease Ryan for screwing up this mission—including some intel on this 'Black King' person."

"That will depend."

"On what?"

"On whether the 'Black King' is as big a fish as Grigori was."

I pray that's the case.

4

Colorbound

The bishop is the only piece that is "colorbound," that is, it can only move on the color from which it started. And since a different color is on both sides, in front and behind it, the bishop must move diagonally.

Imagine how you'd feel if you weren't allowed to leap onto a square that quote-unquote wasn't meant for you! You'd feel as if you were missing out.

At the same time, if breaking the rules meant your team would lose, towing the party line would be worth it. Right?

Don't be so sure.

If life is a chess game, don't settle on being a pawn, let alone a rook, a knight, or even a bishop.

Move through life like a queen.

When we roll into Acme, instead of joining the others in the conference room, I head for what Acme euphemistically calls "the Dungeon."

At the CIA's Farm, we were taught—and underwent—interrogation tactics. Hooding, continuous noise, sleep deprivation, withholding food or water, and stress positioning interrogation techniques are also part of an Acme operative's training. We are taught them here too: deep in the bowels of the innocuous multi-building complex that serves as the company's offices.

In fact, periodically, we must undergo a refresher course. You know what they say: practice makes perfect.

Thus far, Drunk Dude has shown that mind over matter—even that of physical and psychological pain—is achievable.

Before seeing him, I put on the makeup and costume that I wore on the bus. He smirks when, once again, he sees The Little Old Lady. Only, this time, he's as toothless as her, and not because he, too, is wearing black tooth wax. One of Acme's torturers got carried away playing Nasty Nazi Dentist.

As I remove my prostheses and wig, his eyes open wide. "You are Donna Craig!"

"If you know of me, you must also know of my organization."

"I am being held *by Acme*?" His laughter roars through the dungeon. "Such irony!"

"Then you've confirmed my suspicions: that we're on the same side."

"Yes." He lifts his head proudly. "It was I who intercepted the message between the American traitor, Whitlaw, and the Russian spy, Luda Morozova."

Talk about a get-out-of-jail-free card.

I unlock his shackles. "It's time we get you out of the Dungeon."

~

RYAN'S SHOUTS FROM THE CONFERENCE ROOM CAN BE HEARD all the way down the hall.

Note to Acme: time to update our Cone of Silence technology.

I open the door and stick my head through. "So, guess who we've got in the Dungeon?"

Ryan snarls, "It should be you."

"That's not a very nice thing to say—*especially since I'm here to stop you from torturing a U.S. ally.*" I pull our prisoner into the room with me.

Ryan's jaw drops.

"Blimey! Dominic exclaims. "That's Drunk Dude…"

"In truth, he's Kostyantyn Ponomarenko of the *Sluzhba bezpeky Ukrainy.* He's a Ukrainian intelligence operative— ergo, an American ally."

Our guest bows slightly.

"It was my country that hacked Whitlaw's texts," Kostyantyn explains. "My president spoke directly to your highest intelligence officer: Director Branham, about Luda Morozova's rendezvous with Whitlaw."

"If what you say is true, you must have known the United States would have followed through on preventing Luda's mission," Jack points out.

"Because I am stationed here as a recognized diplomat, my president gave me direct orders to monitor the rendezvous. I saw no one from the FBI, so I felt I had to stop Luda myself."

"Wait… you know the Los Angeles bureau's agents?"

"Yes. I have interfaced with them on other covert matters. And I have a photographic memory. What with the bus practically empty—drunks, the fashion plates, and who I assumed was a frail old lady—I felt I had to intercept the pass."

"Kostyantyn jumped off the bus with the intent to follow and stop her when Dominic and Arnie accosted him," I add.

Dominic huffs, "Why didn't he just say who he was?"

The Ukrainian agent sighs. "Because I assumed you were part of Luda's back-up." He searches our faces. "I take it she succeeded."

"She's dead." Ryan's eyes shift my way. "But unfortunately, she'd just passed the intel forward."

Kostyantyn bangs the table with his fist. "Then the Black King has it! He'll expose all of us—*all of you*—to the highest bidder!"

"*You know of him?*" Ryan asks.

"Russia's attempt to decimate our country has been a call to arms. A border cannot stop our fight for freedom. Our assets in Russia are deep." Kostyantyn smiles proudly. "The intelligence Luda secured from Whitlaw was a digital directory of American operatives and assets located overseas. The Black King has already acquired similar intel on the United Kingdom, France, Germany, Japan, Saudi Arabia, China, North Korea, Russia—and Ukraine as well. Eleven in all, each the focus of a different auction event. Whereas the countries must pay to retrieve their digital directories, they are also welcome to bid on their enemies' directories at any other auctions. Once the bids are collected, the Black King will contact the winner with the retrieval location. The data will be placed on an SD card."

Ryan paces the room. "What guarantee will any country have that it will be the sole owner of the dossier?"

Kostyantyn shrugs. "None, of course. Your only hope— and that of the other countries—is that you discover the

Black King's identity and exterminate him before he carries out his plan."

He's right.

A thought occurs to me: "Kostyantyn, you mentioned Russia is also bidding. But knowing Luda was involved, wouldn't it indicate that Putin is the Black King?"

His laugh is mirthless. "Hardly!"

"How do you know this?" Jack asks.

"Because Ukraine has already received an invitation to bid on the Russian directory. And no doubt Russia will bid on ours. I wager your president will soon be notified about the theft of yours. Acme, please understand the severity of this! If the Black King succeeds with his plan, the whole world grovels at his feet! Even Putin will come to realize this." He hesitates, then adds, "Luda certainly did. She was in league with the Black King."

Shocked, I exclaim, "Why would she defy Putin and give the stolen intel to the Black King instead?"

"For good reason. They were lovers. She was his Black Queen."

"Grigori accused her of that," Jack declares.

Ryan looks over at me.

My heart sinks. He now has another reason to keep Luda—or me, as her—in play.

Ryan holds out his hand. As Kostyantyn shakes it, Ryan says, "I'm sure you understand that we must detain you until we verify your credentials. If they check out, you'll be released immediately. I hope you can forgive the stridency of our interrogators. Of course, you'll immediately receive new dental work, courtesy of Acme."

"I thank you. It's a luxury that we can ill afford in our country now that it's under siege." His words come out slow and difficult. To be expected, considering the state of his mouth. "I only wish Luda or Whitlaw had been here in my stead."

"Me too," I reply. "Only we wouldn't have offered them free dental work. I guess their deaths are the one good thing that's come out of this."

"*Amin*," he whispers.

The prayer is universal in any language.

5

Tempo

In chess, the word "tempo" indicates the worth of a piece in your game strategy. Creating the right tempo gives you the impetus to move around the board competitively. For example, a good tempo is getting three moves from a pawn before it's captured.

Strategizing the perfect tempo in other areas of your life can help you achieve success there as well. Start by being honest about how well you play others instead of playing with them.

Let them be your pawns.

Ryan nods to Abu to take Kostyantyn to a holding cell. At the same time, Emma is dialing Marcus's number.

Ryan's eyes seek out ours, one by one. "I don't want to hear any excuses as to why you fucked up the mission." Despite this declaration, Ryan is cool, calm, and collected. Whereas our mission team doesn't exhale its release in unison, shoulders relax. "What I will emphasize, however, is that any more screw-ups will cost the lives of multitudes; not just our overseas operatives and assets, but those stateside too. Each of us will have a target on our back." He rises when Emma signals that he's got Marcus on the phone. "While I confirm Kostyantyn's claim with Branham, I suggest you divvy up the list of countries affected and reach out to your highest-order contacts. Let's see if we can take down the Black King before he does it to us."

Even before he's out the door, Jack is scanning the list. "Donna, you call our operative in France. Dominic, you take England. Arnie, you're tight with one of the Japanese diplomats, right? Call him. Abu, how about contacting one of Saudi Arabia's operatives and seeing what he can dig up? I'll contact our highest-ranking Chinese contact and call on those in North Korea."

"How do we know they won't just pass us misinformation?" Abu asks.

"We'll just have to trust that they see the advantage of telling it like it is. After all, their affiliations with the U.S. means their lives are at stake too."

Dominic leans in and mutters, "Donna, my dear: do me a favor and trade me France for England."

"Why?"

"Well…since Jody came into my life, I've avoided communicating with…with Teddy Twala."

"Is that your way of saying you've ghosted her?"

Dominic sighs. "I suppose it is."

I wag a finger. "Shame on you! Treat her with respect! She's a big girl. She can take it."

He frowns. "Well then…mum's the word to Jody."

"Grow up, Dom. She's a big girl too."

He winces. "If you say so."

But his fingers are shaking so hard that I grumble, "Okay, alright, call France instead. I'll call Daniela in the U.K. She's higher up the tree than Teddy, anyway."

"Thank you!" He kisses my cheek.

I swear! Why are the guys with all the swagger also the biggest jerks regarding their exes? I speak from experience.

One advantage: it made me a better shot. All I had to do was think of my former husband Carl, now deceased, and I hit a bullseye every time.

"Ah! My dear, sweet Donna, I can neither confirm nor deny that MI6 has received such a threat." On the surface, Lady Daniela Baxdale-Cuthbert's purr could be considered the gospel truth.

Damn it! We're all hitting dead ends with our foreign contacts, who say the same ol' thing as if reading from the same script: "I can neither confirm nor deny…"

Having been on the receiving end of Dannie's dry retorts, I know better. "Seriously, old girl? Are you saying that you've never heard of the Black King?"

"No, I certainly know the phrase—euphemistically, that is. I've had a few, I'll admit, in both senses of the phrase. Too many martinis, and who knows where I'll wake up— and with whom? As for my taste in taciturn mysterious men, well, you know it runs deep—admittedly, pun intended."

"Is this how you want to play it, Dannie? My God, both our countries' security is at risk! If there were ever a time to band together, this is it!"

"Again, *old girl:* 'tis not anything I'm aware of."

"Okay, I get it. The word is coming from on high. But

it's kinda silly, don't you think? Your country and mine are cousins. We should have each other's backs—"

"And we do—*when it is convenient.* Times like these are anything but!" Dannie's sigh lingers on the line like fine smoke. "Your man Branham has already discussed this with our Defense Minister. Like me, I'm sure you'll get your marching orders soon enough."

Would shaming work? No time like the present to test that theory: "Dannie, seriously: I'd hope we'd be heel-to-heel, in lockstep."

"You thought wrong, dearie. I'm sure I'll see you soon. Had I heard right—that you and Jack will be vacationing in Narva-Jõesuu Spa soon? Such fun! Its masseur is to die for! Book the four o'clock slot on a Saturday afternoon. It's his last one of the week. He's heavenly. Must run now. Ta!"

I've barely got out my own "Ta" before I hear the line go dead.

What the hell is she talking about? Jack and I take a vacation?

I can only wish...

Ah—

Got it!

I look up Narva-Jõesuu. It's located in Estonia, on the eastern side of the Gulf of Finland. It also borders Russia on the south and is only ninety-three miles from St. Petersburg.

"How are we doing, folks?" Ryan's shout is like the dinner bell at a dude ranch. You dread it even more after a rough and tumble day, knowing you'll be left eating the dregs of your last supper.

I needed grade-A red meat to throw at Ryan. Here's hoping he appreciates the morsel I extracted from Dannie.

"Estonia, eh?" Ryan smirks. "How fast did it come after her 'confirm nor deny' bullshit?"

I shrug. "At least I shamed her into giving me this much."

"Good move. Granted, she stuck to her playbook since it wasn't her country's bid event but ours. That's okay. We'll have confirmation on her intel when Marcus calls me with the who, where, and when. In the meantime, tally up the players on the board while I put in a call to Dannie's boss." All ears prick up in Ryan's direction as he bellows: "Has anyone else gotten beyond a 'confirm nor deny?'"

Jack raises his hand. "After denying that the Black King made contact, my North Korean asset sent me coded text with coordinates that triangulate in Paris: specifically, the Ritz. The event's date is a week from Saturday at twenty-thirty sharp, in Paris. North Korea's representative has been given a code name: 'the Black Castle.'"

"France is going too, but she wouldn't divulge where the bidding event is occurring," Dominic reports. "My, my! It looks like the Black King is ensuring the bidders are far away from their home bases."

"Makes sense," Abu replies. "Keeping the countries' representatives hopping makes it harder on their security teams. By the way, Saudi Arabia is going South of our Border—to Mexico City."

"What's with the code names?" Arnie asks.

I shrug. "My guess: it keeps the bidders anonymous."

"Well, Japan is headed for Mumbai, so we are too. He had no idea where the auction would take place but was told that Japan's bidder is to reserve a room in a specific hotel. It's the—"

"Whoa, wait a minute! Let me write all this stuff on the whiteboard. Let's go with the most recent date and work forward." I grab a marker.

Ryan returns just in time to give us the details on the U.K. bid. "The ministry secretary Lord Such-and-What-Not stiff-upper-lipped me. So I called his mistress, who's married to his shadow secretary. She reads all the communique on both sides of the aisle." He hands me his notes.

I chuckle. "In other words, she's worth every dime we pay her. Did she tell you who MI6 is sending?"

"I asked, but she said they hadn't yet decided," Ryan admits.

I fill in the last blank:

THURSDAY:
White Castle - Germany - Istanbul -
Conrad Istanbul

SATURDAY:
Black Castle - North Korea - Paris - Ritz

MONDAY:
White Knight - France - Singapore - Peninsula Excelsior

WEDNESDAY:
Black Knight - Japan - Mumbai - Taj Mahal Palace

FRIDAY:
White Bishop - China - Brussels – Grand Place Hotel

SUNDAY:
Black Bishop - U.K. - Rijeka, Croatia - Hotel Continental

TUESDAY:
White Queen - Saudi Arabia - Mexico City - Gran Hotel Ciudad de Mexico

THURSDAY:
White King - Russia - Venice - Hilton Molino Stuckey

SATURDAY:
Black Queen - US - Narva-Jõesuu - Narva-Jõesuu Spa
White Pawn - Ukraine - Narva-Jõesuu - Narva-Jõesuu Spa

"The representatives for the country whose directory is up for grabs aren't supposed to reveal who they're sending and where. Otherwise, the winner could be exterminated after they've retrieved the SD card containing the directory du jour," Ryan explains. "After the auction, the winning bidder will receive a separate communication with directions of a location where they are to pick up the directory."

"Is it a coincidence that the Black King has made our country's codename "Black Queen?" I ask.

"Doubtful," Jack replies.

"What about the fact that the bidding representative must also be booked at the same hotel as Lee's competition?" I muse.

"Again, doubtful," Jack answers.

"Why not use one location for all the bids?" Emma wonders. "He could schedule a different one every hour on the hour and be done with it."

I shrug. "I assume the Black King prefers creating inconvenience and chaos."

"Agreed. Not to mention it's harder to hit a moving

target. Every country involved will want his head on a plate, that's for sure." Ryan declares.

Arnie whistles. "With ten countries in play—and all over the globe—the Black King will make a financial killing."

"Beyond showing up for the auction of their own directory, what's to stop operatives from also showing up in the cities where the auctions for their enemy's directories are taking place?" Emma wonders.

"Nothing," I point out. "And if the Black King is demanding that the other bidders also stay at the same hotel, it could still turn into a shooting gallery."

"I'm sure he's figured that out. Maybe it's exactly what he wants," Abu replies.

"As far as our dealing with Ukraine, as a show of good faith to the other countries, Ukraine will only bid on its directory. The U.S. has also agreed that it won't bid on Ukraine's directory. However, since the bid hotel is too close to the Russian border for Ukraine to feel comfortable sending a representative, it has asked our country's bidder to represent it in the Ukraine auction—not that the Black King will know this."

"Who is the U.S. sending?" Jack asks.

"Funny you should ask. Marcus says the Black King's missive specifically requested Mrs. Craig."

I croak, *"What?... Me?"*

More to the point: why me?

THEY SAY THAT YOU NEVER FEEL MORE ALIVE THAN WHEN YOU face death.

I disagree.

Nothing is as exhilarating or makes me appreciate life more than sex with my husband.

In the past seventy-two hours, I almost died twice. During that time, two others no longer walk the earth because of me.

I fought hard to beat the reaper. Had I let him win, I would have missed out on what I live for:

My husband's hungry kisses—damp trails that criss-cross the peaks and valleys of my body, causing me to quake, to ache for him all the more.

He takes me in hand: roaming, probing.

I do the same: stroking, pumping.

Hoarsely, he whispers sweet entreaties.

I answer with my own requests: naughty taunts for him to up his game, to make every precious second count.

A flick of my tongue in the right place is rewarded with a loving smack. When he sucks my nipple to a tight point, my nails press into the small of his back until he groans, "I can't…hold back."

"*Enter me.*" Jack knows better than to read my aching whisper as a gentle request. It's a vehement command.

Now, our mutual goal is to stoke each other's passions. I groan when his shaft fills me, granite-hard and rock-steady. He moans as my muscles clench him tightly. When his arms push off from the bed, my body rises with his.

Jack's deep thrusts find a tempo that I keep too—

And our joy-filled eyes meet as our passion tango erupts in ecstasy.

Yes, I live for this—

And to fall asleep in his arms.

A buzz wakes me: a text on my cell.

I look at the screen. Acme ComInt has relayed a message received by Luda's cell:

Soon we shall be together, my love. —BK

A shiver runs through me. The Black King is writing to her.

Which means he doesn't know she is dead.

Or…

Is he writing to me?

6

En Passant

*In chess, an "en passant" (which means "as it passes")
takes place after a pawn moves two squares forward from its
starting position. When this happens, only on the next move is
its opposing pawn allowed to move into the passed square and
capture the pawn as if it were still there.*

*Your opponent may not know of this rule. In fact, your oppo-
nent may be upset when you use it, even after you point out its
legitimacy in* the U.S. Chess Federation's Official Rules of
Chess.

*At that point, should your opponent be angry enough to
challenge you to a duel, you can answer one of three ways:*

*1) Give back the pawn and chuckle, "No harm, no foul." (We
both know your life is worth at least a knight, right?)*

*2) Call his bluff by pushing back from the board, declaring,
"Pistols, at twenty paces? I am so in! I've got my second on
speed dial. Let me see if he's free...." Then hope your opponent
backs down.*

*3) Run like hell, and pray your opponent doesn't carry his
dueling pistols around just for fun.*

The lesson here: even if you're right, you must measure that against the price of making a stand.

I wake to my children's laughter as they run up the stairs.

In a flash, I scramble into my pajamas. Throwing Jack his flannel bottoms, I nudge, "Sit up!"

Shaking the sleep from his eyes, he mumbles, "Wasn't Aunt Phyllis going to pick them up tomorrow from camp?"

I grumble, "I guess there was a change of plan."

Thank goodness we're decent enough when they knock on our bedroom door.

"Come in," Jack and I call out in unison.

We're surprised to see Jeff and Trisha with our eldest, Mary, and her boyfriend: our ward, Evan. "Aunt Phyllis and Porter extended their honeymoon—yet again," Mary explains. "Since she forgot if you were still on the road, I cut my internship short to pick them up. Mario understood since Evan and I leave for Berkeley in four weeks anyway. And...." She blushes. "We want to take a little getaway before it." She gives Evan a sideways glance. "Not that he won't be tethered to his cell, what with all the government contracts that have come his way in the past few weeks."

"I agree. You both deserve to take some time off ," I declare. "As for Aunt Phyllis, she was wrong on both counts. The kids were due home tomorrow. And I'm afraid we're back on the road again tonight. So, seeing all of you before we go works out perfectly, even if it's only for one day." I nod at Jack. "I only wish our break were longer."

"I know what you mean. It's been a hell of a summer for you, too," Evan declares.

He's not joking. We've had three missions, back-to-back. Evan's assistance was integral. The company he inherited, BlackTech, provided newly developed software to Acme and the DNI that made the capture of terrorists in these past missions possible.

"Mr. Chiffray is disappointed since he needs to hit the road with some international event," Trisha explains. "Janie is going too. I'll miss her."

"Boo, hoo, hoo," Jeff mutters. "Frankly, I think separating you two is a great idea. She's picking up some of your obnoxious habits."

"You're just jealous because she no longer moons after you since Mason moved in," Trisha snickers.

Jack stares at me. Then, to Trisha: *"What?... Mason who?"*

Jeff rolls his eyes. "Ledbetter. You know—the guy the Russians threw into jail, like, forever."

Trisha scowls. "It was four years—and it wasn't his fault! I'd like to see how well you'd do in prison! You'd cry like a baby the first night—"

"Alright, you two, calm down!" Jack grabs Jeff's arm before he can put his younger sister in a headlock.

"How did Mason end up at Mr. Chiffray's?" I wonder aloud.

"I suggested that Mario reach out to him," Mary replies. "The NSA had to find a safe house for him quickly. Something went wrong with the prisoner exchange, so Putin initiated an execution order on Mason. Mario asked Lee if he could stay there for a few weeks until another location could be found," Mary explains. "Jody vouched for him since he's one of her biggest social media clients.

But since Lee's charitable foundation sponsors the International Junior Chess Competition, most of his security detail will be on the road with him as he attends those events. Before he takes off, Mario will have to chase down another estate with top-notch security for Mason's safekeeping. Jody is beside herself. With such strong interest for Mason, she's been doing everything she can to promote his return—not just as a chess master but a human rights advocate."

Suddenly, I feel as if I've been gone forever. "I've never heard of that competition. What's it about?"

"It's sort of like the Goodwill games, only for kids who play chess, which is universal. It's is great for promoting friendships and good sportsmanship," Trisha explains.

"Chess?" Jack's gaze, aimed at me, is heavy with dread.

"Janie is going," Trisha adds. "Mason taught her how to play. She asked if I could come too—and Jeff, especially since the other nerds in his coding camp got him hooked on chess."

Jeff shrugs. "I may enter. I picked it up pretty quickly. Besides, Genghis and Guang are going, and I play better than either of them—"

"Yikes! Yet another mark of shame on the Craig family by way of its nerdy young son!" Trisha teases.

Jack can't stop Jeff this time before he twists Trisha's wrist. She yelps from the pain.

"Where are these games taking place?" I ask.

"All over the world!" Trisha replies. "Singapore, Paris, Rio de Janeiro, you name it."

Jeff chimes in, "The winners of each of the first eight events' board games will face in the final tournament in some place I've never heard of. Heck, if I can pronounce it…Narva…Narva…"

"Narva-Jõesuu," I'm so stunned that I can barely get the name out.

"Yep, sounds about right." Jeff shrugs.

Oh…

Shite.

"Mom, Dad, I'll start your pancakes first—" Mary tells Jack and me as we fly by her to the shower.

Not to disappoint our daughter, but it's not the food we have on our minds. Like me, Jack knows the competition's dates and places are too much of a coincidence.

As I shut the bathroom door, I hear Mary exclaim, "Wow! I didn't know they thought so highly of my cooking."

Evan responds, "The fact that they ran out of the room isn't a good thing. Seriously, babe: have you actually eaten your own flapjacks?"

The next thing we hear is Evan's yelp.

Someday, he'll learn: If you can't say something nice to your beloved, don't say anything at all.

"Damn it, you're right!" Ryan scowls at the whiteboard in front of us, which, to our dismay, proves our assumption:

Every city where a Black King auction is to be held is also hosting the International Junior Chess Competition on the same day and place.

"He's got to be using the competition as a cover for the auction," Jack reasons.

"With chess being one of the events, it certainly plays into his theme," Emma adds.

"The only piece missing is the one detail that hasn't

been passed forward to us by any of our contacts: when the auctions are to be held," Ryan says. "If it isn't in the same hotel, we'll have a better chance of capturing the Black King without collateral damage."

"Wouldn't he have thought of that too?" Abu asks. "My guess is that he'll make it as difficult for us as possible. A throng of unsuspecting families makes a perfect obstacle course for a getaway."

"We know of one locale: Dannie mentioned the Narva-Jõesuu Spa," I point out.

"Which, according to Marcus, is where the U.S. auction is to take place," Ryan informs us. "It was good of her to warn us."

I frown. "I don't like that our auction is last."

"It's the Black King's way of keeping all bidders in play until the bitter end," Jack guesses.

"I hate to say it, but I think you're right," Ryan concedes.

"Ryan, there's something else you need to know about the Black King. He reached out to Luda via her cell."

His eyes widen. "Was it a text or a call?"

"A text. All it said was 'soon we shall be together, my love,' and signed 'B.K.'"

"Apparently, he didn't get the memo," Dominic sniffs.

"Which validates our contention that he's a lone wolf," Jack reasons, "And that she secured the Russian directory for him."

"If he trusts Luda, we must keep her in play." Ryan looks pointedly at me.

Tag, I'm it—

Yet again.

"Yeah, okay, whatever. But regarding Lee's event, we must warn him that the Black King may be crashing his soirée. If something goes wrong, the lives of innocent children and their families may be at stake." I pick up my cell.

Ryan puts his hand over mine. "Let's not be too hasty."

Jack grimaces. "What do you mean?"

"The goal is to take out the Black King. If he realizes we've figured out the when, why, and how, if not the who, he may go underground until all of this blows over," Ryan points out.

"Ryan, if we don't let Lee know, he'll never forgive us," I insist. "Remember, he'll be there with his children and hundreds of other innocent people."

Ryan sighs. "You're right. Okay, I'll set up a meeting right now. Donna and Jack, you'll come with me to tell him in person."

OUR ARRIVAL AT LEE'S PALATIAL ESTATE, LION'S LAIR, IS marked by an odd silence. Usually, we're greeted by the friendly patter and ecstatic giggles from Lee's daughter, thirteen-year-old Janie, and her seven-year-old brother, Harrison.

Having been informed we've driven up by his Secret Service detail, Lee meets us at the door with his assistant, Eve, and beckons us into his downstairs office.

"Where are the kids?" I ask as I sit beside Eve on one of the two couches perpendicular to Lee's desk. Jack and Ryan grab the other couch.

Our host chuckles. "Take a guess, and the first one doesn't count."

Jack rolls his eyes. "The Craig homestead."

"Yep, their home away from home. Jody took Mason there as well. He's been teaching Janie how to play chess.

She's so into the game that she's wanted him to coach Trisha too."

"Jeff played while he was at coding camp these past few weeks," I reply.

Eve smiles. "Apparently, he's a natural. Janie just texted me that Mason is quite impressed. In fact, he's encouraging Jeff to enter the International Junior Board Game Competitions."

Lee smiles. "The more, the merrier. We need all the bodies we can get! Despite worldwide outreach to middle- and high school students, sign-ups are just half what we'd need to break even." He hesitates. "As much as I love the concept, without a big-name draw or a deep-pocket sponsor who won't mind a less than stellar crowd, I may scrap it."

"You can't."

Ryan's voice is adamant enough to make Lee frown. "Something tells me this isn't just a friendly drop-in."

"Unfortunately, your right." Ryan sighs. "Lee, the national security of ten countries is at stake, including ours. Each has had its diplomatic intelligence directories hacked. The perpetrator calls himself the Black King. He's scheduled the auctions on the same days, and in the same towns, as your competition."

"We think he's using your event as the cover for his own," I point out.

"If you call off the competition, we don't know what, if anything, can be done to retrieve the directories before they're sold to enemy states," Jack adds.

Lee nods slowly. Leaning back in his chair, he declares, "I know more than anyone the importance of your mission. I thoroughly understand why you want the competition to go on. But the one thing I can't condone is putting the lives of the attendees at risk: the children, their families, those who are there for the love of the game and to support the players."

Ryan nods. "May I present a possible solution?"

"By all means," Lee replies.

"Whereas we don't know if the Black King plans on holding the auction in the same hotels as the ones you've booked, we assume this may be the case. In any event, we'll err on the side of caution by informing you and the event's staff when we know the time and place of each auction. That way, if the competition coincides in the same location, your players and their fans can be moved elsewhere."

"We do have some free time activities built in throughout each event day, as well as the day before. And we could alter some of the competition's schedule." He glances at Eve, who measures him with a nod as she takes notes.

"Part of the event's mission is that the players make new friends from other countries," Eve explains. "To further that effort, we've scheduled excursions: to museums, plays, and various outdoor activities. In one location, it may be rock climbing. In another, it may be fishing or water sports. It makes losing less heartbreaking, too—especially if you enjoy the company of a competitor."

"I take it, then, you feel comfortable moving forward with your plans?"

"Yes—because I'll also beef up the event's security team." Lee's grin is half-hearted. "If we're lucky, it'll intimidate the Black King into moving his bake sale elsewhere."

"Lee, you mentioned that a big-name draw may pull in more competitor applications and spectator ticket sales," I point out. "Have you thought about asking Mason if he'd participate?"

"In fact, I had. The conversation didn't go well. He slammed it down, then offered to leave if it was a prerequisite for staying. I assured him it wasn't, that I was honored to have him stay. Donna, he's like a wounded animal since his incarceration. It's a shame since Jody has been inundated with requests for speaking engagements. Thus far, he's turned them all down."

"Do I have your permission to try to change his mind?"

"Frankly, should he say yes, I'd be ecstatic. But don't hold your breath, Donna. The poor man has been to hell and back. Even knowing that interacting with Russians is part of your mission may relieve his post-traumatic stress."

"I'll tread lightly."

Lee smiles broadly. "Then go for it. I've always considered you a miracle worker. You know that."

Ryan rises. "Thank you, sir, for your flexibility."

"Just don't make me regret it." Lee looks at me when he says this.

All I can do is look away. He couldn't be more worried than me.

7

Zugzwang and Trébuchet

IN CHESS, THERE MAY COME A TIME IN WHICH A PLAYER ENDS UP with a "zugzwang," which means they have absolutely no good moves at all.

Well, too bad. You've got to move one way or the other, even if it means losing the moved piece—or, for that matter, the game.

Just like real life.

Another chess term to remember is "trébuchet," which is a move that creates a reciprocal zugzwang for the opposing player.

Should your zugzwang cause your opponent to trébuchet, this may lead to a stalemate.

Is that preferable to a loss? It is, in chess.

In real life, it may also be for the best.

Except in divorce. At that point, don't give up any pieces except pawns.

IT'S LATE AFTERNOON WHEN JACK AND I PULL INTO OUR driveway. Our great room is quiet except for an occasional thoughtful grunt, the errant ecstatic squeal, and one solicitous murmur: "Checkmate." I attribute the lack of rap music, television chatter, and the usual kid-snark and counter-jibes to Mason. The kids are enthralled with chess, thanks to him.

Janie is now paired with Genghis, Trisha with Guang, and Jeff plays Mason.

"The harder you lose, the more you learn to win," Mason insists.

From their thoughtful but aggressive moves, they've certainly taken this motto to heart.

Jody gives me a grateful nod as I refill her coffee mug. After a sip, she scoots her chair a few inches and cranes her neck to look down the hall. Noting the players' contentment, she sighs happily, tipping her mug toward mine in a salute. She no longer questions her decision to have accepted Lee's offer to host Mason at Lion's Lair until the press has cooled its heels over the chess master's release. She sees proof of this in Mason's face. The hollow stare that the news cameras have caught upon his return has finally been replaced by a steady, attentive gaze. Once pale, it now sports a ruddy glow from his morning jogs through the estate's private golf course.

Usually, it's turned in Jody's direction.

Don't think Dominic hasn't noticed. For instance, today, he barely waited an hour before stopping by to see what Jody and Mason are doing here. "To borrow Jack's lawn mower," he insisted.

Dominic—*doing yard work?*

Yes, because it pleases Jody. He only recently released his manservant, the last vestige of his previously pampered life as a British lord.

Jody felt it was overkill. "He doesn't do anything you can't do for yourself," she teased.

"Manual labor isn't my style," he huffed.

She countered, "How can you claim to be self-sufficient if you can't even use a leaf blower?"

Right now, he's trying Jack's patience with all his mower usage questions. Jack is no fool. Dominic keeps his eyes pried to see how often Jody and Mason's paths cross.

Today, it's pretty often. Every now and then, Jody, who's been fielding texts and emails in the dining room, will walk over to Mason to whisper something in his ear: Since his return, every news organization wants to interview him. At the same time, speakers' bureaus are calling with offers to lecture, partake in a panel, or give a speech. But Mason always shakes his head, giving her a firm no. She nods but always turns her head away so as not to show her disappointment.

Unsurprisingly, his time in the Russian prison has put him in an emotional tailspin.

From what I can tell, teaching the children the game that is his passion gives him solace.

Now that Jody has taken a break from her Mason must-do list, I beckon her to join me outside on the veranda. This makes Dominic happy—

Until Jack informs him that Ryan has strict orders for them to avoid us until I ask Jody the question on Ryan's mind: is Mason well enough to be used as the bait for us to trap the Black King?

"What's so important that you needed to get me away from the two most important men in my life—my boyfriend and my biggest client?"

Ah, so Jody's on to me…

I laugh. "I thought you'd appreciate a break from their male posturing."

"You're right. At first, their mutual jealousy was flattering, but now it's getting old." Jody twists her hair behind the nape of her neck, my usually self-assured friend's only nervous habit.

"It's a matter of national security—one in which your opinion about, and influence over, Mason would be invaluable."

"Sounds intriguing. How would it involve Mason?"

"I understand he rejected Lee's proposal to participate in the International Junior Chess Competition."

"Do you blame him? Its final game takes place on the banks of the lake where he lost his freedom–not to mention four years of his life!"

"Is there some way you could encourage him to reconsider? Without a major American headliner, the Russian and Chinese delegates will glide to the finish—that is, if they feel the event is worth even showing up for. Ticket sales are sluggish as is. Even with Lee's offer to underwrite the exhibition, the broadcast sponsor has threatened to pull out. If it does, there goes its major source of visibility."

Jody sighs. "Look, I get it. Mason sells tickets. But from what he's told me, he's traumatized at the thought of traveling—even within this country! That said, I don't imagine he'll consider Europe, let alone any cities that border Russia."

"Acme would be honored to provide around-the-clock security. I promise we'll never let him out of our sight."

Jody is silent for a long while. Finally: "I assume it's a matter of national security?"

"I won't deny it. But I'd prefer if you didn't divulge that to anyone, including Mason."

Jody frowns. "Keeping him in the dark wouldn't be fair! Remember, at least three exhibition games are in countries adjacent to Russia. All of those venues are just meters away from its border! If Mason does, or says, something—even unwittingly—that provokes retaliation...." As her voice fades, she shudders. "You know all too well that Russia isn't against poisoning those who thought they were out of reach! I'm sorry, Donna, but I can't ask that of Mason!"

"Ask me what?" Jody and I freeze at the sound of Mason's voice.

He's staring at us. His steel blue eyes pierce my soul with naked defiance. His face is still handsome despite being lined with the fatigue and the pain of his imprisonment.

I can only imagine the anguish this man has been through. And yet, he survived one of Russia's worst prisons. His mind, shrewd enough to beat every competitor he's played professionally, was put to good use in strategizing every minute of his survival, never knowing if he would ever get out from hell on earth.

"We were just talking about the youth game board exhibition. Donna was wondering if you'd reconsider attending...."

Seeing Mason's stunned reaction, Jody's voice trails off.

Slowly he sits down. He's shaking.

"I'll be honest with you, Mason. Without your participation, the event may be canceled," I explain. "Lee wouldn't have mentioned it to you, but the camaraderie it generates between students worldwide is an important consideration." I'm being cruel, I know, to lay this at his feet.

Jody's sidelong glance chides me to add, "And…there are diplomatic incentives to be gained as well."

Mason buries his head in his hands. His sobs bring Jody to his side. Her glare warns me I've said enough.

I, too, walk over. It seems like an eon before his convulsions subside. In time, his body slumps against Jody.

The silence is deafening.

Finally, he sighs. As if it takes all his strength, he struggles to his feet. He pulls off his shirt and turns around so that we can see his back. Wide welts crisscross it, top to bottom. Some places are raw, stripped of all skin.

"The torturers love to hear you scream and beg for your life. The deep cuts—the ones with the burns—are from live electrical cords. The wider ones are from a razor belt." He holds out his right arm so that I can see the number tattooed there. "See this? I'll always carry the mark of IK-2, the penal colony for political agitators and rights advocates. *I will always be marked as Putin's prisoner.*" When Mason sits down again, it shows me the bottom of his feet. Though healed now, welts are still visible there too. "They cripple you so that you can't walk. Instead, you crawl through your own piss and shit." Shamed, he drops his head again.

I take his hand. "I'm so sorry, Mason. I had no right to ask it of you."

Still, he doesn't look up.

I take my leave.

BY THE TIME I MAKE IT OVER TO JACK AND DOMINIC, JODY has taken Mason inside.

Jack asks, "What did he say?"

I give the answer with a shake of my head: Mason won't help us.

"It's for the best," Dominic declares. "If he'd said yes and then sometime during the exhibition if he had an emotional break, it could jeopardize the mission."

"I guess you're right." Jack shrugs. "Better he should stay here and get on with his life. Jody will take good care of him."

Dominic's back stiffens. As he walks off, Jack calls, "Hey, don't you want to take the mower with you?"

The traditional British version of the American gesture for "fuck you" is two fingers, not one: the middle and the index, the other digits curled in, and the palm facing out.

In other words, the American sign for victory.

Not in this case. We haven't begun the mission, and yet we've already lost.

8

Touch-Move Rule

Oops! While thinking through your next move, you touch one of your pieces. Well then, according to the "touch-move rule," you must now play that piece in a legal move.

Accordingly, if you touch your opponent's piece, they can capture your piece if it can be done legally.

A simple way to avoid these dilemmas is to keep your hands to yourself.

Isn't that what your mama told you?

Once again, she was right.

The International Junior Chess Competition commences next week. It's been three days since the Black King wrote Luda. Since then, not a peep.

To get my mind off the mission and the fact that it's the hottest day of summer, Jack, the kids, and I head over to Hilldale Creamery, our gated community's sweet shop renowned for its one-hundred-and-one ice cream flavors.

No surprise—all of Hilldale is there too. "The line hasn't moved in a quarter-hour," a mother with two toddlers on leashes grouses.

"It's because that felon, Cheever Bing, is sampling every flavor in the joint!" retorts a father pulling a wagon with three-year-old twin boys. "He's testing all the new flavors since his quote-unquote egregious incarceration."

Ah, some things never change.

Jack mutters, "I thought the Feds had locked him up and tossed the key."

"He's only sixteen. He wasn't tried as an adult," Jeff reminds him. "And apparently, he got out early for snitching on another kid dealing vapes on his detention floor."

"Commendable," I mutter, "And unsurprisingly, a typical Cheever move."

As Jack, Trisha, Jeff, and I take our place at the end of the line that snakes two blocks beyond the shop, we come across Janie, Lee, and Mason. The girls squeal their mutual joy at their reunion. When Janie pulls Trisha in line with her, I wave her off.

"Me too?" Jeff asks.

"Sure, the more, the merrier." Lee winks at me.

On the other hand, Mason frowns.

I can take a hint. The last thing I need is to set off his post-traumatic stress.

I shake my head. "Nope, sorry, Jeff. If we jump the line, we may start a riot."

He grumbles but follows Jack to the back of the cue.

I'm about to join them when I see something odd: an older gentleman, walking with a cane, has lost his footing and is toppling over—

Onto Mason, who doesn't realize they're about to collide.

Quickly, I grab the man under the arm and pull him away. Collision avoided.

You'd think he'd thank me, right? Instead, angrily he shakes me off. When he lifts his cane, I see why:

Its bottom has a needle-thin tip.

It would have spiked Mason.

The Russian overseas extermination method of choice is death by poison pinprick containing a Novachik nerve agent. Usually, the victim is struck with the tip of an umbrella. But carrying a 'brellie in sunny southern California would have made the assailant stand out like a sore thumb.

Mr. Cane shrugs off my grip and takes off into the crowd.

I head after him.

Instinctively Jack follows me.

The crowd is so thick that I motion for Jack to go left while I go right. "He's silver-haired, over seventy, has a goatee, and carries a cane. Khaki slacks, white button-down shirt, sleeves rolled up to the elbows."

Jack nods and takes off.

I go another block, scanning left and right. I'm about to give up when I see the man heading toward a courtyard created by a trio of shops.

I peek into the first one: a bookshop. The clerk, immersed in a rom-com, doesn't even look up. I glance around. She's alone.

I pass the second store, Penelope's Bing's Cum and Get It, is a sex shop owned by Cheever's mother. She was my carpool partner when the kids were in elementary school. Having starred in the first and only season of the salacious reality television show — *Hot Housewives of Hilldale* — the store is how she's parlayed her claim to fame.

Or should I say shame? She debased herself on-air in so many ways that I can't remember them all.

(Okay, yeah, Jack and I were also part of the cast—but only because our mission was to root out a terrorist who wanted TV exposure for a sensational act of violence.)

A CLOSED sign hangs on the store's doorknob. Figures, since Penelope's Instagram demonstration reels have been a bust.

Still, I test the knob. The door creaks open…

So I step inside. My eyes must adjust to the small amount of light coming in through the front window when I hear something beside me.

Quickly, I dodge to my left—

And just in time. Instead of stabbing me, the man's cane deflates a human-sized sex doll.

I grab the cane from the middle, but he holds firm to its handle. As we grapple, I trip over a spanking bench—

And topple into an open bondage cage.

Before I can get on my feet, he's turned the lock. "Now I'll be infamous for killing the notorious Donna Craig! What a feather in my cap!" He tightens up on the cane, holding it in his fist—best for stabbing me in the heart.

I move as far away as possible until I'm in the back of the cage. It's up against a wall displaying all sorts of sex toys.

I grab something, too: a hot-pink taser gun.

This time when his arm juts into the cage, I zap it.

The man's eyes roll back into his head as the charge races through him. But when I release the trigger, the surge doesn't stop.

Shite! Only Penelope would be stupid enough to sell defective merchandise!

Finally, the charge burns out. Mr. Cane stares at me through dead eyes before dropping to his knees. Falling sideways, his head smacks the floor.

It takes me a few moments to catch my breath. I text Jack CLEAN UP ON AISLE FOUR and the cipher for the address.

I drop the taser into my straw bag—not as a souvenir but because I see no need to leave evidence of my extermination lying around.

TEN MINUTES LATER, I HEAR VOICES. I RECOGNIZE JACK'S—

And Penelope's. She must have been heading this way from the ice cream shop too. The way she's always had a crush on Jack, I'm not surprised she's chatting him up—especially since he's right in front of her shop. It gives Penelope a perfect excuse to suggest that he sample her merchandise—on her.

In her dreams.

Just as I duck behind a circular display of dildos, the door opens. Penelope exclaims, "A gift...*for Donna?* Hmmm... I never pegged her as anything but a prude. But maybe we can awaken the vixen within her." There's a pause, then: "Oh my God! I must have forgotten to lock the door last night, silly me."

She turns on the light: really, it's a black light. At the same time, a disco ball twirls on the ceiling.

"Classy," Jack mutters.

"I thought so too! Like minds!" I peek out in time to see

her stroke Jack's cheek. "It gives the place a retro groovy vibe, doesn't it?"

As he moves out of range of her hand, his eyes scan the shop. Catching my quick wave, he nods pointedly in the opposite direction before turning to Penelope with a smile. "Tell me, what's that on the back wall?"

"*Ooh,* you naughty boy! That's my bondage wall!" She pulls him toward it. "I know what you're thinking: Donna deserves to be taken down a notch. Someone needs to show her who's the boss—and boy, oh boy, do I agree! I can personally guarantee the quality of all my paddles. In fact, if you want to test out a few on me—to see if they fit your grip...." The thought makes her giggle.

I think I'll throw up.

Better yet, I should take a swing at her.

With a Louisville Slugger.

Too bad she's not running a sports emporium.

I slip out just as she asks him, "How about a cat-o-nine-tails? That'll have her purring...."

I could use that ice cream now.

No. Really, I could use a drink.

A half-hour later, Jack comes home with a hot-pink bag blazoned with the words PENELOPE BING'S CUM & GET IT in a bright yellow girlish scroll.

"*Ooh,* toys!" I fake a gleeful clap.

"The things I won't do for my wife—including carrying this bag through town. You should have seen the sly winks I got from a group of Hilldale's Women's Club members." Jack tosses the bag to me.

I catch it with my free hand. The other is holding a dry dirty martini—though, I'll admit, I'm curious enough to see what he bought to put it down. It's my third one, anyway.

I spread the bag's contents on the kitchen counter: A naughty nurse outfit. G-Spot stimulating serum. His and hers edible undies. "What, no fuzzy pink handcuffs?"

"We carry real ones. It would have been a waste of money."

"What happened when Penelope found the body?"

Jack looks skyward. "Exactly what you'd expect. She screamed, then swore on Cheever's life that he wasn't one of her exclusive clients—which I take it to mean that some of our neighbors have signed up for her in-home discipline demonstrations. Like Tupperware parties, but a helluva lot more painful."

"She admitted that to you?"

Jack smirks. "Not just to me, but to the cops who took her statement. By the way they rolled their eyes, I take it she makes more home deliveries in Hilldale than Amazon." He looks in the bag. You forgot to open the best gift of all."

"Really? What did I miss?" I grab it back and pull out a pink velvet sack tied with a black ribbon. It contains a bondage bunny mask—something Catwoman would wear but with longer ears. "Is this it? Your fantasy is to be spanked by the Easter Bunny?"

"Nah. But who knows? It may come in handy. Maybe it'll stop the Black King in his tracks—whoever he is."

"If only it were that easy." I put it on over my head. "How do I look?"

Jack shows me with a kiss. "I wish I'd bought the fuzzy tail, too," he murmurs.

It's my turn to smile. "Is that a carrot in your pocket, or are you happy to see me?"

"Let's find out." He scoops our new toys into the bag and takes it—and me—upstairs.

I'm scouring the pan that held our roast beef dinner when my cell buzzes. Jack's mobile rings at the same time. Pulling it from his pocket, he stares down at it. "We're being summoned for a sermon on the mount."

He turns his phone toward me: it's a text from Ryan asking that we head up to Lee's place.

No explanation as to why.

It's been three days since the ice cream incident. We haven't heard from Lee, Jody, or Mason in all that time. However, Dominic reports that Mason has quit his daily runs on the beach. He sticks to circling Lee's eighteen-hole golf course.

And although Jeff and Trisha have been invited to Lion's Lair, the same invitation hasn't been extended to Jack or me.

It was to be expected.

I sigh, then motion to Jeff that he take my place at the sink. At the same time, Jack tosses his dishcloth to Trisha so that she can dry what's left of the dishes in the drainer.

"If you're going up to Lion's Lair, why don't you wait until we're done?" she grumbles. "That way, I can go too."

Jack rustles her hair. "It's a work call. Trust me on that."

"We can play chess with Janie and Mason," she insists.

"Sorry, champ. Another time."

She pouts, but she knows when to stop. She reads it in Jack's face: no one's playing games tonight.

At least, not the kind she likes.

LEE'S SECRET SERVICE AGENTS NOD AS WE GET OUT OF THE car. Eve stands in the open doorway. We follow her to Lee's downstairs office.

When he rises to greet us, his eyes glance at one of the Chesterfield wingback chairs in the seating area in front of his massive desk:

Mason is seated there.

Jody is in the chair's twin.

Jack and I nod to them, then sit on the couch between their chairs.

No one says anything. Finally, Mason clears his throat. "Donna, thanks for saving my life."

"You're welcome."

"I assume Lenkov never made it back to the motherland, and it was Russia's retaliation?"

I nod.

"Thank you for your honesty. It's helped me make up my mind.: Mason stands. "I realize now I'll always be looking over my shoulder. Russia's goal is to intimidate me. To crush me. Well, I won't have it." His face seems set in steel. "I'll be the chess competition's guest speaker."

"I'm… so happy." I reach over to take his hand.

Jody smiles up at Mason. "You're a brave man, my dear friend."

Thank goodness Dominic isn't with us. Hearing her would send him into a jealous fit.

Lee chuckles. "I guess that means my chess instruction will be on hold for a while."

For the first time, I notice the chess game on the table by the window. I walk over.

A king is down.

I ask, "Who won?"

"You did." Mason isn't smiling.

It doesn't feel like it.

9

Time Control

In a time-controlled chess game, each player makes a specified number of moves—or all of his moves—before his game clock buzzes.

Liken it to all the tasks you must complete in a typical day:

• You must wake up and dress yourself and your children before getting them to school, and you to work. (Give yourself points for shoes that match, or if you gloss within the lines of your lips!)

• You must slip past your boss before he notices you weren't already at your desk so that you can pretend you got to work on time.

• You must make all project deadlines before stopping to snarf down your homemade lunch at your desk.

• Then you pick up your children from school before the after-class program closes for the night. (Bonus points if dinner wasn't a drive-thru pickup or yesterday's leftovers!)

Some days, you win. Some days, you lose. What you can count on is that your time will always be controlled.

Is this what winning looks like?

LEE'S PRIVATE JET—A BOMBARDIER 8000 WINGING ITS WAY ON the thirteen-hour flight to Istanbul, Turkey with Jody, Mason, Lee, Eve, and the children—will arrive a few hours after Acme's much smaller ride: a Dassault 2000LXS.

Our Acme team—Abu, Arnie, Dominic, Jack, and me—are sitting in a conference space comprised of six captain's chairs surrounding a large monitor as we confer with Emma and Ryan. "Germany is up first," Emma reminds us.

"Who at the BND drew the short straw to play the White Castle?" I ask.

Our handheld devices show a photo of a voluptuous blonde in her mid-twenties. "Hanna Bleichner is an intelligence agent with the Bundesnachrichtendienst."

"Is she based in Istanbul?" Abu asks.

"No. Her cover is that she's a communications assistant with the German consulate in Toronto. She'll fly out of Canada. It's a ten-hour flight," Emma adds.

"This makes it even odder that she was the BND's choice," Jack muses.

"More than likely, the Black King requested her. And based on the distance she has to travel and that she doesn't speak the language, I imagine it's yet another way he gets the upper hand," Ryan reasons. "By demanding who each country sends as its bidder, he controls each auction from every angle."

"Hanna's cover is that of a tourist," Emma adds. "She arrives two hours after you land, so you have plenty of time to intercept her."

"What if the Black King has already made contact with her?" I ask.

Jack shrugs. "Beyond telling her where to stay? I doubt it. His goal is to control everyone and everything."

"We'll just have to hope you're right about that," Ryan replies. "Either way, we have a new toy for you: an ultimate tracking device, as it were. Abu, hand them out."

Abu lifts a suitcase onto the table, opens it, then hands each of us a new cell phone.

"I assume you've heard that the Israelis have developed undetectable dynamic surveillance spyware?" Ryan asks.

"Of course," I answer. "It's called Pegasus. Supposedly, it hacks a cell within minutes, just by being within a few feet of it, and can harvest all sorts of intel: passwords, texts, email addresses, you name it. No phishing necessary. Mexico and Thailand have already used it against their civil rights advocates."

"That's the one. As it turns out, BlackTech has its own version: It's called Achilles," Emma says.

"Like the great warrior with mummy issues. Apropos!" Dominic nods approvingly.

Jack smirks, "You're thinking of Oedipus, genius."

Dominic puffs up. "Not at all! Those of us who have studied the classics at Oxford, raise a hand, please!" Only his shoots up. "I thought not. As I was saying, Achilles' mama made the mistake of holding him up by one heel during his Styx River baptism. It never healed, ergo, 'Achilles' heel.' It is truly a great name for the program, metaphorically speaking."

I laugh. "Evan and his tech team have been busy little bees."

"Unlike those countries, our president vows never to use it on our citizens. Besides that, it's against U.S. law for our government to spy on its citizens without due cause and a court-authorized search warrant," Ryan adds. "But Acme isn't a government agency. Despite that, we've vowed to President Kentfield that we won't use it stateside."

"Evan asked us to beta-test Achilles," Emma adds. "One flaw it has when compared to Pegasus is that its activation takes a bit longer: eight minutes. He's working on that. In the meantime, the spyware has to be within five feet of the target's device to activate."

"Ideally, we'll initiate activation immediately after Hanna lands," Abu replies.

"After a long plane ride, many women head for the lavatory," I point out. "It's a long shot. I can approach her there."

Abu laughs. "Eight minutes is a long time to trade make-up or travel tips. Let's hope she gets off the plane with irritable bowel syndrome."

I stick out my tongue at him.

"Give it a try anyway, Donna," Ryan replies. "If you fail, Emma has more reconnaissance on Hanna's habits that may be helpful."

"For example, she enjoys hotel bar pickups," Emma tells us. "She's even been known to seduce a bellhop or two."

"Ah! Well, Jack, old boy. Your rough-hewn charms are a perfect fit for the role." Dominic reaches over and pats Jack on the back.

Ryan snarls, "Dominic, we've already discussed your sudden propensity to play coy about this duty. Face it. You're a designated honeytrap. The Craigs don't belly-ache about it, so you can live with it too."

Jack and I exchange sidelong glances. Like me, he's thinking, *doesn't Ryan comprehend the heartache it causes us?*

Dominic nods slowly. He mutters, "At the very least, flip a coin for it."

Ryan shrugs. "Sure, go for it."

"Heads, Dominic takes it on. Tails, I do it. Okay?" Jack asks.

"Sure, works for me." Dominic's voice drips with disdain.

Jack pulls out a quarter, flips it, then slaps it onto his wrist.

"Heads. Sorry, old man." He shows it to Dominic.

I breathe more easily.

Dominic shrugs. I wonder if he's discussed this portion of his job description with Jody.

He leans into me and murmurs, "Mum's the word, right ducky?"

I have my answer.

"Until Achilles is activated, you'll also have hotel rooms adjacent to Hanna's to set up other eyes and ears. Godspeed, people." Ryan and Emma sign off.

Sulking, Dominic moves to one of the side captain's chairs.

Jack smirks as he flips the coin in his hand. When it's airborne, I grab it.

And slap it on my wrist.

Heads. I do it again. And again, it lands heads up.

I flip it over. Like I'd suspected, it's a weighted coin.

Just as I open my mouth, Jack claps his hand over my mouth and whispers, "I don't know if you're going to laugh like a hyena or if your conscience is kicking in and you're going to rat me out. Either way, remember: *I did this for us.*"

I nod slowly.

He releases his hand.

Sighing, I hiss, "I assume you've also got a weighted tales coin for the next time you bet Dom?"

Jack smirks. "Hell, yeah. I'm no fool. I stole it from Trisha, who took it from Janie."

"Smart boy." I groan. "Sometimes I wish I didn't know you so well. Now I'll feel guilty if I don't activate Achilles first."

"Let Dominic know that. It'll make him feel better."

"He'd feel better quicker if you told him you tricked him. Or at least agree to a do-over and use a real coin."

"Admit it: wouldn't you be upset at me if I lost the toss-up—and at yourself for insisting I play fair?"

"Okay, yeah," I admit. "But should he ever find out, be prepared to lose his friendship." I take the coin. "Hand me the other one too. From now on, all's fair in love and warfare."

Jack grimaces but hands it over too.

Dominic can be arrogant, self-centered, irritatingly condescending, and lazy. On any given day, Jack or I have threatened to wring Dominic's neck.

And yet when the chips are down, he has never failed us, professionally or personally. He even allowed us to move in with him when we had to blow up our home before an FBI raid. Seriously, who else would have done that? None of our other Hilldale neighbors. Trust me, after that antic even my usual community picnic offerings— three of my award-winning cherry pies—were reluctantly accepted by the Hilldale Women's Club.

And only after I signed an affidavit that it contained no poisons or explosives.

So, yes, we owe him.

~

I drop into the seat next to Dominic, who's staring out the window, glassy-eyed.

Finally, he looks at me. "I may quit."

I nod, then sigh. "Do you mean to tell me that Jody has no idea this is part of your job?"

"We've never discussed it."

"She has some knowledge of Acme's role as a government contractor. Surely, she's suspected."

"I'm sure she has. And to her credit, she's never asked outright—I assume because she knows I took a vow not to tell anyone the duties I undertake in my position."

"I understand why you're concerned. Should she not be forewarned…" I pat his arm. "Perhaps it's time to have an honest conversation. I think she'll intuit the gist without going into details."

"And what if she can't accept the gist?"

"At that point, you must decide: is staying with Acme worth losing her?"

Dominic buries his head in his hands.

"Look, Dom, maybe I'll be lucky, and you won't have to go through with it."

He sighs. "All appendages crossed."

10

The Fork Play

IMAGINE A TAG TEAM ATTACK! A TYPICAL PLAY IS MOVING A knight and a pawn against the opposing piece.

Why call it "the fork play?" Because the squares used resemble a fork, silly!

THE ISTANBUL HOTEL HOSTING THE YOUTH COMPETITION IS part of a five-star international chain. It's located in the town's Old City, within walking distance of the Grand Bazaar and the historic Hagia Sophia mosque. When we arrive, it's already buzzing with the teens participating in tomorrow's competition.

Before Hanna's plane lands, we have a few hours to position ourselves in the hotel. Emma has arranged for Arnie and Abu's room to be on one side of Hanna, and Jack and mine are on the other. Dominic's room is on another floor. Because Hanna registered as herself and put down her consulate position and telephone information at check-in, she'll think nothing of Dominic's solicitous inquiry into her personal needs while at the hotel—

If I fail to activate Achilles beforehand.

Arnie and Abu do fast work bugging the video monitor in her suite's living room and bedroom for visual and audio reception. We then head back to the airport to wait for her plane.

The flight from Toronto arrives right on time. We're alerted by Emma when Hanna appears in the middle of the jet-lagged throng.

My mission team spreads out around her, armed with Acme lenses, earbuds, empty travel bags, and our cells sporting the Achilles app.

She skips a lavatory stop.

Darn it.

Instead, like most who have departed the flight, she gets on the moving sidewalk, moving at the same leisurely pace as those in front of her.

Abu is already on it too, but standing still, letting others move around him. In a wig and glasses, Dominic walks behind her on it, but out of her peripheral vision. Jack, immediately behind Hanna, is keeping pace with her.

Suddenly Abu whispers, "Yo, Jack, have a nice trip."

Jack responds, "Ditto. See you next fall."

The next thing I know, Abu is bending down as if tying his shoe—

And Hanna trips over him.

Jack moves quickly to help her onto her feet. When she takes his hand, he pulls her into him slightly, flashing his hundred-watt smile. At the same time, Abu apologizes, untangling his bag from hers and handing it over.

Something tells me she'll find no reason to leave Jack's side, even after Achilles has been activated on her cell.

I don't need my earbuds to confirm my suspicions: Hanna is smitten with Jack. I'm fluent in the pantomime of flirtation. Even as she waves off Abu's apology, Jack fixes the tucked-in collar on her coat, allowing his eyes to linger on her until she blushes.

Grrr…

They talk—no. Really, they flirt—until they reach the end of the moving sidewalk.

Thankfully, Emma declares, "Target's Achilles signals are live."

I should breathe easy, except I don't like what I hear: Hanna's full-court press for Jack to share a ride. Though he lies and says he's headed in the opposite direction, she suggests they grab a drink somewhere.

He continues to flirt—or I should say tease her—as they walk to the taxi stand.

I hold my breath until she gets into her taxi alone, and it drives off.

A moment later, I join Jack curbside. Soon Arnie, Dominic, and Abu drive up in a van.

"Much obliged," Dominic whispers to me. He has never sounded so humbled.

"YOU'RE AWFULLY QUIET." JACK, WHO KEPT UP A STEADY flow of conversation in the van while we were with the others, waits until we're alone in our hotel room—next to Hanna's suite, which is flanked on the other side by Abu's and Arnie's—to address my sullenness.

That he can read me like a book can be charming sometimes and annoying at others. In this case, I wish he wasn't so intuitive. After all, I encouraged him to play fair with Dominic.

And now I'm regretting it.

"I'm just glad that all's well that ends well with Hanna."

"She's still in play, which means we are too."

"Yeah, okay, I get that. But now that Hanna's signal is live, you have no further reason to bump into her."

Or up against her.

"I know what you're thinking."

I stare elsewhere. "Am I that transparent?"

Jack turns my face so that we're eye to eye. "Five minutes would be a world record even for a bad lover.

"That's your worst trait in the field: you're too good at....*it.*" I shrug. "If that's your way of saying, 'Achilles made me do it,' I'll just have to grin and bear it. But that doesn't mean I have to like it."

"I don't enjoy it either. You know that." He scowls. "And I hate it when you're up to bat."

"Awful analogy, dear sir. For me, it's not a sport. It's war."

"We're of like minds. We are screwing the enemy, literally." He strokes my cheek. "Now that Hanna is no longer the issue, what say we channel our emotional frustration into a celebratory love fest? How do you say 'I want you now' in Turkish?"

Why declare something when you can show it?

It takes less than ten seconds to strip off our clothes. I'm sure it could have been quicker if I hadn't already put Jack in a lip lock, but some things can't wait.

We've just climbed under the sheets when our cells buzz. We groan but look at the screens:

Oktoberfest drink is on its way.

That's the code informing us that Hanna's bidding event is about to start.

Some things must wait after all. I guess that's why they're so precious to us.

THROUGH HER CELL, WE'RE ABLE TO FOLLOW HER BID AND those of her enemies:

Hanna starts at a million dollars. Since all bids are anonymous—given in the bidders' assigned code names— she doesn't know who has just taken it to ten, just like that.

Hanna—a,k.a. White Castle—counters with twenty-five million.

Another bidder, Black Castle—North Korea—doubles it.

It goes on and on like this: doubling, quadrupling—

And then China hops in with a bid of a billion dollars.

Russia doubles it again.

What else can Germany do but keep it in play?

Hanna's bid goes to five billion.

No one counters.

Hanna squeals, elated to learn she's saved her fellow BND operatives.

A moment later, she gets a missive from the Black King" in German. Emma translates it:

Congratulations on your winning bid!

Your superior confirmed the directory's legitimacy via the sample sent.

As per future bids to be placed by your country:

Was it an oversight that the U.S. directory wasn't on your bid sheet? If not, this is your last opportunity to be included. Counting down the seconds from ten...

Hanna takes a moment to consult with her superior. With only three seconds remaining, she replies:

Ja

Ryan's curses ring through our earbuds. "I'm calling Branham now."

As he rings off, the Black King responds to Hanna:

Your interest is duly noted.

At the proper time, you will be notified where the U.S. bid will take place.

In the meantime, you may pick up your winning bid at Hagia Sofia. The middle arch of minbar, high wall, center.

Ryan calls us. "President Kentfield is apoplectic, to say the least. Her directive is to retrieve Germany's directory once it's in her hands and duplicate it so that the U.S. can use it as a show of good faith if the Germans follow through on bidding against us."

"Would it be wiser to intercept Hanna's retrieval?" I suggest. "That way, we have the leverage to convince Germany to stay out of our auction."

"POTUS has given us our immutable orders: in no way shall we interfere with an ally's auction or bidding," Ryan warns. "Furthermore, to circumvent the BND's retrieval of intelligence that is rightfully theirs would open us up to retaliation."

"Whereas duplicating it is hunky-dory in the Spy versus Spy Official Rule Book?" I can't keep the sarcasm out of my voice.

"Germany's representative must retrieve what Germany paid for. Am I making myself perfectly clear, Mrs. Craig?" He's so loud that I must hold the phone away from my ear.

"Yes, sir."

"Mr. Craig, after their operative has secured the item, your mission is to duplicate the SD card. Use any means possible to do so."

"Sir, yes, sir."

Ryan's line goes dead.

Emma sighs, "Dominic, since you're now on surveillance, swap rooms with Jack and Donna in case—that is, *since* the inevitable will happen—if Hanna insists on using Jack's room instead, we wouldn't want her to know he was next door all along, let alone have them bumping into each other after the fact." She signs off.

Hanna, sleeping in my bed? And with my husband?

My husband gazes over at me.

Nothing I can do but shrug.

I'll cry later.

By hacking Istanbul's ubiquitous CCTV, our team can track Hanna as she slips out on her retrieval mission. Assuming she may be followed, she takes no chances: doubling back, ducking in stores through the front door, then out the back into alleys, and making subtle changes to her appearance in the process.

We're also able to access Hagia Sophia's webcams, following her, scarfed and shawled, as she says her prayers in the mosque before slipping into the arch beneath the minbar. If she retrieved it, we can't see where she hid it.

She entered through one door but left through another, moving through the Old City's thick crowds.

The only hint that her mission was accomplished is the sly smile when she enters the Conrad Instanbul's elevator and takes it to her room.

⌇

WHEN SHE GETS BACK INTO HER SUITE, THE FIRST THING SHE does is strip naked and get into the shower, but not for long. She slips on a hot pink off-the-shoulder body-hugging mini-dress, then steps into stiletto heels.

"No room in that get-up to hide even an SD card!" Arnie opines.

"So, she's left it in the suite," Jack replies.

We watch via hotel security as she heads back to the elevator and down to the lobby.

"If Jack takes her to her room, he won't be able to search it," I point out. "But I can if he keeps her in the bar."

"On it." Jack is out the door. He skips the elevator. Instead, he goes down the stairwell—

And into the hotel's lounge—

Where Hanna finds him, nursing the scotch rocks the bartender has just placed in front of him. She struts over, leans in, and strokes his cheek.

He grins. "I was hoping I'd find you here. I'd have

stayed just a few more minutes, then given you up for lost."

"Ah, ye of little faith." Her head tilts up, and her lips find his.

"Donna, move fast," Abu mutters.

11

Pin

To "pin" is to use a back chess piece (usually a rook, bishop, or queen) to attack a piece guarding one that is worth even more.

Should the protected piece be your opponent's king, then huzzah! You've accomplished what is known as an "absolute" pin.

Pat yourself on the back because your opponent is immobilized; in game parlance, "in check."

A real-life example of pinning works well for keeping away that pesky neighbor who likes to enter your home when you're gone on the pretense of borrowing a cup of sugar:

Purchase a large snarling watchdog trained to attack if the trespasser attempts to move in any direction.

"Checkmate" would be an apt name.

～

"One double old-fashioned down the hatch...." This is how Dominic gauges Hanna's return to her suite.

Hopefully, alone.

That I'm dressed in black is not a reflection of my mood. It took me ten minutes to find the locker room holding the maids' uniforms and another five minutes to break into the storage room holding their towel carts.

Finally, I arrive at Hanna's door. I knock twice and call out *"Temizlik…"* (housekeeping). Leaving the cart in the hall, I open it with my universal key card and walk in with towels and soaps.

I try the safe first. The SD card isn't there. I'm doubly frustrated because even after watching and rewatching the videos from her suite's living and bedrooms, Abu informs me that he can't identify when and where she laid down the SD card.

It's got to be in the closet, her suitcase, or the bathroom.

"A second old-fashioned ordered," Dominic warns me.

"Tell Jack I need time," I mutter. I slip into Hanna's closet.

She packed light: a couple of dresses, two pairs of slacks, and the jacket she wore at the airport. I check all pockets: nothing. I feel every inch of the items for a wafer-thin square disk: nada. Next, I tackle her suitcase. The fact that she locked it gives me hope it's in there.

I look first in the outer zipped pockets. As suspected, it's not there. After jimmying the lock, I feel the sides of the case for the SD card: nothing. It's not in any interior pockets, either. Nor can I feel it through her nicely folded clothes, damn it.

"She's on her third double old-fashioned. Man, this chick has hollow legs!" Arnie hoots.

"Tell Jack to get her to milk it," I retort.

Arnie chuckles. "She wants to milk something, alright!

The way her fingers work over his nipples, you'd think it was a cow's udder."

Gross!

Onto the bathroom.

My hands roam through the towels still folded on the shelves: nothing.

I look through her toiletry case: all vials are filled with liquids or lotions. None have false bottoms or tops. The case itself has no secret compartment.

Nothing in the cabinet drawers, either.

A hairbrush is on the counter. No secret compartment there, either.

I circle back through the suite, going high and low through every surface. I start in the living room. There is no SD card attached to the lampshades or taped to the underside of the lamps.

Not in the sofa or chair cushions, either.

Now the bedroom: it's not taped to the bed's head-board or frame, between the mattresses, under the pillows, or tucked into the sheets. There are no tiny rips in the drapes or the bed's comforter. No gaps in the floor or ceiling molding. I take note of the glass of water on Hanna's bedstead. Her contraceptive pill case is beside it.

A long shot, I know. Still, I've looked everywhere else…

I've just opened it when Arnie screeches, "Mayday! Mayday! They're leaving the lounge!"

The case holds a foil card with slots for twenty-eight tiny pills, each encased in a plastic bubble. Eighteen have already been used. Through the empty slots, I see the SD card.

It seems like a hundred hours before its contents are finally uploaded into Acme's secure cloud. Then I run as fast as I can to the front door. I'm just about to open it when I hear voices coming down the hall—

And stopping outside Hanna's suite.

I've got to hide! Behind the couch, maybe?

I'm there for a moment…

No one enters. *Hmmm….*

I can't stand the suspense. In a flash, I'm at the front door again, looking through the peephole—

To see them going into the room directly across the hall. *Why not here?*

Mine is not to reason why. Mine is to get the hell out of there…

I TAKE THE SERVICE ELEVATOR TO THE STAFFING FLOOR WHEN I realize it's going up, not down. No matter which buttons I push, nothing stops its trajectory.

When it opens, it's on the top floor: *inside the Presidential Suite.*

The Secret Service detail looks at me—really, through me. One mutters to the other, "About damn time! Eagle needed those towels, like, half an hour ago." He motions for me to follow him down a hallway.

Oh, heck, I hear squeals and giggles. The girls are back from dinner already. Thank goodness they're so busy gossiping that they don't even look up when we pass their door.

Before I know it, one of the agents gives two sharp raps on the hall's final door: Lee's suite, I assume.

Which is opened by Lee: in a bathrobe.

His double-take is vaudeville worthy.

He waves off the Secret Service agents but beckons

me and my towels forward, shutting the door behind us. His eyes take me in, top to bottom. "If your skirt were shorter and tighter, I'd be flattered. Instead, I'll accept reality—that somehow my order for extra towels to replace the ones Janie and her entourage stole from my bathroom waylaid you from your formal duties. If you must hurry out, I'll be heartbroken, but I'll understand."

"As a matter of fact, mission accomplished."

"Another Acme triumph, then."

"At least, my portion of it." I shrug. "We won't know if it was a complete success until Jack finishes his call of duty. Or, I should say, his 'beyond the call of duty.' But, hey, he's yet to fail in that department—with any target."

"Ah… gotcha." Lee shakes his head. "I don't know how you—or he—does it."

"At times, we don't know either." I sigh. "At least you know *why* we do it, Lee. I hope it mitigates your revulsion."

"My opinion doesn't count—nor should it."

I look down at my feet. "You're a dear friend, so of course it does."

Gently, Lee takes my hand. "Donna, I'd never judge you. You know that."

"It means the world to me."

We're silent for a while. There is comfort in knowing I don't need to entertain him, nor he, I. We trust that should something need to be said, the other person will be there to hear it, to give loving counsel.

No judgment. Just concern.

In time, he says. "Have a drink with me. You look as if you need one."

"I shouldn't, really." Not on an empty stomach.

And not when I'm so pissed at Jack that I only want to cry.

"I'll give you two great reasons. Both Jeff and Trisha won their chess matches."

"Oh… wow! That's…it's awesome. I should have been there to see them play." I drop onto the couch, hoping he doesn't see my tears.

"Don't beat yourself up. You had your hands full. And they know you well enough to understand why you weren't there."

I nod. But from Lee's concern, he knows he hasn't convinced me.

As he heads to the suite's bar, he vows: "I'll text you their game times when we get to our next destination, Paris. Promise."

Lee grabs a bottle of champagne buried in a silver bucket filled with ice. While gripping the cork and its cage with one hand, he uses the other to rotate the bottle's base. When we hear a gentle *pfffft,* he tilts it at a slight angle before releasing the cork. Not a drop spills until he pours the fizzing liquid into two Tiffany flutes.

I laugh. "Mr. Chiffray, you missed your calling. You'd have made a great bartender."

"That's how I paid my way through college."

I shake my head in wonder. "How did I not know this about you?"

He comes over and hands me a glass before he sits down. "There are times when you surprise me too—when you *astound* me—and I think exactly the same thing. And then I remember the cruel and unusual circumstances in which we met."

"Good old Babette." He hears the malice in my voice. "To deflect her ties with the Quorum, she did everything she could to make Acme suspect you of being one of its assets."

"I was a fool for loving her. Even after I realized we were a mistake, I protected her." Lee sits back. "Donna, you saved me from myself."

"Not before it was too late for her to put you in Carl's path." I lean back too. Bubbly on an empty stomach makes me lightheaded. I can't remember the last time I ate. This morning, on the plane? Maybe. "Well, if we've proven one thing to each other, it's that it was worth taking the leap of faith to trust the other, even when all the warning bells were ringing."

"The loudest of all regarding Babette." When Lee's head lolls in my direction, it touches mine.

"She left you with two things wonderfully irreplaceable: Janie and Harrison," I remind him.

He tilts my face toward his. "Had circumstances been different, imagine the children we'd have had."

A world in which I'm not an assassin, let alone a honeypot.

A world in which I've never met Carl, let alone Jack.

No, Lee, don't go there. That place doesn't exist…

Because I loved Carl—until I knew who he really was.

And I love Jack—

No matter what our jobs entail.

Just as he loves me.

My silence speaks volumes. Lee rises. I take his outstretched hand. But as he pulls me up, I avoid looking him in the eye.

This doesn't stop him from kissing me—

On the forehead.

"You and Eve—how is that going?"

"It's not." Lee looks away. "I think she saw herself as a consolation prize."

"If you think it would help if she heard it from me… you know, that we're just friends—"

From his pained look, I realize it's the last thing he wants to hear. Gruffly, he declares, "It doesn't matter now. She's moved on with someone else."

"Oh!…Anyone I know?"

"Yes, in fact. Mason."

"Wow!" Truly, I'm flabbergasted. "They've only known each other for, what… a week, tops?"

"With what he's been through, I can imagine his view of his time on earth differs from the rest of us. You could see it in his eyes the moment he met her."

I've seen that look in Eve's eyes, too… for Lee.

"Mason is good-looking," I concede. "Not to mention brilliant—and charismatic; inspiring. But let's face it: he's no Lee Chiffray."

Lee's laugh is hollow. "Maybe that's the attraction. While I want for nothing, Mason is digging himself out of a deep emotional hole. He's been through hell, and yet he sees Eve for who she is: someone with such a big, nurturing heart—"

"So do you," I argue.

"She wants to feel appreciated."

"She must know you feel grateful to have her at your side—"

"You don't get it. Eve is happiest when she's with someone who lets her know he can't live without her…." His voice trails off.

"*You need her.*"

"I do. But I took her for granted, so now I've lost her." Lee sighs. "He's asked her to marry him."

"What? … And she said yes?"

Lee nods. "Eve has already given her notice. She'll stay on four weeks beyond the competition and help me vet her replacement." He walks me to the cart. Grabbing three large towels, he holds them up. "Thanks…for these."

I have to lighten the moment somehow. "It's all part of the service."

He doesn't smile.

If possible, he looks even sadder.

Two hours later, Jack is back in our room.

"Wow, that was quick. A real 'slam-bam, thank you, ma'am.'" He knows I'm being sarcastic.

When he flops onto the bed, I shove him off. "At the very least, take a shower."

"I did it…with her."

"Yeah, I know."

"Showered, I mean."

"Oh? Well then, I'm sure you're squeaky clean." I shrug.

I want to taunt him with my visit to Lee's suite. But then I think better of it. As much as I'd like to hurt Jack, his jealousy of Lee has gotten him kicked off a past mission. We need all hands on deck for this whirlwind tour, so I'll save him from thinking the worst of Lee.

Of me.

"Since Hanna didn't know I was already staying here, she asked that I get a room for us," Jack explains. "Obviously, she wanted to keep me out of hers, which must have worked in your favor."

"In *Acme's* favor, yes."

He ignores the frost in my voice. "Ah, good! I'd hoped to buy you the time needed to finish the job."

"All's well that ends well—though I'll bet the boys are disappointed they missed seeing you in action."

"I'm not a performing monkey," he growls.

"You were with Hanna half the night. I'm sure she'd beg to differ."

"Don't do this, Donna. It could have easily been you with some…asset. Some ass-*hole.*"

Or someone who cares enough that, if I loved him back, he'd never compromise himself.

Lee.

I can't go there.

Instead, I reply, "Speaking of asses, was hers as cute out of that dress as it was in it?"

"Hard to say. She wasn't wearing it long enough for me to make a comparison. Imagine how fast she'd have shed a bathrobe."

Wait…*What?*

He stares down at me as if waiting for me to say something.

I don't know what he wants to hear.

I just know what I want him to say:

That, once again, I've been blinded by my jealousy;

That, like me, what he does for love of country repulses him;

That acknowledging I must do it too cuts him to the quick.

That only with me does sex give him pleasure;

That every time he does it, his heart breaks.

And that he knows he's breaking mine too.

But no: he doesn't lash back at the silliness of my jealousy so that we can both pout it out and then apologize—

and then move on to that always bittersweet *fait accompli:* make-up sex.

Instead, Jack gets up and walks out the door.

Perhaps to the room he just left, where he slept with her.

My only solace is that she'll probably lose her job when her bosses find out that their directory was further compromised by her oversized libido.

I'll give Jack credit: he didn't bring her to *this* room—

Into *our* bed.

12

Section

In some chess tournaments, players are paired based on how they have been rated in previous competitions. In fact, "sections" are further divided by rating classes and whether they've played scholastically or not. If they have played scholastically, some levels additionally rate them.

The rated players are also separated by the unrated.

That doesn't mean that an unrated player may not be capable of winning against a rated player. It means the unrated competitor is late to that party known as 'competitive chess play."

Don't expect a kegger—at least not until the tournament is over.

"Ah, Paris! The perfect town to be with the one you love." Dominic and I are standing on his terrace, looking out onto the Jardin des Tuileries. He waves to Jody, who's crossing into the park with Mason, where they're scheduled to meet with journalists. Not only will he talk about his recent incarceration, but then segue into his excitement about the competition, which should make Lee happy.

"I take it you're no longer upset that Mason is tagging along."

Dominic smiles supremely. "Righto, ducky! Had I known he had set his sights on Eve all along, I'd have done somersaults."

I chuckle. "That would have been a sight to see. Well, I'm glad you two lovebirds talked it out. It's the only way to find longevity in your relationship—"

Dominic guffaws. "Says the woman who'd rather cry on the shoulder of the one man she knows her husband despises."

"What are you talking about?"

"Why, your little nighttime tete-a-tete with Monsieur Chiffray!"

"How did you…"

"Darling Donna, the whole team had eyes and ears on you! Not that I'm complaining. Had you not forgotten to turn them off, I'd have never known Mason wasn't wooing my Jody but Lee's Eve. Poor man! Sadly, when it comes to l'amour, some gents just don't know how to express themselves, eh? Albeit, Lee certainly found a way to tell *you* what you wanted to hear." He wags a finger in my face. "Insecure and tipsy is a bad combination in a desperate, love-starved woman."

Jack saw us too.

It's why he mentioned a bathrobe.

Specifically Lee's.

Oh…

Crap.

And why, on the plane ride here, he ignored all my

attempts to converse. Or, more importantly, to make up for being stupidly jealous.

In our line of work, the law enforcement motto is bastardized to "protect and service," preferably with a come-hither simper and open arms—

Not to mention open legs.

And there I was, teasing Jack that our mission team was living vicariously through him! Who'd a thunk Hanna's hardcore rub-a-dub tug wasn't half as popcorn-worthy as my soap opera melodrama?

Because Dominic is casually leaning onto the balcony, it's a piece of cake to shove him over it. His arms flail as he grabs for anything.

A mere second before he finds himself flatter than Parisian sidewalk mérde, I grab his belt buckle.

Just at that moment, my cell pings with a ciphered text—

From Arnie:

The bidder is now identified. Details in 5, my room.

Oh, mon Dieu!

Alas, the dread of coming up with some coherent explanation to our boss for Dominic's four-story fall trumps my anger.

As I yank my British colleague over the rail with all my might, he yelps from the inevitable nut crunch and then drops to his knees, whimpering.

I growl, "And by the way, being smug, stubborn, and clueless is bad form for a man desperate to hold onto the best woman to have walked into his life—and stayed, though Heaven knows why! A bit of relationship advice: get into the habit of expressing your concerns openly with

Jody. Oh, and while you're at it, instead of eavesdropping on your friends, turn off your own damn eyes and ears."

Dominic follows, still groaning in pain.

Jack has already joined Arnie in his suite. Following Ryan's directive, my suite and Dominic's are on different floors from Acme's rooms on either side of the one we know is already assigned to Black Castle—a.k.a. the North Korean bidder.

"Who will be behind Door Number Two?" The edge in Dominic's voice is palpable. This is understandable since he may have to trap the target.

"His name is General Jung Ji-ho, of the KPA—the Korean People's Army," Emma explains. The man's picture appears on the monitor: a short, brawny man, mid-fifties, slightly bald.

Dominic breathes a sigh of relief.

On the other hand, Jack tips his hand to me.

"He flew into CDL on a private plane that came in through Mumbai—something our North Korean contact couldn't give us a heads-up about," Emma continues.

"In other words, we missed our opportunity to initiate Achilles activation at the airport," Ryan says. "We'll just have to intercept him at the hotel before Black King's bidding instructions are relayed."

Jack nods in my direction. "How is Mrs. Craig to make contact?"

Abu and Arnie's eyes open wide. Like me, they'd rightly deduced that Jack has adopted Ryan's frequent use of my married surname—not as a sign of deference but to indicate my current status in his eyes: hog-tied in the woodshed for having committed some random act of egregiousness.

"What little we know about the general is that he speaks English fluently—he was educated in Cambridge—is a teetotaler, lives alone, and keeps to himself," Emma explains.

"That's not much to go on," I grumble.

"We also know he's a very heavy sleeper. If the auction starts soon, this should work in our favor since he's probably jet-lagged," Ryan adds.

"How high will I be authorized to bid?"

"Twenty billion," Ryan informs me.

Emma whistles. "Well, there goes the millennials' Social Security protection!"

"Since North Korea is an enemy state, should Jung win the bid, are we to duplicate the SD Card?" Jack asks.

"Yes, by all means! And believe me, he'll win at any cost. Otherwise, he'll be executed the minute he returns home—if he dares to go back," Ryan declares.

"If he's on his way here already, why don't I get into the elevator with him?" I suggest. "If Arnie stops it between floors, I'll have time to activate Achilles."

"Sure, that works," Ryan replies. "And your elevator contact may give you an opening to visit his room later that evening."

"Since Mrs. Craig is also the United States' designated bidder, is that wise?" Jack asks. "If we win over North Korea and somehow he's been tipped off about that, it may put her in jeopardy."

Hearing that Jack cares about my safety gives me hope.

And yet, because he's doubled down on calling me "Mrs. Craig," perhaps I shouldn't expect him to be the first person through the door if Jung puts me in a chokehold.

Ah, well. If Jack isn't, I'll have all the proof I need that our honeymoon is over.

"Mrs. Craig can take care of herself," Ryan retorts.

Oh…kay. Somehow I'm not feeling the love from Ryan either.

"Jung is now half an hour from the hotel," Emma informs us.

"Showtime, folks." With that, Ryan signs off.

I SPOT JUNG IMMEDIATELY: IN KHAKIS, A NAVY JACKET, AND glasses.

My frock is Carolina Herrera: a lime green bateau-neck silk faille cocktail dress. I've accessorized it with a matching broad-brimmed hat, kitten heels, and sunglasses in the same color. I'm also toting luggage: Louis Vuitton. I move toward the elevator, arriving just before Jung. Immediately, Abu and Dominic, dressed as bellmen, run interference with a couple headed toward us so that General Jung and I can get on the lift before they can join us.

Jung's room is on the fifth floor. Mine is on the sixth. The mirrored elevator stops between the third and fourth floors. As if annoyed, I push the emergency button several times, then sigh.

Most people try hard not to make eye contact, especially if their elevator's walls and doors are mirrored. The general says nothing, but his eyes never leave mine.

Strange.

Seductively I pull out a gloss stick and line my lips. Jung watches intently, but no tantalized smile or lascivious smirk rises on his mouth.

"Activated," Emma whispers in my ear.

The elevator rises again.

When the door opens on Jung's floor, he walks down the hall to his suite but turns around before the doors close on me and tips his hat.

Bingo.

~

"A present." Abu is waiting in my room. He hands me a dress bag. Inside is a maid's outfit, hat, and apron. "Your room key is coded to open all doors as well."

"Well, this certainly makes things easier going forward, if not with Jung." I look around. Jack's suitcase is nowhere in sight.

Noting my surprise, Abu says, "Jack's bunking with me tonight."

"Oh." I think I'm going to throw up. I gulp hard so as not to gag.

"Don, listen…" Abu puts a hand on my shoulder. "Just give him time to cool off."

"Sure, okay, of course I will." My voice sounds strange, even to me. "Abu, you saw what happened too. He has no right to be mad at me! When Lee pressed me—"

"*You did nothing wrong.*" Abu is adamant. "Heck, what you did and said to Lee could have been a conversation with any other close friend, including me: shared a drink, reminisced about our mutual history, commiserated about the woulda-coulda-shoulda."

I sigh. "The big exception is that you wouldn't have fantasized about what it would have been like to have kids with me."

"You're darn right I wouldn't!" Abu scoffs. "Hey, I've

been around your hellions. If anything, I'd suggest putting them up for adoption."

Now I'm laughing—but just to keep from crying. "Admit it! You love them too."

He nods. "I do. It's an honor to be in their lives and watch them grow up. Had Khrystyna lived..." Abu shrugs. "I know I would have changed my mind about rugrats."

Khrystyna Vashchenko was an asset Acme used as my body double. A professional masochist, she doubled as me when I was summoned to do the now-deceased U.S. President Bradley Edmonton's sexual bidding. My subservience to Edmonton was the only way to save Jack, who had killed a U.S. Congressperson, Elle Grisham, at Edmonton's behest, assuming she was a Russian agent.

She was. Then again, so was Edmonton.

Edmonton threatened to have Jack imprisoned for her murder if I didn't join his administrative staff as his personal exterminator.

Ah, good times.

What turned Edmonton on was chaining and then beating women. He almost killed me. Instead, he took Khrystyna's life.

Had he not, she and Abu would have gotten married.

"Donna, everyone you meet—especially those of us who cherish your friendship—has some history with you, including Lee," Abu explains.

"Then why won't Jack accept that?"

"Because Lee makes it all too obvious that he wishes it were more."

"And Jack knows I've told Lee, time and time again, that it'll never happen. Heck, I said it to him again last night! Jack must have seen that."

"He did. But it doesn't mitigate Lee's persistence. Or your close friendship with him."

"I know it must be awful for him," I admit.

"Now, imagine how you'd feel if the dear friend were his."

Shuddering, I mutter, "I'd hate it too."

"Correct. Still, in the back of Jack's head, he wonders if you'd give in to Lee if he caught you in a vulnerable moment—like, now, when you're frustrated with Jack's—well, let's call them job duties—even though knowing that, like him, you're adept at tuning out the part of yourself that feels anything but disgust when you bed traitorous strangers."

"You're trying to tell me that I have no reason to be jealous, but that Jack does."

"Yes."

"Well, you're right." I wipe away a tear. "Not that it matters now. I'll still be sleeping alone tonight...after...*my job duties*, if it comes to that."

Abu groans. "For both your sakes, I hope it doesn't. I was left with the short straw. And for my sake, I hope Jack doesn't snore. Otherwise, he can sleep with Dominic and Arnie."

"Sheesh! *Dominic agreed to bunk with Arnie?* I'm surprised he's not begging me to take Jack back!"

That's only because he knows he hasn't been dumped by Jody. Her door is always open to him." Abu walks to the door. "I tell you, Acme is morphing into *Vanderpump Rules!*"

The words are barely out of his mouth before our cells buzz.

Abu looks at his screen. "Ah, hell, the auction is starting. We'd better go back to Jack's and my room."

I wince at that.

And pray that Jack cools off soon.

Should I lie to Abu and tell him Jack snores?

GENERAL JUNG DOESN'T MESS AROUND: TEN MILLION DOLLARS is his opening bid.

Black Bishop—that is, U.K.— counters with twenty.

White Castle, a.k.a. Hanna, pipes up with thirty million.

White Knight—that is, France—doubles it to sixty million.

The White Bishop—China—takes it to a billion.

U.K. raises to two billion.

Saudi Arabia ups it to five billion.

Jung's bid goes to ten billion.

No one counters.

I do: at the limit I was given: twenty billion.

Jack groans. "Sheesh! Talk about giving away the bank!"

Seeing the panic in my eyes, Abu murmurs, "Look, what she did was fine. Jung must be sweating bricks. Now he has to put up or shut up."

"But...*what if he doesn't?*" The words stick in my throat.

The silence is deafening. *Is it over?*

And then:

BLACK CASTLE
   Thirty Billion

Relieved I've been outbid, I drop to the floor.

Then I remember I also have to duplicate the SD card

from General Jung, a man whose record of kills is notorious: not just personally, but because he has so callously commanded the death of millions of innocent victims.

And Ryan has no doubt I can handle him?

Well then, that makes one of us.

13

Fool's Mate

There just so happens to be a checkmate that can be achieved by Black's second move. It's called the "fool's mate" and is the quickest possible move, bar none—

So yes, you want to learn it!

Again: it can only be made by the black opponent. And for it to happen would be serendipitous because the white player would have to be even worse than you. I mean, JUST TWO MOVES! So, yeah, your opponent would have to be really bad.

Here's how it happens:

First, White moves their f3 or f4 pawn, leaving their king open to a diagonal attack.

Next, Black moves their e-pawn (also known as the king's pawn) ahead to e6, which allows the queen to move diagonally. At the same time, the king is still defended.

Then White moves their g-pawn to g4. (Dumb move, you're thinking. So, really, try not to smirk.)

Finally, Black moves their queen to h4...

And voila—checkmate!

Should fate play in your favor, try to be a gracious winner.

By that, I mean don't leap up and do a victory dance. Your oppo-nent may be the fool, but you like him enough to play a game that's usually a few hours long, which makes you that fool's mate—

So act like it.

THE BOOKSTORE BESIDE THE SEINE IS CLOSED. THE SIGN ON the door says it will open again tomorrow morning at nine. Through Paris' webcams, we watch General Jung follow his coded directions: to reach into the wild ferns growing behind the stall. There, he'll find a small tin canister containing the SD card.

His route was espionage tradecraft at its best. He zigs and zags through the undulating masses: mostly the tourists who fill Place Vendome at all hours. That hour in particular—the shank of the afternoon—was a shoulder-to-shoulder throng. At one point, General Jung joined a group of Asian tourists. He's fully aware that, to unworldly eyes, it's the best way to hide in plain sight.

Not mine. The look he gave me is one I'll never forget.

After a twenty-minute circuitous route, he's back in his room.

A FEW HOURS LATER, ACME VALIDATES HIS SLUMBERING STATE. After augmenting my maid's outfit with a blond wig, deep blue contacts, a nose prosthesis, and a beauty mark, I walk into his room holding four large towels and a few of the hotel's signature pillow chocolates. That way, should I get caught, I at least have a valid excuse for being there.

With a tap of a card, I enter his suite. Thankfully, Arnie has silenced its gentle buzz.

The bedroom monitor's infrared camera shows that Jung's bedroom door is closed. His snores, rocking his bedroom, come at me in stereo via my earbuds. Still, anxiety has unleashed shudders of cold chills and damp sweat. Should I go bump in the night and alert him to my presence, this renowned killer knows the cruelest ways to make me pay for my trespass. Death would be a blessing.

A search of the suite's living room—walls, drapes, paintings, pillows, furniture—turns up nothing. I move on to the bathroom, which also opens up directly into the bedroom.

I go through his leather toiletry bag, opening lids to make sure these items contain the contents described: toothpaste and toothbrush, floss, antacids, disposable razors, comb, hair gel, aspirin, aftershave, jock itch spray, talcum powder, lip balm, petroleum jelly—

And condoms. Lots of them.

He also has a photo of a young woman: perhaps his daughter?

I take the picture out of its plastic frame:

The SD card falls out—

Just as the lights go on—

And I'm slammed up against the wall. Jung has his forearm against my throat. As I struggle to stay conscious, he stares at me—

Then strips off my fake nose.

"Ah, I thought it might be you." Slowly, he eases his arm off my throat. "From the elevator. Donna Stone, of Acme. Am I right?"

I nod. "You know of me?" The question comes out as a raspy whisper.

"You're on my country's ten most wanted list." Noting my grimace, he adds, "Not to worry. I have different plans for you."

I shake off my tremble. "And what would those be?"

"I want you to kill me."

"Beg pardon?"

"Fake my death, as it were. Since I've already transmitted this intel to my country's supreme leader, giving it to you should be worthy of asylum and a place in your Witness Protection Program."

Jung's hotel phone rings.

"It's Ryan. Ask Jung to take the call on speaker," Emma whispers.

I tell the General: "It's for you. Put it on speaker."

"Sold," says Ryan. "General, your death will be announced within twenty-four hours: a heart attack. In the meantime, you're to be held in custody until we verify that the directory is, in fact, the one you retrieved. Two State Department representatives are on their way now to escort you to a safe house. You'll be sent to a black site if the directory is fake. If it's real, we will honor your request."

"My wife and daughter are to join me in Witness Protection," he insists.

"From North Korea?" Ryan asks.

"No. They're already stateside. My wife…we were never formally married in North Korea. When she and her family escaped nearly two decades ago, she was pregnant with my daughter. My communique to her goes through a holy man: my brother is a Buddhist priest."

"So, she knows you will soon join her?" I ask.

"Yes. Each year on our daughter's birthday, I've sent her three mugunghwa—you know them as hibiscus plants or the rose of Sharon—as a show of my love, fidelity, and constant vow to return to her. The price I've paid to honor this vow is high: too many crimes against humanity to count. I recognize this. But it was necessary to earn the trust of Our Respected Comrade Secretary General. And in doing so, I was chosen for this mission." Jung's declaration is tainted with sadness. "What I've done here today is the first step in redeeming myself before leaving this life."

We hear a knock on the door. I open it to two men who introduce themselves as representatives of the U.S. State Department.

As they enter, I leave.

I GET OUT OF MY MAID UNIFORM AND CLEAN UP ANY TRACE OF my escapade before knocking on Abu's door. When he opens it, I see he's alone. "Where's Jack?"

"He should be downstairs by now. Trisha's competition game has just started."

Yikes! Already? I run to the elevator.

I get to the competition hall just in time to hear my daughter say, "Checkmate."

The crowd circling her table—including Jeff and Janie —goes wild.

Anxiously, Trisha scans the throng. She sees Jack first, off to my right, and joyfully beams. Then she sees me. "Mom! I did it! I can advance with Janie and Jeff!"

Darn it—

I missed Jeff's game!

By the time I reach Trisha's side, Jack is already there, as is Mason.

My husband ignores me. His icy eyes stare through me, then beyond me:

Only then do I realize that Lee now stands beside us.

Seeing me, Jeff pulls me over to Trisha, Lee, and Janie. But Jack ignores Lee's nod to join in the photo op.

When Mason hands Trisha her trophy, she hugs him. I know I should smile, but it's not easy to do when one's heart is breaking.

The photographer insists we look at the camera. When he finishes shooting, I wipe away the tears clouding my eyes.

By then, Jack is gone.

I'M PACKING TO CATCH OUR FLIGHT TO SINGAPORE WHEN Emma texts me:

CC NOW

I call into Acme's secure line. Immediately, I'm put into a call with the rest of my team.

Ryan begins: "Good work, mission team. Albeit, it may have been smart to have assisted Donna before General Jung could have caused her to pass out—or worse yet, crush her larynx."

"Not to worry. I was on the other side of the door," Jack assures him. "When I saw she had the matter under control, I felt it was best to leave it in her capable hands."

"I would have done exactly the same, Mr. Craig," I purr. "Especially had I, like you, known our daughter's match had started."

"One loving parent had to be there. Wouldn't you agree, *Mrs. Craig*?" Jack spits out the words.

"Oh, sure, no better way to ruin her high than breaking

the news, "By the way, sweetie, mommy isn't here too—*because she's dead.*"

"Alright already!" Ryan bellows. "Can we leave it there and get on with our mission notes?"

Yep, that shuts us up.

"We've verified the bidder representing French Intelligence—that is, DRSD, also known as Direction du Renseignement et de la Sécurité de la Défense," Ryan continues. "It's Philippe Legrand."

"Ah, yes! Consistently a top three SPILF candidate." Dominic offers.

"What the hell is that?" Ryan growls.

Dominic declares, "It stands for 'Spy I'd Like to—"

"I get the picture!" Ryan runs his hands through what little hair he still has left. "What relevance does it have here?"

"None," Abu declares. "Other than being Dominic's *forte*—saying *petite amusements* at inappropriate times."

"*Tre bon, Mon Ami.* Using two French phrases in one sentence earns you *beaucoup* brownie points," I point out.

You've just bested me with three, *Mon Cheri*—"

"*Au, mon Dieu!*" Ryan hollers. "Keep to the task at hand, folks!"

"The point I was making is that I doubt the Frogs will be bidding for the U.S. directory," Dominic sniffs. "After all, they fought with the Colonies against the Union Jack."

"Unlike you, POTUS doesn't base her assumptions on a two-hundred-and-fifty-year-old grudge," Ryan declares. "If the German bid proved anything, it's that the U.S. has to be prepared that our directory may appeal to any country—if only to be used as a bargaining chip with an adversary who may have deeper pockets but is willing to trade up."

"Then it's settled. Should Monsieur Legrand proffer the winning bid, Mrs. Craig must duplicate the SD card," Jack declares.

"Don't be so anxious to toss her to *that* wolf, old boy," Dominic warns. "His appetite is voracious. He'll devour her and all that implies."

"She's a big girl. She can handle it." I cringe at Jack's flippancy.

"Then it's settled," Ryan replies.

Not.

"Emma, what else do we know about him?" Abu asks.

"As with the previous bidders, he was told to book himself at the competition's hotel: in this case, the Peninsula Excelsior," she replies. "And he's ordered champagne to be placed in his room before arrival. He's also ordered one of the hotel's famous in-suite massages."

Dominic chuckles. "You mean 'infamous.' The masseuses have fingers that do things most patrons can only fantasize about."

"That's your point of entry, Donna," Ryan declares.

"Ouch," Dominic murmurs. "Bad choice of words, considering Philippe's appreciation for getting—and giving—deep, probing massages."

Had he and I been in the same room, I'd have punched that pretty face of his. Instead, I ask, "Does our plane get in early enough for us to intercept him at the Singapore Airport?"

There is silence on the line.

"The Acme plane does, yes," Ryan responds. "Okay, you can all sign off now—except for Donna."

Hmmm. I don't like Ryan's tone.

Even after only he and I are left on the call, Ryan's

pause is long enough to set my teeth on edge. Finally: "
For the rest of the mission, you'll take Lee's plane."

I can't believe my ears. "But… why?"

"Jack feels your focus might be better if you take a break whenever possible. The kids are a great distraction."

"You know what you just said is not only sexist but demeaning, too, right?"

"Feel free to file a complaint with Human Resources."

"Ha! As if that will do any good! I'm a sparrow, remember? They'll snicker, pull out their tiny violins, then tell me to suck it up—literally."

"Granted, they're a jealous bunch. Completely understandable since they push papers all day long dealing with all the infractions you field agents so regularly and callously break. Really, their derision is proof you do your job no matter the consequences."

"Legal or personal," I mutter.

"What was that?" Ryan growls.

"I said, 'Aw, gee, thanks for the backhanded compliment,'" I coo. "As for your irrational rationale for why I'm being relegated to the kiddie plane, I respectfully decline the offer."

"You have no choice in the matter, and here's why: *Jack is your team leader.* I must take him at face value that he's doing what's right for the mission."

As opposed to our marriage.

I sigh. "You know what this is all about, don't you?"

"Are you asking if I give a flying fuck about your personal drama despite it having nothing to do with this chance to save the lives of thousands of our fellow spooks? No, not really."

I sign off.

Then I throw my cell at the wall.

And then I cry.

Jack has never let our personal lives get in the way of a mission. Why now?

When I reach the tarmac, Jerry Cabot, Lee's pilot, beckons me aboard. Taking my bag, he says, "Mr. Chiffray is honored that you're joining us. Can one of the attendants get you a libation?"

It's on the tip of my tongue to say "a good cab, and leave the bottle," but then I think better of it. The only reason my kids have only seen me sober is that I'm a mean drunk.

14

Double Attack

When a single piece is under attack by two of the competitor's pieces simultaneously, it's called a "double attack."

Liken it to both of your kids berating you for something they want despite hearing you say no a million times.

So, what do you do? Stand your ground.

Better yet, attack back. (Threaten no dessert after dinner. It works every time.)

I smile—because Trisha throws herself into my arms.

I laugh—because Jeff is acting goofy to get Janie's attention.

I bury my sadness—that Jack isn't here to enjoy this too.

I stay away from Lee. When he moves closer, I throw myself into a conversation with anyone else within reach.

It's a fourteen-hour flight. I'll pretend to sleep through

most of it. Still, eventually, I'll have to say something to him.

Just not now.

Instead, I corner Eve, knowing that Lee will not come over to us because he finds it difficult to hide his heartbreak when she's around.

The first thing I do is congratulate her on her betrothal to Mason. "How did it happen?" I ask.

She breaks into a broad smile. "I guess you'd call it serendipity. Early one morning—while I was taking my usual sunrise walk on Lion Lair's grounds—I came upon Mason, who'd been out for his run. He'd found a baby bird that had fallen out of its nest and was placing it back where it belonged! When he turned around and realized I'd seen this simple act of kindness, he felt silly for explaining why he was up in the tree. I was incredibly touched by his concern for the bird's survival. After that, it was as if we'd been old friends forever."

"But friendship is a different type of love from passion and trustworthiness, especially in an untried relationship."

Her smile goes flat. "You think we're moving too fast."

"It's not for me to say," I admit. "The first man I loved, I trusted with all my heart. It was passionate immediately. We married in less than a year and were together for five more. Only after he left did I learn everything he'd told me was a lie. This made it harder for the man I now love—Jack —to win me over, though everything he did was trustworthy—although there were times I doubted it because what we do professionally is on a need-to-know basis. Despite this, his actions always proved him worthy of my love."

"It's true that nothing has yet to test ours," Eve admits.

"Then all you can do is let time prove your conviction.

Heaven knows this event must be testing both of you mentally, physically, and emotionally."

"You better believe it." She leans back against the headrest. "I can't wait until it's over."

"Eve, Lee … he'll miss you terribly."

She shrugs. "He'll be left in good hands."

"Yes, he told me you'll stay to help vet a replacement. But I don't think anyone will fill your shoes—professionally or personally."

"That's kind of you to say. If I believed he felt the same way…" She looks out the window. It's dusk, and we're just skimming cotton candy clouds in a darkening sky, turning from pink to indigo.

"His feelings are deeper than merely professional. Surely you must know that. You share mutual trust, respect, and appreciation. He loves you!"

"Yes, I do. And yet, he's not *in love* with me, Donna. You know that better than anyone." Her tone has no bitterness, only resignation.

"What if you're wrong?"

She turns to face me. "I'd have to hear it from him."

So, there's still time.

"Hear what, from whom?" Mason wants to know.

How long has he been standing behind us?

Eve sets her lips into a smile and invites him to join us on the sofa by patting the available seat. "Donna feels I'm wrong to encourage Jeff to keep playing in the competition. She feels he'll be tremendously disappointed should he lose the next game."

I blush—not because what she says puts me on the spot but because she'd prefer to lie than tell Mason the truth.

But since this is good news for Lee, I go along with it. "From what we know of who he'll be up against next, I feel he should quit while he's ahead. That way, he's always a winner."

Mason frowns. "True, the level of play gets harder if, in fact, those who enter later may be better players. For example, his Russian competitor, Mikhail Sokolov, is ruthless. I know this because his father, Pavel, is the director of Russia's Federal Penitentiary system. He went easier on me when I finally agreed to coach Mikhail in chess." Mason's lips curl into a smirk. "Like Jeff and the other players, he can enter one or more competitions. My guess: Mikhail will jump in when we play in Venice."

"And because of his training with you, Mikhail would be Russia's best shot."

Mason nods. "It's the logical way for his father to impress his superiors—other than the vile treatment of his prisoners."

"Specifically, Putin," I reply. "However, if the Russian child loses, are you saying it could cost his family their lives?"

"You know your adversary well, Mrs. Craig."

Hearing my surname, I stifle a wince. At least this time, it's not meant to be a slur. "Please, call me Donna."

"Donna, it is." The tension disappears from Mason's face. "If Mikhail wins in Venice, it will be interesting to see if he shows up for the next game, which is also the final one."

"Yes, in Narva-Jõesuu." Cautiously, I add, "I know you were reticent to join the event. Will you hang in until we get there?"

Mason nods stoically. "I promised Jody—and Lee. As uncomfortable as it will be—so close to Russia—I feel I owe my host, well, everything, in fact." he nods at Eve, who is deep in discussion with Jody; I assume they're talking about Mason's press schedule while he's in Singapore. "If you're wondering if I know about Eve's history with him beyond the professional, I feel you're close enough, both to her and me, to tell you I do. Though I would never hurt Lee, I have to follow my heart. I'm grateful that Eve feels the same way. She knew I felt guilty for coming between them. But then she divulged that Lee's love for you is genuine and too strong for anyone else to matter."

"Eve said that?"

"Why wouldn't she? Eve loves Lee, and she views you as a friend. I thank God she's clearheaded enough to recognize her opportunity for love with me. I'll make sure she never regrets it." He lifts my chin. "How about you, Donna? It's obvious to everyone who sees you together that you have strong feelings for Lee." Mason rises. "And if Jack is willing to walk away, maybe it's because he sees the writing on the wall. Life is too short for regrets. We both know that firsthand."

"Yes, well..." *No!* The last thing I want is for this debacle to be laid at my feet!

"If it hadn't been for Lee taking me in, I'd have never met Eve." He pats my hand. "And if it hadn't been for you convincing me that I should participate in Lee's event, Eve wouldn't have had the opportunity to see me as a stronger person—someone who has something to offer the world and, at the same time, give her the love she deserves."

He rises and heads toward Eve. When he puts his hand on her shoulder, she pats it. This is all the invitation he needs to kiss her.

Lee notices this too. He leaves the cabin.

I don't follow because I don't want him to get the wrong idea, that I see it as my role to comfort him.

Mason can tell himself what he wants to believe: about Lee, Eve, and himself.

As for me, he's got it all wrong:

I love Jack, and I always will. I'll never walk away from him.

Even if Jack thinks otherwise.

I'll just have to convince him of that.

By the time I land, Acme has already activated Achilles on Philippe Legrand.

Whoop—de-doo.

"Piece of cake," Arnie crows. "It happened while he was in the airport men's lavatory. The guy pisses like a racehorse—so long, in fact, that we could have set up Achilles twice over."

"Yes, well, it's a trait for those of us who are over-endowed, as it were," Dominic pronounces.

Abu snorts. "That's an old wives' tale!"

Miffed, Dominic, retorts, "The older women I've pleasured can enthusiastically vouch for it."

"Wishful thinking," Abu mutters.

My team arrives in plenty of time to set up surveillance of Philippe's room too.

Within half an hour of getting to my room—where I'll sleep alone unless Philippe insists on joining me here—the French bidder receives the Black King's text that the bidding for the French operatives' directory is open.

Curiously, Philippe's isn't the first bid. That honor goes

to North Korea. Apparently, General Jung's replacement wants to prove to His Respected Comrade Secretary-General that he's no slouch and bids ten million.

From there, it doubles to twenty million (Saudi Arabia) and doubles again to forty million (China) before Russia stops the nonsense by taking it to a billion.

At that point, Philippe bids two billion.

He and Russia play leapfrog until it gets to fifteen billion.

At that point, Russia goes radio silent.

A moment later, the Black King texts:

Congratulations! You may now go to the Lau Pa Sat Hawker Center, to Stall 52: Whampoa Nanxiang. Pick up a "special order" in your name: the Dragon Roll Special.

That's one of Singapore's famous food markets." Arnie's fingers fly on his laptop keyboard. "I'm looking up Whampoa Nanxiang now… *Hmmm,* there's no 'dragon roll' on the menu."

"Duh! That's what makes it 'special,'" Emma explains.

Philippe writes back:

AFFIRMATIVE

The Black King responds:

Question: You omitted the United States from the bid sheet. Please confirm now that his directive holds. It's your last chance to do so. You have five minutes.

Like me, my team waits silently for his response.

Four minutes later:

Nous participerons.

The Black King responds:

As with your other bids, you'll get the auction invitation at the proper time.

"Blimey! Now the Froggies have turned on America!" Dominic is incensed. "What more proof do you need? There's no trusting them!"

"Get over it, Mr. Fleming. It's not like we didn't antici-pate it." Ryan growls. "Well, that does it. Donna, stay with Monsieur Legrand as long as it takes Jack to get in there and duplicate the intel."

The faint pop of a champagne cork can be heard in Philippe's room.

Damn it, he's already celebrating.

Every street corner in the city sports a webcam, courtesy of Singapore's strict vandalism laws. (Ask anyone who's ever been caned for stealing a street sign.)

Between those cameras and those inside the labyrinthian Lau Pa Sat Hawker Center, we can track Philippe's moves as he follows the instructions. He finds the SD card not in the dragon roll but in a small plastic sleeve between the Styrofoam food box and its paper bag. He slips it into a hidden pocket. Immediately, he goes back to the hotel room—

With a half-hour to spare before his scheduled massage.

During that time, he transmits the intel to his superiors. After they verify receipt, he takes a shower.

Seeing him naked, I see why Dominic is so jealous: the man is a stallion.

I'll time the massage long enough for Jack to find and duplicate the SD card, then leave.

Nothing more.

It's the only way to avoid Jack's derision.

15

Backward Pawn

SOMETIMES, A PAWN FINDS ITSELF ALONE ON THE BOARD, OUT of range of the other pawns in its color, let alone other pieces that might save it from capture. Nor can it safely advance.

Should this happen to your pawn, your best bet is to create a weakness for your opponent. If they are on the defense, you may find a way to defend your pawn.

This lesson can be used in other areas of your life. If you find yourself on the defensive, turn the tables on those who may use it against you. For example, you attend a sale at your favorite department store because the designer purse you've had your eyes on all season is now forty percent off! But—oh, no—there's only one left. Just as you reach for it, another woman does too. Neither of you is going to let go.

Be gracious enough to offer her the difference between the bag's old price and the sale. You can PayPal or Venmo the money. If she takes you up on the offer, of course, she'll need to text you her cell number to do so—

Which means she'll have to release the coveted purse—

And that's when you run like hell.

Finders, keepers. Losers, weepers.

PHILIPPE OPENS THE DOOR CLOTHED ONLY IN A TOWEL THAT covers his waist, hips, and…well, you get the picture.

I smile brightly, making a point to bend seductively as I pick up my folded massage table and carry it inside.

"Monsieur, shall I set up in the…bedroom?' My tone is deferential.

Still, he reads the inference of my pause. With a wide smile, he too answers in English: "My thoughts exactly."

He follows as I roll the table through the suite. When we reach the bedroom's threshold, he pats my ass to guide me in.

Under my uniform.

When I flinch, he roars with laughter.

I'm glad someone finds it funny. "Shall we start with you, face down?"

He looks down at his hard-on. "That may be somewhat uncomfortable."

"Trust me," I purr. "It'll be worth it."

He groans but does as he's told. I spread his legs just a bit then open a vial of heated oil, which I pour on his calves, kneading it into his skin down to his feet, then up to his thighs.

Through my lenses, I see that Jack is slowly opening the front door.

'Bout damn time…

"I'd like you to work my back—below my waist. Knead it harder," Philippe demands.

I rub more warm oil onto my hands, then lay them onto

his buttocks, massaging gently at first; then pressing deeper, harder.

Just as he groans, Jack passes the doorway, on the way to the bathroom. He stops to watch, throwing his head up in a silent guffaw. I lift a hand for a single-finger salute.

Now…please…a thumb massage."

Ugh…

And ruin an acrylic? Not gonna happen.

I look around for a substitute and find it on the night-stand: a Sharpie pen. But the massage table is in the way. Still, if I climb on top of Philippe, it'll just be within reach…

He grunts with pleasure when I put my knee on his back. Then, with an outstretched hand I grab the pen—

And insert it, very gently.

"Deeper," he commands.

O…*kay.*

When I shove it further in, he moans ecstatically.

But then it disappears in the great beyond.

Hmmm. Well…

There are numerous ways in which to pleasure the human body. Huzzah for Philippe for knowing his eroge-nous zones. When the time comes for nature to take its course, I'm sure everything will come out fine in the end.

As a precaution, though, I add two bowls of oatmeal with prunes to his room service breakfast.

"My upper back," Philippe murmurs. "Straddle it and massage my neck…"

To accommodate, I must swing around—

But my left hand is so oily that it slips off the table—

And I find my face on his neck. "Ah, now you're ready to earn that very generous tip, eh, *mon ami?*" he whispers. "Why don't you start by licking me there?"

I do as he asks.

"Now, put your tongue in my ear."

Yuck. Still, I do it.

Suddenly, I feel Philippe's hand: snaking up my thigh and between my legs. Two fingers slip beyond my panties. They yank them down—

But instinctively, I retaliate by twisting his neck: swiftly, to the right. The crack is loud. He lets loose with a blood-curdling scream.

Jack runs to the doorway. I motion him to stay out of Philippe's line of sight.

Not that it matters. His body is convulsing.

His final breath comes with a sigh.

As nature would have it, the pen finds its way out of his body on a flow of putrid flotsam and jetsam.

I roll off the table and push Jack away so that I can heave into the toilet.

ABU, DOMINIC, AND ARNIE COME IN THROUGH THE DOOR that connects Philippe's room to Jack's. While Jack, Dominic, and I look for the SD card and Arnie takes care of all evidence of Acme's hack, Abu looks over the body. Finally, he lets out a soft whistle.

"Don't leave us in suspense," I retort.

"You pinched a nerve in his neck."

"That shouldn't have killed him!" I point out.

"It didn't. But something caused his heart attack. My guess is a blood clot, probably dislodged during the massage."

Jack opens up Philippe's toiletry bag. After rummaging

around, he holds up a pill vial. "You're probably right. He was taking a blood thinner."

"The mini-fridge is stocked with all kinds of fancy French cheeses, too, so, maybe not such a great diet for someone with a heart condition." We can barely make out what Arnie is saying, what with his face stuffed with a wedge of hard cheese.

"Let me see that toiletry bag," I say to Jack.

He tosses it to me.

As I suspected, there's a roll of condoms. Upon closer inspection, one of the wrappers holds something much harder: the SD card.

"Eureka!" I hold it up for Jack to see.

"What made you look in there?"

"Hanna kept her SD card in her birth control case. It was a shot in the dark, but still…"

He smirks. "I guess Acme never got the memo to consider contraception for something other than…well, contraception." He looks at his watch. "Guys, how much longer will it take to clean up Donna's mess?"

Asshole.

"I've pulled all our cameras. Now, all I have left to do is erase any webcam evidence of Donna, and do the same of our departure from here," Arnie replies. "I can do that in my room."

"And I'll be done as soon as you help me get Philippe off this table and move him over to the bed," Abu adds. "That way, he'll be found having died a peaceful death—a novelty in our business."

Together with Jack, Philippe is moved onto the bed. Only the towel covers him.

Dominic lifts it for a peek of the dead man's renowned

fifth appendage. Shuddering, he mutters, "So this is what it comes down to: *'la grande déflation.'*"

We slip out of the suite by way of Jack's adjoining door.

I don't follow the others out into the hall. Instead, I take Jack's hand. "We've got to talk."

He jerks it away. "No, we don't."

"What you think you saw…It was nothing like that!"

"With Lee, it never is, Donna. I get it: that's your story, and you're sticking to it." He stalks the room. "Look, I heard what he said to you! Hell, Donna—he wants to have children with you!"

"I'll admit Lee said something extremely inappropriate. He apologized for it."

"Until the next time." Jack glares at me. "He's a guy. He's testing the waters, seeing how far you'll let him go."

"There won't be a—a next time!"

"Why? Are you going to end your so-called friendship?"

"No!… I mean—he loves Eve…"

"Bullshit! Then why did he let Mason walk away with her? Why doesn't he stop her from making the biggest mistake of her life?"

"What do you mean?"

"Mason is a…a broken man. And he… Damn it Donna! They—Lee, Mason, Eve—they aren't the point." Jack shakes his head. "You don't get it! You're Lee Chiffray's wet, hot fantasy. As long as you're within sight, he's going to pant after you—and you know it. Worse yet, *you like it.*"

"You're wrong! You're the only one I want panting after me! You're the only one I want to love me—to be *in love* with me!" This time, when I take his hands, I don't let him shake me off.

"If that's what you really want, cut Lee out of your life."

"Are you crazy?" I back away. "Forget that I feel as close to Lee as I would a brother, and that he's always been there for me—and for you—at some of the darkest moments in our lives. Would you honestly do that to Trisha—have her cut ties with her best friend since childhood?"

Jack's cold granite stare sends a chill of dread through me. "I'm not asking Trisha to break off her friendship. I'm asking you. If you want to save our marriage, you'll do it."

"Are you implying that I've made love with Lee? Jack, I swear to you: never have we—"

"I know you haven't fucked him." His voice is barely above a whisper.

"Then what is this all about?"

"Don't you get it? The fact that Lee is in love with you isn't what drives me crazy. *It's that you don't mind.* Worse yet, you don't tell him to cut it out!" Jack stares away. "I guess it's because you love it too much."

"As if that will fix everything that comes between us! What's wrong with us goes much deeper than your jealousy of Lee!" I wipe away the tears streaming down my face.

"I suppose you're referring to how you feel knowing that I have to fuck other women—just like you sometimes have to fuck other men."

"Yes, I am."

"Don't you understand? I fuck them. *I don't love them.* What's more, I'm not even making love *to* them!"

"And when I'm in the same predicament—doesn't it make you angry too?"

"Angry, yes. But jealous? No. I feel empathy for you.

And I accept that, like me, you'll go as far as you can to accomplish your mission." The longing in his eyes breaks my heart.

And yet, Jack doesn't walk toward me. He doesn't take me in his arms so that he may comfort me, or kiss me, or make love to me.

Instead, he walks to the door.

When Jack gets there, he stops, but he doesn't turn around. Instead, he says, "Let me know your decision by the time the mission ends. If you need Lee's love—his adoration—then you don't need mine."

16

Unrated vs. X-rated

A CHESS COMPETITOR WHO HAS NEVER PLAYED A RATED GAME *or whose rating has not yet become official within their second month in the U.S. Chess Federation is considered "unrated." Ergo, any games played will also be considered unrated and won't go toward their ranking.*

Interestingly enough, the federation has yet to contemplate the ranking of an X-rated player: one who strips naked during the game or proceeds to act lasciviously.

However, the organization's regulations do have Rule 20G, which asserts: "annoying behavior (is) prohibited," and also Rule 20G1 regarding "inadvertent annoying behavior," which further clarifies that any penalties for such acts are at the discretion of the competition's director.

Which begs the question: should neither the opponent nor the director object, can the naked player's indiscretion continue with the others' approval?

At the very least, T.V. ratings would hit the roof.

~

"You've been avoiding me." Lee's voice comes from behind me.

I'm watching Trisha play Jeff and Janie at the same time. Not to be outdone, Jeff is also playing Genghis, and Janie's other game is with Guang. This is the kids' new thing: playing two games at once.

"It's something Mason says will sharpen our skills," Janie explained. "We're thinking in double-time."

I look up at Lee and attempt a smile. "I've been preoccupied."

"The mission, eh?"

"Yes…No…Partially."

"Ah." Lee rolls his eyes. "Let me guess: Jack is upset because you're flying in style on Air Chiffray."

"You're half right. I've been banished to this posh purgatory because… Well, let's just say Jack felt we'd be less distracted on this op if we weren't in such close proximity."

"The fool. I agree that you're a distracting presence, but it's for all the right reasons."

To all the wrong people.

I can't admit this to Lee since he's the person in question.

"I'll take that as a compliment."

"You should." His eyes roam to the next cabin, where Mason and Eve snuggle on the couch. "Sometimes I wish I could jump ship. Do you think Acme would make room for me?"

"Lee, I don't think…." I stop myself, only because I don't want him to feel blamed for Jack's stupidity. "I'm trying to say that I don't think you should dismiss your feelings for Eve—at least, not yet."

"Why?" My words bring a glimmer of hope to Lee's eyes.

Suddenly I feel guilty. My little white lie is backfiring. Even if I told him he'd be welcomed on Acme's plane with open arms, he'd know I was lying.

Worse yet, it would only make him think less of Jack.

I'm saved from explaining myself by the buzz on my phone: Ryan.

"May I use your office?" I ask.

"Of course. Take as long as you need." He hands me the key.

Surprised, I exclaim, "I didn't know you've taken to locking it."'

"We have precious cargo onboard. I want to keep it that way. Jody's made up for lost time with the press coverage, but it's a double-edged sword. Now, with all the reporters covering our event, we can't afford a tracking or communications leak."

I assume he's talking about Mason's whereabouts.

Despite having lost Eve to him, Lee can still be gracious.

Lee is truly a great man.

Why can't Jack see this?

ACME'S MEETING, A VIDEO CONFERENCE, ALLOWS ME TO SEE all of my Acme team.

So near, yet so far.

I slip on an earbud. Though Lee built the room to be soundproof, old habits die hard.

"The Black King has contacted Japan's bidder," Emma announces.

The face of a beautiful young woman appears on the monitor. "Her name is Himari Enomoto. Officially, she's an investment officer under the Foreign Direct Investment to Japan. In reality, she's an operative with the *Jōhōhonbu*—that is, Japan's intelligence agency."

"Ah!… Well, yes, on occasion, Himari and I have met up," Dominic exclaims.

"In what capacity?" Ryan asks.

"Um… the typical lunge and parry over intel vital to both our countries. 'The Geisha' is her nickname for a good reason. She aims to please."

Dominic's smug smile says it all: she's a honeypot.

"So, I take it you're bowing out yet again?" Ryan's question drips with sarcasm.

Dominic throws up his hands. "Can I help it if I'm better known with *les femme fatales* than Jack? He's been out of commission for quite some time now. Someone had to pick up the slack!"

I scoff. "Is that what you call our marriage—and *the past five years of our lives*—'out of commission?' I beg to differ. He's had his fair share of…of 'lunging and parrying.'"

Staring right at me, Jack declares, "No problem, Dom. I'll intercept the Geisha."

"I say, old man, much appreciated!" Dominic pumps Jack's hand.

So, this is how it's to be from now on?

We'll see about that.

Innocently, I ask, "Who will be meeting her plane?"

"You will," Ryan replies. "She'll be on a JAL one-stop from Tokyo to BKK in Thailand, then onto Mumbai."

"Got it. I assume she's also booked at the Taj Mahal Tower."

"Correct."

"Emma, any luck on tracking who's planting the SD cards for the winners?" I ask.

Emma sighs. "Thus far, no matches. My gut tells me that the Black King is paying couriers to plant the intel for him, which is why we can't make a match."

"A shame, but I'd have done the same," I reason.

"Any other questions?" Ryan asks.

"I've got another," I reply. "Am I'm still relegated to the kiddie car?"

Ryan sighs. "Yes, Mrs. Craig—*until further notice.*"

"Works for me. I'm in great company."

Jack flinches at that.

Serves him right.

Himari Enomoto's limo driver is late because I called in his license plate to have his car towed.

A few of Mumbai's notorious pickpockets stand near the airport's arrival area. They are easy to spot. Three of them—no more than ten, maybe twelve years old—are scouting out the more naive tourists whose purses or bags are an afterthought to their expensive, overpacked luggage.

I point out Himari, already harried and incensed that her limo driver is nowhere to be found, and promise them five thousand rupees—about a hundred U.S. dollars—if they steal her purse and give it to me.

They swarm her and are gone before she knows that they've done it. She panics. But she has no cell to call anyone, so she searches for a security officer.

Twenty minutes later, I find her giving an earful to a

disinterested policeman. I tap her on the shoulder. "From the passport photo, I believe this may be yours? It was over there, by the trash can."

Of course, the currency is gone, but her passport is still there, as is her mobile phone.

Only, now it's armed with Achilles.

She can't thank me enough. Her English has a posh British lilt.

By now, Trisha and Jeff have joined me curbside. We're just about to walk off when her driver shows up too, effusive with apologies. When Himari realizes we're headed in the same direction—and to the same hotel—she offers us a lift.

My children quickly boast of their tournament successes: two wins and one loss each. They invite her to watch their game tomorrow. She demurs. "Alas, I have meetings scheduled throughout the evening and will be gone tomorrow morning."

Through the night, eh? Has Jack already made contact?

Knowing who she is, how will our kids feel should they see her in the hall or an elevator, clinging to their father's arm?

I pray they won't.

I want to blame the Black King for putting us in this predicament, but I know better. Jack and I choose to do it for our country.

Still, I don't want our children to be the collateral damage of our play-acting for Uncle Sam. I don't want my marriage to break up over it, either.

So now I sit and smile pleasantly, listening to Jeff and Trisha explain their favorite chess moves.

The traffic is lousy. By the time we finally get to the

hotel, being pleasant is wearing thin on the Geisha as much as it is on me.

While she's letting off steam with Jack, I, too, will be steaming: about the fact that my husband is with her, not me.

"Good work, Donna," Ryan declares. "Now, take it easy."

He doesn't need to ask twice.

Because this is a travel day, the tournament doesn't start until tomorrow. Lee, Janie, and Eve join us for dinner. "Where are Jody and Mason?"

"Press interviews." Eve rolls her eyes. "No rest for the weary."

Through the meal, I smile and try to seem engaged, as if I haven't a care in the world—despite knowing that, via my earbud, at this very minute Himari has opened the bid on Japan's spy directory at a very reasonable half a million dollars.

Saudi Arabia doubles her bid.

Russia doubles that one.

Not to be outdone, China follows suit.

North Korea now raises it to five billion dollars.

China goes up by half that.

When no one counters, Himari raises it to twenty billion.

China stays silent.

Himari wins.

Well, surprise, surprise. A moment later, she gets a text inviting her to bid on the U.S. directory. After a quick consultation with her superiors, the Japanese show their true colors. No matter the reason—to use the U.S. directory as a future negotiating chit or because it sees its resale value—the *Jōhōhonbu* has elected to participate in our auction.

It doesn't matter. Her goal is to safeguard her colleagues, even at our expense.

And because we feel exactly the same way, Acme isn't going to let it happen.

Jack will make sure of that.

WHAT IS IT ABOUT WINNING AN AUCTION THAT MAKES ONE SO horny?

Is it the fact that you've spent billions of dollars—none of it your own—that makes it such a great aphrodisiac?

When Jack hits on Himari in the hotel bar, she doesn't waste time suggesting they continue their flirting in her suite, where the hotel's complimentary bottle of champagne has been chilling on ice.

From the moment the door shuts behind them, he shows her no mercy: no sweet come-ons and compliments. Only cruel barbs and snide asides. No gentle kisses, sweet caresses, or love pats, but slam-bam-hurt you, ma'am, rough stuff.

I feel sorry for her…

Nah. The Geisha deserves what she's getting. She's living up to her moniker, submitting herself to all he doles out.

It's brutal—yes, for her, but also for me. The cruder Jack is, the more titillated Himari becomes.

And the angrier I get—

Because she's enjoying it.

Begging for it, in fact.

It's distasteful. Demeaning.

Disgusting.

Especially when he spanks her—*really, beats her*—until she cries.

Still… Himari is a sparrow, and all that implies: sexy, yes. Submissive, sure. But also devious at the sport of sex. In espionage, love is part of the game. She knows what it takes to win, and stoops—sometimes on all fours—to conquer.

So, why would she put up with such cruelty from a perfect stranger? Is it because he supposedly doesn't know who she really is?

So what? Neither do the targets she turns—

Or kills.

Does she like it? Possibly. Does she feel she deserves it? My guess is yes.

I feel dirty just thinking about it.

I need a shower.

No, a bubble bath.

I take my complimentary bottle of champagne with me. Maybe, as my grime and dirty thoughts go down the drain, so will my urge to kill them both.

I thank my lucky stars that I'm nothing like her; and that I don't let the filthiest part of my job get to me to the point that I punish myself.

Or worse, that I feel I *deserve* to be punished.

At least, that's what I tell myself.

I'VE JUST CLIMBED OUT OF THE TUB WHEN I HEAR A KNOCK ON my door.

Now some idiot is pounding on it.

What the…

Quickly, I grab my silk robe and tie it at my waist. Instinctively, I grab my gun too.

I hope it's some drunk. With the day I've had, I'm ornery enough to make him dance down the hall to a bullet polka. Granted, it would be *petite amusement*. But, hey, right now, I so desperately need something to laugh about.

But no, it's Jack.

"Go away!" I shout.

The pounding only gets louder.

I open the door through the safety chain. "I said, go—"

The chain's bracket tears from the wall when he kicks it in. I step back with a yelp, just in time to miss being smacked by the door. Still, I'm shocked enough to drop my gun. I'm about to pick it up—

But Jack grabs me.

The next thing I know, he's pinned me to the wall. While one arm braces my chest and his mouth grinds into mine, his other hand works doubly fast: opening his pants zipper, lifting my robe—

And then his hand moves between my legs. Two fingers probe and pump until I'm damp enough—

And then he enters me, slamming into me again and again. But he doesn't allow me to match his rhythm. Instead, he distracts me: fondling my breasts, biting my lip, clenching my ass.

When I retaliate by grabbing his haunches, too, he heaves both my legs to his waist so I'm walking with him.

And then I feel us falling—

Onto the bed. He pins my arms above my head as he

grinds into me. His hand is over my mouth, stifling my moans. I'm climaxing—

But then he pulls out—

Only to turn me over. "I want you on your knees." His whisper is a command.

Apparently, I don't move fast enough, so this time, the slaps to my exposed bottom come with an open palm—

And hard—

Again and again.

My primal instinct is to escape. I rise to my knees—

Which is precisely how he wants me.

And how I want him.

~

I FEEL EVERYTHING:

The sweat covering our bodies. (His? Mine? Does it matter?)

The pulsating throb when you feel like you're being torn in half. (In a *good* way: when every inch of you is heightened by that euphoric sensation only felt during sex.)

His rapidly beating heart. (I know mine beats quickly too. Like the rest of me, it feels as if it's about to burst.)

And I hear everything:

His cascading grunts of anger. (At me? Or at himself because he was too stubborn to admit he was wrong about his accusation?)

His dark curse. (At me. At himself. And…Aw, hell! He just mentioned Lee too! *For God's sake, let it go!* My unspoken prompt is to clench him tightly so that, at the very least, he can finally let…*that…go…*)

When Jack orgasms, he gives an anguished bellow. I

hear my name used in vain. I'm okay with that. If I'm the devil that made him do it—lean into his worst instincts, especially about me—then so be it.

Was this to be some sort of punishment?

Would he be disappointed to know it was pure, unadulterated pleasure?

Whatever it is, my Jack is back—

With a vengeance.

EVEN WHEN WE'RE SPENT OF OUR LUST, I CAN'T QUIT smiling…

Until he gets out of bed.

And zips up his pants.

And heads for the door.

What the…

I sit up. "Hey—where are you going?"

"I think I proved my point."

"What the hell point do you assume you made?"

"That, like most men, I can turn off my feelings during sex."

"Seriously? You didn't *feel* that?"

"Well…I know *you* did."

"Uh—yeah. So, why are you disappointed about that? It was the perfect way to apologize for your little misunderstanding—"

"Is that what you think this is, an apology?" He's laughing so hard now that he has to wipe away tears. "Wow!… Well, so much for women's intuition."

"Then… what was 'this' exactly?"

"Fucking. Plain and simple. Like an op."

"You're comparing *that* to a mission fuck?"

"Exactly." Jack frowns. "What did you think it was?... Jesus! Don't tell me you took that for... *for makeup sex!*"

"No!... Well... Not exactly." I try to tamp down my anger. "I mean, sure, you were rougher than usual... Okay, yeah, you were cruel. Hurtful. Mean. Uncaring. Selfish—"

"Exactly! There you go. That's how my targets feel when I'm with them. You've always wondered, haven't you?" He watches my face, looking for a telltale sign of...

Of what? Relief? Contrition? Gratitude?

I don't move a muscle. I say nothing. I won't give Jack the satisfaction of knowing how deeply he's hurt me—

For being so good at his job.

Suddenly, it dawns on me: what he did to her, and then to me, were variations on a theme:

Conquer. Dominate. Humiliate.

And do it in a manner that allows his conquest to assume it's her fault, not his.

That, because of her innate sensuality, she's driven him crazy in lust.

And leaves her wanting more.

"Lucky ladies," I mutter.

"Wait... You really think so?" Jack reels back as if I've cut him to the quick. "Gee, I guess I shouldn't try so hard to be so...well, bad at it." He watches my face for validation.

If only.

Not that I'll let him know it. "Yeah, work on that, why don't you? It would help if you weren't... I dunno; such a savage, maybe? Oh, and here's a thought: can you make Little Jack go limp? Now, *that* would be cruel." I turn my back to him.

"Sure... I'll work on that. But—well, you know: Mother

Nature has her own mind…Or, I should say Little Jack does."

I fake a snore, hoping he'll take the hint to get the hell out.

"Hey, let me ask you something," His voice, softer now, has lost its hard edge.

"Sure, go for it."

"Do you think about Lee when we do it?"

I turn to stare at him, all the while grinding my teeth to keep from screaming at him. "You aren't being serious, are you?"

"Just…*be hones*t."

"Honestly? Okay." I prop myself up on my elbow. "Jack Craig, I can't hate you more than I do now."

He smirks. "Since you've always been great at deflection, I'll take that as a yes."

"No surprise there. It allows you to keep pouting about something that never happened—*and never will,* as far as I'm concerned."

I see it in his eyes: a glimmer of trust.

I've missed it.

I never want to lose it again.

But when Jack shrugs and walks out the door, I realize I've imagined it.

All I can do is cry.

Because I've lost him for good.

17

Threat

A 'THREAT' IS ANY MOVE THAT CAPTURES ONE OF YOUR *competitor's pieces or is aggressive toward one that is undefended. To mitigate threats, you should:*

(a) Be on constant alert for your opponent's possible moves;

(b) Triple-check your moves; and

(c) Always be more aggressive than your opponent.

The same thing goes for half-yearly sales!

(a) Before the sale day, you should memorize the layout of the store's merchandise, specifically the aisle where you'll find those skinny jeans you covet;

(b) On the day of the sale, get there first, grab them, and run like hell to the cash register.

(c) Wear sneakers, not heels, in case another shopper has the gall to snatch them from your hand. That way, you'll run fast enough to tackle her.

Talk about beating her at her own game!

I TRY TO SLEEP ON THE PLANE RIDE TO BRUSSELS: NOT EASY TO do, considering Janie, Trisha, and Guang's playful chatter.

Sitting in the captain's chair across from me, Genghis grouses, "Why are they winning more games than me? I take it seriously, whereas they're just having…well…fun!"

Hearing him, Mason walks over, taking the seat beside me. "Maybe that's part of the problem. You need to lighten up; to remember that it's just a game."

Genghis nods at Jeff. "He's just as driven as me."

"True," Mason concedes. "But he doesn't act like every bad move or lost game is the end of the world. He shrugs it off, learns from it, and preps for his next competition instead of wallowing in the pain of the last one."

"I don't know if I can turn it off like that," Genghis admits.

"The best way to do it is to channel your energy elsewhere. Before and during competitions, I watch videos of those I'll be competing against. I analyze their moves. What did they do right or wrong? Would I have done the same thing had I been in their seat? Did you know every chess organization has a YouTube channel where you can access previous competitions? In fact, Lee has been recording our event's games so that future chess players can study them too."

Genghis slaps his forehead. "Aw, just great! For the rest of the time, everyone can see how badly I play!"

"Maybe they'll see how greatly you've improved." He nods toward Jeff. "He's watching it now. You should too." Genghis walks over to Jeff and plops down beside him. So that it's easy for him to also see what's on his iPad, Jeff mirrors the game on the cabin's large monitor.

"Hey, so I have a question for you." Mason's cheeks pink up. "While in Paris, I snuck away to Tiffany and grabbed a couple of wedding rings I hope Eve might like. Can I get your opinion?"

Instinctively, my eyes scan the room for Lee. He's sitting with Eve. Their heads are together as they go over something on her computer.

"I…I don't know, Mason! I mean… I really don't think that's a good idea."

"Hey, look: if you're worried about Lee taking it as an indication that you're being disloyal to him, you're wrong. He's accepted that Eve is already out the door. Frankly, from what he told me, he's relieved she's found someone who loves her with all his heart," Mason insists. "Lee never felt that way about her. Only about…" He stops himself in time.

From saying something that I already know, but really don't want to hear spoken aloud:

Lee's feelings for me.

Mason shrugs. "No problem, Donna. I know her well enough to guess she'll flip over both." He winks at me.

That's his way of telling me I'm being silly.

Well, he's right. "Let me see them."

He pulls two ring boxes from his jacket pocket.

I open the first one. Three rings of brilliant round diamonds are mounted on a wide platinum band. I can't help but whistle.

Mason laughs. "Wait until you see the next one."

"Give me a second!" I tease him. "I still have the glare in my eyes from this one."

The second ring is more modest: a gold band surrounded by tiny diamonds. Its center is tapered so that the ten-carat multifaceted diamond on its band nestles into it.

"Wow!… Just… wow," I murmur.

"So, which will it be?"

"Which is the one you think she'd like best?" I insist.

"I think she'd go with the first…but I hope she picks the second."

I nod.

From my bag, I pull out Jack's weighted heads quarter. I hold it up for Mason to see. "Let's say heads, you give her the second ring."

He laughs. "Sure then, flip the coin."

He laughs even harder when the coin lands and he sees he's won.

"Okay, wish me luck. Tonight, at dinner, I'll know if she likes it too."

Elated, he walks off—

Right past Lee, who has been watching us.

I feel my face heating up.

It's still warm by the time Lee reaches my side.

"I hope you were helpful." His tone is flip and frosty.

Well, hell, I deserve it. I sigh. "Are you putting me in the doghouse too?"

"What do you mean by that?"

I shrug. "I'm already getting the cold shoulder from Jack. Now, to get it from you too—"

"Jack's a fool." Just as flip. Just as frosty.

"Don't… *don't say that about him.*"

"Now, you're defending him?" He takes the coin out of my hand. "Let's play a game. Heads: you leave Jack for good. Tails: you go back to him."

"That's… a lousy game!"

"All of life is a lousy game." Lee's eyes move to Eve, who has Mason at her side.

"Come on, Mrs. Craig. The odds are even. So what will it be?"

But the odds aren't even. When I flipped it for Mason, I gave him what he wanted. If I flip it now, Lee gets what he wants—or what he thinks he wants.

But it's not what I want at all.

I want Jack.

I want his love, his trust, his fidelity.

And he'll get the same from me too—

If he still wants it.

I look up to find Lee staring down at me. Hearing his steely laugh, Eve and Mason look over.

"Don't worry, Donna. I already know how you'd answer." He sighs. "Jack is one lucky guy. I hope he admits it to you soon. Otherwise—"

My cell buzzes with Ryan's ringtone: *Chopin's Funeral March.*

"Apropos," Lee mutters. He hands me the key to his office.

Meekly, I ask, "May I have my coin back, too?"

"Heck, no! A weighted coin is always useful, especially if you ask the right question."

"You knew it was weighted?… But…how?"

"Janie lent it to Trisha last week—who lost it for a while. Thank goodness she found it again, just in time for Janie to win it back from her." He thinks for a moment, then hands it back. "Keep it. Heaven knows you need it more than anyone. But don't tell Jeff the girls had them. Otherwise, he'll figure out why he never got to move first on the board."

"IT'S VERY KIND OF YOU TO JOIN US, MRS. CRAIG." Ryan's annoyance booms loud and clear through my earbud.

"So sorry, Chief."

Ryan groans at my meekness. Is there anything I can say or do that won't get me in hot water with the man?

Jack is smirking.

Well… fuck him too.

This brings to mind our last liaison.

Which puts a smirk on my face…

"I just got word that The Lotus Blossom will be the Chinese bidder," Ryan informs us.

"My Lord! The infamous Lotus Blossom!" I've never heard Dominic so reverential.

"I'm not familiar with this operative," I admit.

"You're showing your ignorance, ducky!" he chides me. "Lotus Blossom is… well, she's legendary!"

"What do we know about her?" Jack asks.

"See? I'm not the only one who's never heard of her," I exclaim.

"Not much," Ryan concedes. "Except that she cut her teeth—and a few throats— in the last few years of Chiang Ching-kuo's presidency and has navigated every Chinese regime since."

"In what capacity?" I ask.

"The usual," he replies. "Diplomatic Envoy was her official title, but in some cases, mistress or sparrow was implied. Her biggest claim to fame is the brainchild of a so-called charm school for female Chinese intelligence operatives. Like herself, she demanded that admission criteria include perfect English and college educations from top-notch schools, usually with degrees in economics. Most of its graduates were born either stateside or in the U.K."

"Do we have a photo?" Abu asks.

"Unfortunately, no," Emma admits.

"Age-wise, by now, she must be in her early to mid-sixties," I reason.

"That does narrow it down considerably," Emma replies.

"Any other known habits?" Jack asks.

"Let me see…" We hear Emma tapping away on her computer. "Ah, well… I don't know if this helps, but an operative who was once interrogated by her remembers one distinguishing feature during his three days of torture by her: she drank a rose-flavored tea that was sold by the East India Tea Company."

"How did he discern that?" I ask.

"He recognized the smell: roses. She taunted him that it was the only good thing to come out of his country."

Abu whistles. "Where was he from?"

"Iran."

"That's not much to go on," Dominic mutters.

"Sorry," Emma huffs. "It's all we have."

"It's a ten-hour flight for us," Arnie reasons. "If she's coming from Peking, it's also a ten-hour flight. If she comes from Beijing, it'll take a couple more hours beyond that. So we should be in place before her."

"That doesn't help us. An airport intercept is out since we don't know when she'll get to Brussels. And for all we know, she may already be there," Abu points out.

"You'll be staying at the Hilton Brussels Grand Place Hotel. ComInt has already hacked the hotel's security system and is analyzing all guests' features, particularly those with Asian characteristics," Emma explains.

"The biggest issue we face is whether we can activate Achilles on her cell before the auction begins," Ryan reminds us. "The sooner we identify her, the quicker we can address that problem." He sighs. "You'll be on the ground in another seven hours, so get some rest, folks."

BY THE TIME WE'VE LANDED, COMINT STILL HASN'T IDENTIFIED any hotel guest who might be Lotus Blossom.

Not good.

We've just arrived at the hotel when Emma calls a conference. "Okay, well, a guest who could be her just checked in under the name of Miranda Smythe-Barrington. I'm uploading the photo we got from the hotel security cams now."

The woman in the photos is slim and tall, about the right age, and dressed in couture. Her platinum blonde hair is fashioned in a chignon.

Her eyes are almond-shaped but light.

"Her features aren't Asian, per se," Jack points out.

"Neither was Faina Chiang Fang-liang, who was the First Lady of China as the wife of Chiang Ching-ku," I point out. "She was born in the Russian province that is now Belarus and orphaned at a young age."

Arnie's mouth drops. "How do you know that?"

"When Jeff was in the eighth grade, I had to quiz him on that portion of a world history test." I pat his arm. "You'll be doing the same for Nicky."

He rolls his eyes. "I can't wait."

"As if," Emma mutters. "Mama to the rescue."

"Thanks, hon." Arnie is genuinely relieved.

"Why would you think she's our target?" Jack asks.

"Because she ordered a tea service, but she said she'd brought her own tea, and to just bring hot water."

"Since we've got nothing else, at the very least, we

should give it a shot," Ryan says. "Dominic, since you're the only one who knows how to serve a proper tea, you're on deck for the Achilles activation portion of the mission. If she wins, we'll play it by ear as to who copies the SD card of the Chinese directory."

Dominic sighs with relief.

Not me. This means Jack will act as the raven.

Unless she asks for a second tea service.

Fingers crossed.

Emma called it: Ms. Smythe-Barrington is delighted with the hotel's tea service: "Goodness, it rivals the Saville's!"

Acme has secured only one room adjacent to Lotus Blossom: thankfully, the one with the adjoining door. Unfortunately, we've had no time to set up surveillance in Lotus Blossom's suite, so we can only watch her reaction through Dominic's lenses.

"If Madame has her preferred tea, I will be delighted to play Mother." Dominic's tone is both deferential and polite.

From her QEII-sized purse, Lotus Blossom takes out a tea tin labeled Rose Buds Infusion made by the East India Tea Company.

Emma's guess was correct: she's our target.

"By all means." Lotus Blossom hands him the tea.

Dominic takes his time. He dips a tiny scooper into the tin, taking just enough loose leaves to fill the strainer, which he places into the malachite teapot.

As it steeps, he offers elaborate descriptions of each of the delicacies on the Mackenzie-Childs three-tiered stand:

tiny sandwiches (cucumber, beef, chicken, and Burford Brown egg), savories (caviar, smoked salmon, and lemon cream cheese for bagels; tomato, pesto, and basil on brioche) and various sweets (lemon curd tarts, hot gaufres, chocolates, and tiny frosted cakes) as well as freshly baked scones with Cornish clotted cream and strawberry preserves.

Every now and again, Miranda exclaims, "How scrummy!" Finally, after perusing the veritable feast, delicately with a manicured finger she points out those items that have caught her fancy so that he can prepare two plates: one sweet, the other savory.

Or is it Dominic causing her to salivate?

He'll soon find out since she has requested that he buttle her room service dinner later this evening.

When Arnie gives Dominic the all-clear on Achilles' activation, he's out of there in a shot.

Before he reaches the elevator, Ryan declares: "Tonight, let me encourage you to be as solicitous as possible and all that implies."

CHINA DOMINATES THE BIDDING, STARTING OFF IMMEDIATELY with fifty million dollars.

The United Kingdom raises it to seventy-five.

Japan takes it to one hundred million.

Saudi Arabia doubles that to two hundred and fifty million.

"Be a shill and double that," Ryan encourages me.

I do as he insists. We're playing with house money since China will hold onto it one way or another. Still, it'll be fun to watch China sweat it out.

China holds onto it for two hundred billion dollars when all is said and done.

Lotus Blossom is told to pick up a dozen roses being held under her code name at a local florist shop.

Acme tracks her via Brussels' webcams as she strolls to her destination. A few minutes later, she emerges with a long thin box.

Half an hour later, Emma intercepts Lotus Blossom's room service order: filet mignon, rare, a bottle of Moët & Chandon Dom Pérignon—oh, and a tall crystal vase.

"Dominic, you're up," Ryan declares.

By the time I slip into Lotus Blossom's suite, my colleague has already sweet-talked her into the bedroom.

Now is the perfect time for the maid—*moi*—to deliver fresh towels and pillow chocolates.

From what I can see via his lenses, Lotus Blossom asks him to "pop her bubbly." He nods silently and takes the bottle he brought for her. She pulls one hand away. By putting it on her breasts, she makes it clear she has something else in mind.

She puts her hand on his bottle rocket when he freezes at the inference.

Looking down through his lenses, all watching can see she's succeeded: he's ready to pop.

He can't help it. His body naturally responds to the expert fingering of a femme fatale whose ability to purr, stroke, and fluff is the stuff of legend.

By the time I've copied the digital directory, their sounds indicate that they've moved on to rougher stuff. From what I gather, she's bound him to her bed's posts with sheer chiffon scarves. Her naughty talk prompts his coarse growls.

I'm just about to sneak out the door when I realize something isn't right. Usually, while doing the horizontal tango, Dominic talks oh so pretty: Shakespearean sonnets that, when he orgasms, rise to stentorian decibels. Instead, I hear gasps, then choking.

Fighting my gag reflex, I take a peek inside Miranda's boudoir:

The object of her affections—or, I should say, torture—isn't Dominic.

It's Jack.

But one of the scarves that have him tethered to her bedpost is now tied around his neck.

He's red-faced and choking.

I bite Lotus Blossom's wrist, breaking her grip on the scarf—

And wrestle her off the bed.

Scrambling up, she grabs the champagne bottle from the table and breaks it against the edge of the chiffonier, leaving its neck jagged.

By now I've leaped up, too, feinting left when she jabs right. Her next parry is straight at me. But I dodge it, leaving her low and moving fast enough that a hard kick slams her into the wall—

And she blacks out.

I don't waste any time. Pulling one of the long scarves from around Jack's wrists, I bind her hands behind her back before tying them to her legs, leaving her hogtied. Then I drag her into the bedroom closet and lock the door.

By now, Jack has untied his ankles and is dressing.

"You're welcome," I declare as I walk out.

YES, I'M EXPECTING A TAP ON THE DOOR.

I open it through the chain. "If you kick it open this time, don't expect me to save you again."

Instead, he passes me one of Lotus Blossom's long-stemmed roses.

He's got the vase filled with the rest of them too. "Peace offering," he murmurs.

I unchain the door. "Accepted." I motion him in.

He steps in reluctantly.

Okay, I get it: all business. "What tipped her off to you?"

"Lotus Blossom teaches a course at her charm school on known enemy assets. I'm one of the course's trading cards. So is Dominic."

I snicker. "You're kidding, right?"

"I only wish I were. I now feel as if I have a target on my back." He frowns. "Donna, I think you're also in her deck of cards."

"If that's the case, the U.S.'s digital directory is a treasure trove of America's Most Wanted spies." I sit down on the bed.

But Jack keeps standing.

Ah. So, even after saving his life, nothing has changed between us.

At least, not as far as he's concerned.

All I can do is shrug it off. "What does Ryan want us to do with Lotus Blossom?"

"Believe it or not, he says to let her go. Better that China thinks she safeguarded its directory. And besides, she'll be too ashamed to admit she may have compromised it. They're pretty rough on operatives who fail."

"In that case, maybe we can turn her."

"Funny you should say that. Ryan thought the same thing." Jack smirks. "He thinks Branham can play this altercation to our advantage, perhaps arrange another run-in between her and me—as if it's unplanned, of course."

"You two looked as if you were having fun. I'm sure she'd enjoy convincing you she could be turned."

He shakes his head. "Doubtful. In China, there's no way to retire gracefully. From day one, its agents are pitted against each other, like *Game of Thrones*. But knowing how they treat defection, let alone treason, she wouldn't dare. You've got to stay in the game or die trying. However, because of her reputation, she may possibly convince them she could be a triple agent."

"Interesting thought," I murmur.

He hesitates as if he wants to say something—

But instead, he walks out the door.

From now on, is this how it's to be between us: frigid formality? Friendly but not familiar?

Maybe *I* should consider retiring.

As soon as I think about it, I shake off the thought.

Without Jack, what would be the purpose? I'd just be lonely.

And bitter.

Like I was before we met.

I may be lousy at relationships, but at least I'm good at something.

18

Isolated Pawn

---

*A*N *ISOLATED PAWN IS ONE WITH NO OTHER PAWNS WITH ITS same color in any adjacent squares. Thus, being alone, it is vulnerable to capture.*

Think back to the time, perhaps in elementary school, when you had yet to make friends and were an easy target from all sides.

Now you get it.

Should your pawn get captured, the good news is that should one of your other pieces—even another pawn—reach the back row of your competitor's, you may be able to replace it with another captured piece, even your queen.

Sort of like how you felt when you walked into your ten-year class reunion and realized you were much more successful and prettier than your other classmates.

Now you get it.

～

For once, I'm glad I'm not on the Acme plane as it wings its way to our next destination: Rijeka, Croatia. Even holding my earbuds at arm's length, I can still hear Ryan bellowing at Dominic.

The dressing-down—for shirking his duty when it came to Lotus Blossom—comes with a warning: "come hell or high water, the next Achilles activation is your mission. And if you pass on it, you're out on that refined arse of yours, got it?"

"But…MI6 has Teddy doing its bidding! She and I… we have a history!" Dominic declares.

"All the more reason the target will be yours," Ryan insists.

"She'll know why I'm there: to steal the intel," Dominic warns.

"You're full of shit. Remember, you have every right to be there. Your girlfriend is running the youth chess competition in the hotel, for God's sake," Ryan reminds him. "You can act pleasantly surprised that Teddy is in Rijeka too. Hell, with Jody as your cover, you can even play hard to get."

"Ah!… Righto." By Dominic's tone, it's obvious that he's still not onboard.

I chime in, "Ryan makes an excellent point, Dom. By introducing them, you show both women that neither is a threat to the other. Exes don't like it when the current girlfriend is suspicious for absolutely no reason."

"But of course, you're right! Why, Jody would never assume I'd been anything but faithful!" he insists. "Because, unlike you, I don't lead astray those who pine after me with salacious inferences of sweet nothings—"

What a pompous oaf!

I fume, "Just what exactly are you implying?"

Dominic shrugs. "Why, nothing at all, darling Donna. Far be it from me to pass judgement on your nonstop flirtatiousness—"

"You're calling *me* flirtatious? Well, now, that's truly something! Talk about the pot calling the kettle black—"

He continues, "And then there's your desperate attempts to cling to any show of friendly affection, no matter how benign—"

"You bet it's benign!" I stare pointedly at Jack. "What?....Wait! I do not 'cling desperately'—"

"Sweet lady, take the compliment!" Dominic chides. "What I'm saying is brava for owning your self-indulgent silly behavior! It's the first step toward moving away from it—especially in light of your current marital upheaval—"

I sputter, "Wait a gosh darn moment! How did Ryan's dressing-down of you suddenly become about me?"

The others quickly find reasons to look elsewhere: anywhere than at me.

I expect it of Jack. The smirk on his smug mug shows he's enjoying my dressing-down. As for Arnie, he's perpetually clueless. But at the very least, Abu should be standing up for me!

As if reading my mind, Abu pipes up, "Come on, Dominic, cut her some slack. It's not as bad as all that. When women get to a certain age—you know, when they aren't as cute and…well, as *perky* as they once were—they can get desperate for compliments. Any little show of attention is catnip to them—"

I'm no longer…*perky*?

I sit up straight. "Thanks, pal—*for nothing*."

"Guys, seriously, the last person who we should pile on is Donna. I mean let's face it. This hasn't been the easiest mission for anyone, not the least of all her." I'm touched by

Jack's empathy. "I'm not just talking about that whole 'bloom off the rose thing' either—though I'm sure that's what's made her even more desperate for affection from anywhere she can find it—"

"How dare you, Jack Craig! You know better than anyone that my…my 'bloom' is very much still, er, rosy—"

"Perhaps, milady, thou doth protest too much?" Dominic's stare implies he actually believes this.

"Don't you 'milady' me! When you see me next, you better run in the other direction, and fast, because I'm going to—"

"Goodness! I'm feeling better already about introducing Teddy to Jody! Having me in common is a perfect introduction to what could be a lifelong sisterly bond—"

"If one of them doesn't kill you first," I mutter. "I may beat them to the punch."

"—not to mention they are two peas in a pod!" Dominic exclaims. "Women with such refined taste have no need for jealousy. Neither is attracted to men with the Neanderthal tendencies exhibited by the distastefully oafish men *you* seem to attract—"

At the same time I shout, "How dare you!" Jack mutters, "Hey, wait a minute, asshole—"

"*If you allow me to finish*, what I am attempting to say"—now Dominic is practically shouting—"is that you have no need to feel guilty over your past behavior, no matter how unsavory. Mrs. Craig, one anticipates it—more to the point, *one expects it*—from someone with your…shall we just call it a lack of distinction? It's why you do your job so well. You so completely embody the trollop, the wench, the whore, the harpy—"

"Ryan, did you hear that? He just called me a—"

"—and with such aplomb! Sadly, as we're witnessing,

your adeptness at the role has a wee downside on the rest of your life. Which brings up a delicate question: considering the present circumstance of your marriage, would you feel more comfortable if we went back to addressing you by your maiden surname?"

It's this very lack of distinction that causes me to shoot him a one-finger salute before hanging up.

I'll let the boys handle this mission on their own.

I need a drink.

But not in front of the kids.

I smuggle a bottle of Zin from the galley and head for Lee's office.

~

THANK GOODNESS NO ONE ELSE IS THERE.

At least, I'm not aware of anyone, until I hear a sob—

And notice that Lee's desk chair is facing away.

Softly, I murmur, "Hello?"

This elicits a long sigh. Then, slowly the chair turns around:

I'm facing Eve.

"I'm so sorry! I didn't know…" I walk backward toward the door.

"No…please! Stay! I…" Eve buries her face in her hands. "I…I just don't know what to do." From her lap she pulls out the two ring boxes. "I need to decide."

"Oh!… Well…" Should I tell her that Mason had already shown me the rings to get my opinion?

Nope, that won't do! The last thing she'd want to know is that he asked my advice, of all people—

The one person who Lee had been pining over, all these years.

The one person who stood in her way of happiness…

Until now.

Until Mason.

So then, why isn't she happy?

"I would choose the one that you love most."

"But…I don't… I don't want to hurt him."

I walk over and take her hand. "Believe me, Eve. Mason will love whichever ring you choose."

She stares at me. "The ring?… Oh… No! I meant… I'm afraid of hurting *Mason*!" She drops her head to her lap. "Donna, I'm… *I'm still in love with Lee.*"

With Lee.

"I…I couldn't be happier to hear it!"

"Do you really mean that?"

"Yes. Because… I know how Lee feels about you."

"As opposed to how he feels about you?" She looks me in the eye.

"He loves you, Eve. He was heartbroken for having foolishly waited so long to tell you how he can't wait to spend the rest of his life with you."

"He told you that?"

I nod. "Truly, the decision is yours."

For the longest time we sit silently while her tears fall in her lap.

In time, she rises. "I must find Mason."

I nod. "You're doing the right thing to call it off now. Had you let it drag on—"

"You don't get it." Her frustration comes with a shake of her head. "My last mistake was that I waited too long for someone who couldn't see me for who I am. Mason knows me. And unlike Lee, Mason knew the moment he met me that he loved me. And he'll do anything to make me happy. I owe it to him—"

"The only one you owe is yourself. Don't spend the rest of your life with someone out of obligation. I watched Lee do that with Babette—supposedly for the children, the country, and though he won't admit it, to assuage his pride. Are you sure that isn't what you're doing now: assuaging your pride?"

She wipes away her tears. "I...don't know. I only know that I'd rather be with someone who loves me unconditionally, who loves me for being his reality than one who'd rather wait for his fantasy."

I have no comeback for that.

Especially since I allowed Lee's fantasy—of me—ruin my perfect reality.

AFTER SETTLING INTO OUR SUITES, THE KIDS HEAD DOWN TO one of the massive convention rooms, where other children who've come from all over the world have already congregated, playing impromptu games of chess. Many of Lee's moderators and event coordinators meander around, answering questions when called upon.

Jack, Abu, and Arnie are hanging out at the hotel's bar.

Dominic has shuttled Jody to a little out-of-the-way restaurant: ostensibly for a romantic dinner for two. In reality, he's already been tipped off by Emma's team that Teddy is there as well, having dinner alone.

Like the rest of my team, through Dominic's eyes and ears I hear and see it all:

He has his arm around Jody's waist: better to steer her toward Teddy's table and into her sightline.

Teddy looks up. Her eyes widen when she recognizes him, and then they narrow when she sees his sweet kiss on

Jody's cheek. A moment later, his eyes scan the room, only to catch Teddy's eye. Dominic fakes a double-take, breaks into a grin, and leads Jody over to her, murmuring something in her ear that has her smiling.

Teddy's response is a wry grin. She holds out her hand. As Jody takes it, Dominic makes the introduction: "Ah, the two women who are nearest and dearest to my heart! Jody, my sweet, this is Teddy Twala. She was once the love of my life. In fact, she's the only woman besides you who can claim that…Well, except for one other who shall go nameless, since my infatuation was never reciprocated."

Needless to say, his audacity astonishes Jody. But instead of being hurt, she laughs as if she's been just told a hilarious joke and pats the hand she now holds. "I guess we're in rare company, Ms. Twala."

"Please, call me Teddy."

"Then I hope you'll call me Jody."

"It would be my pleasure." Teddy motions for them to sit. "Tell me, Jody: shall we compare notes?"

I HATE TO ADMIT IT BUT DOMINIC IS RIGHT: COMPARED TO Jody and Teddy, I'm immature and insecure.

For the next hour and a half, no stone is left unturned. One moment they are laughing at his pick-up lines, the next they are comparing his most annoying habits.

They coo over the random acts of kindness he demonstrated (for Teddy, boxes of her favorite French chocolates; for Jody, exquisite lingerie) and compare notes on their handling of the hissy fits he threw over inconsequential slights. (Jody laughs at him, whereas Teddy had walked out.)

Both are impressed by his sexual prowess, but Jody warns him that should his eye ever wander, he need not come home to her. She'll be long gone.

Is Twala thinking of what might have been had she chosen Dominic over King and country?

Will Jack soon make the same choice? Only time will tell.

As she takes her leave, Twala says, "Jody, you are exactly who Dominic has been looking for all his life. In my native country, Tunisia, we have a saying: 'If the full moon loves you, why worry about the stars?' Your light is so bright that Dominic's heart will never again know darkness."

And then she kisses both Jody and Dominic goodbye.

Dominic's wistfulness is understandable: he treasures his memories of Twala. By activating Achilles on her phone, he's betrayed her.

All may be fair in war, but not in love.

I WAIT LESS THAN A MINUTE BEFORE FOLLOWING TWALA BACK to the hotel, always keeping her in sight.

Suddenly, in my ear, Ryan exclaims, "Damn it! Hanna is here! Her Achilles ID just went live with news to her superiors: her bid in the U.K's auction wasn't high enough!"

"If so, then the auction was happening while Twala was eating with Dominic and Jody," I reply. "Teddy is just making her way back to the hotel now, and she's in no rush. In fact, she's window shopping."

"Then there must be another MI6 operative involved," Abu reasons.

"We're running facial recognition software on guests who have checked in within the past eight hours against the MI6 operatives already in our database," Emma explains. "But if it's not someone we already know—"

"It is," Jack declares. "Daniela Baxdale-Cuthbert has been sitting in a high booth in the back of the hotel's bar. I didn't notice before because she's wearing dark glasses and a scarf over her head—"

"Got her spotted," Emma assures him. "We'll follow her via the city's SecCam network to the pick-up point."

"Jack, when she returns, you're up at bat," Ryan commands.

"Not Dominic?" I express this disappointment without thinking.

"He's done his bit," Ryan replies. "And…so has Jody."

Jody's threat resonated with our boss.

Lucky her.

Lucky Dominic.

As if reading my mind, Ryan adds, "Donna, take the night off. Abu, after she retrieves the directory, you're to cover Lady Baxdale-Cuthbert's pillow chocolates."

"MAY I JOIN YOUR PITY PARTY?" LEE'S VOICE COMES FROM behind me.

I got to the hotel bar long after Dannie left on her retrieval mission. In fact Jack and the rest of my team are already gone too.

Thank goodness! While wallowing in drunken grief, I prefer to be alone.

For Lee's benefit, I point to the martini glasses in front of me: Another four, lined up behind it, are empty. "Only if you're buying. Can you believe it? The bartender has cut me off! I guess he doesn't like my singing. And he snubbed my idea of turning this joint into a karaoke bar."

"The nerve of the guy." Lee sits down beside me. "Don't tell me you're drinking on an empty stomach."

I nod. "Olives only. If I want to stay a svelte femme fatale, I've got to cut calories somewhere."

"It's not the only thing you're qualified for, you know."

"Isn't it? I mean, let's face it: would you want me to take your customer service call?"

It's good to hear Lee laugh again, even if it's at my expense.

He gets serious too quickly. "The barkeep is right. Remember, Jeff and Trisha have early games tomorrow. You wouldn't want to sleep through them. Or worse yet, show up hungover."

I frown. "That's no way to win a girl's heart: shaming her into sobriety."

"I'm not trying to win your heart. I'm just trying to keep you from regretting your inevitable hangover."

"You're right on both accounts. I will have a hangover. And I'm not your girl, so it's a good thing your heart is elsewhere."

"I'm your friend, though, so allow me to save you from yourself." Lee tosses a few big bills at the bartender. "And to walk you to your room."

I don't argue with him—but only because it means opening my mouth, and I'm afraid of what might come out of it:

Rants over losing Jack.

Rants about loving Jack regardless.

Rants about hating one of his old girlfriends—one whom I'd assumed was my friend.

Instead, I keep my mouth shut—but only because I'm afraid I'll throw up if I open it.

At least, that doesn't happen in the elevator ride up to my floor.

Or while Lee walks me to my door—

Which just so happens to be down the hall from Dannie's.

I only know this because Jack is kissing her in front of it while I fumble to find my room card.

Just as Lee gives me a chaste peck on the forehead, Jack looks up.

And that's when I throw up.

19

Perpetual Chess

When one king cannot escape an endless series of checks
—and yet, cannot be checkmated, the situation is known as "perpetual chess."

In the past, this resulted in a draw. However, the hardcore chess competitor will opt for either:

(a) the threefold repetition rule, in which a draw can be declared if the same position occurs three times during the game; or

(b) the fifty-move rule, where if, after fifty moves, neither player gets a checkmate, the game ends in a draw.

Then there are those who don't play professionally and eventually want to get on with their lives. If you're in this category, let me make a suggestion:

There's no shame in a draw.

Just like in real life.

∿

179

Lee is right about one thing: others don't need to feel—let alone see—my pain.

So I turn inward.

It's buried under wordless smiles and benign nods. I don't speak but listen, trying to take in everything around me.

To strangers, my detachment is alluring. Men turn for a second glance. They go out of their way to make contact: they try to catch my eye or murmur a flirtatious come-on as they pass me.

I smile back, but that's as far as it goes.

Any one of them could be the Black King. He's here somewhere, hiding in plain sight.

When he's ready, he'll reach out to me.

When that happens, I'll kill him, plain and simple.

Or he'll kill me.

At least one of us will get on with our life—whatever is left of it.

"I LOVE WATCHING MY KIDS PLAY CHESS," I EXCLAIM TO Mason as we roam the convention hall together. "I owe that to you."

"Well, then we're even because I owe you my life."

His words take me by surprise. "What do you mean by that?"

"Think about it. If you hadn't introduced Jody to Lee, I would have never met Eve."

"Jody is truly the connective glue for all of this, not me."

"Don't sell yourself short, Donna. You're one fierce lady. I've met a few in my time. Granted, not all in places

I'd want to revisit." Mason shivers as if a ghost has walked on his future grave. "I'd put you up against any of them— not to mention a legion of men I've met."

"I'm sorry fate put you in their path."

Mason shrugs. "Chess did it. My love and domination of the game is a double-edged sword. It allows me to travel all over the world. It provides me with financial success. It gives me celebrity. You'd think that a person who makes his living anticipating the actions of others would learn to watch what he says publicly, especially in the presence of those who thrive on the repression and domination of the masses, right? Sadly, it's my Achilles' heel."

Did he notice how I flinched at the word describing the software that has sent us worldwide?

No…he's deep in thought.

"In what way?" I ask.

"My big mouth got me thrown into IK-2, the hellhole where all dissidents end up. I was one of the lucky ones. I got out. Not that I deserved to be traded! What's a lowly chess player compared to a journalist reporting on Putin's atrocities or the patriotic operatives of the CIA who risk their lives every day?"

I shrug. "I hate to admit there was a time I would have agreed with you. But now, knowing you—and what you've done to publicize this very worthy event, I can attest to why it's important that you were indeed the right person to bargain for. Chess may only be a game, but it unites people the world over by challenging them to take part in intelligent discourse. On the other hand, the man you were traded for—the arms dealer Grigori Lenkov— was all about monetizing death and destruction."

"All the more reason Putin was bound to retaliate against me when Grigori disappeared. You changed my life, Donna. Someday I hope to pay you back. In the mean-time, I'll channel my thanks into Jeff. Right now, he's the guy to beat in his age group. I want to keep it that way—especially when the Russian competitor shows up."

"Jeff idolizes you. He won't let you down."

"I know he won't."

His confidence encourages me to ask, "Hey, Mason, are you acquainted with any of the competition's judges and monitors?"

"Some, yes, though not many."

"Can you make a list of the ones you know? That way, I can cut them from my list of possible suspects and focus on the others."

"Great idea." He glances around the room. "The skinny, tall guy over in the corner? He's been on the circuit a long time." Mason scans a different section of tables. "Oh…and the bulky man in the ill-fitting jacket. He's another moni-tor. I've known him for years."

"Thanks! I'll cross them off my list."

"I better take off. Jody's waving me over to meet with the press. Tell you what: I'll take a few selfies with the ones who have raised my radar and have you check them out. Will that work?"

"Like a charm."

He trots off.

Lee is right. I should channel my depression into my job and make it my release.

Until Jack comes to his senses.

Soon, I hope.

"Saudi Arabia's bidder just flew in," Emma tells us. "Abu got approved as his limo driver, so the Achilles activation is happening as we speak. They're already on their way from the airport to the hotel. He's reserved the whole floor, which encompasses the presidential suite."

"Who is it?" I ask.

"Prince Hamza al Fahd. He's a second cousin once removed from the current King on his mother's side," Emma explains.

"What else do we know about him?" Jack asks.

"Early forties, Oxford-educated; he's a real party animal and has always been; only travels with his posse, never with any of his seven wives," Emma replies.

Ryan adds, "In fact, should Saudi Arabia proffer the winning bid—"

"Which it will," I mutter.

"—The celebration party will already be in progress when he gets back," our boss continues.

"So, when are we supposed to duplicate it?" Jack asks.

"You, Dominic, and Donna will be part of the catering staff. Arnie worked through the night rigging several tiny surveillance cameras throughout the rooms, which he'll also monitor for your team. Emma will take on Donna's bidding by mirroring her phone's signal. After he retrieves it, hopefully, we'll see where Hamza hides it. During the party, one of you will take the SD card, duplicate it, and put it back while the others cover for you."

"On it," Jack says.

I breathe easier. With all the arm charms floating around the party, I don't need to play honeypot.

WHILE THE AUCTION IS HAPPENING, HAMZA ENJOYS A blowjob on the suite's circular sofa. As his thumbs tap out his bids and he groans with pleasure.

"You'd think he'd find her, I don't know—*distracting,* maybe?" The awe is evident in Arnie's hushed murmur.

Jack, icing down the champagne magnums, mutters: "Nah. This is, like, the seventh auction, right? He's an old hand at it by now."

"Hey, I recognize her!" Arnie exclaims. "She's in the *Teacher's Pets* porn series! She plays the girl who always turns in her homework late, which means she has to 'stay after school,' if you catch my drift—"

"This isn't *Rotten Tomatoes*. No need to give it a review," Ryan huffs.

After the canapé platter in my hand is empty, I walk back into the suite's kitchen and whisper, "Does anyone else find it odd that Hamza doesn't hold on his bids but counters everyone else's, and with a bid three times the latest proffer?"

As Jack shakes out a martini for one of Hamza's bros, he mutters, "Apparently, his goal isn't just to secure his country's directory but to bid it up so that he can claim to his uncle that the world views it as the most valuable one to have."

Emma snickers, "And the winner is…Well, what do you know—it's Hamza! I've got to give Russia and North Korea credit for their aggressive bids…Ah! And he's confirmed that he wants in on the U.S. bid fest."

"Why am I not surprised?" I whisper.

"Hamza has just summoned me to pull the limo around to the front," Abu declares.

"Keep your eyes open," I warn him.

"Watch your back." Jack's tone sends a shiver up my spine.

What does he expect will happen?

ABU'S EYES AND EARS ALLOW US TO FOLLOW HAMZA'S rendezvous. During the ride, a different party girl takes over with more deep-throat action.

Hamza's bodyguard has pulled down his visor so that he can watch in the mirror. Whereas Abu's eyes stay straight ahead, the rest of us are allowed a webcam's POV of Hamza's backseat sexploits.

I pass on the honor.

Not all of my colleagues are as discerning. Arnie, for one, whistles, then exclaims, "With all the crazy drivers in Mexico City, it's a wonder she doesn't get dizzy and barf all over him."

Dominic is less than enthralled, perhaps because there's more to see back at Hamza's suite. "I say! Orgies are going on in every room of the prince's suite!"

"I'll ask Marcus if he wants us to snag the suite's webcam footage. It may be useful before the next OPEC negotiations," Ryan reasons.

Hamza's orgasm couldn't be more ill-timed: just as Abu pulls up to the retrieval location: a church next to a large central plaza.

Hamza taps on the limo's backseat privacy window. "You, driver: I need you to...to pick up something for me, in there...." His sputtering words can barely be heard, what with his date's vigorous mouth motion. "Third confessional on the right...an envelope...behind the statue of Mother Mary."

"Shouldn't I go?" the prince's security guard asks.

"And leave me here, unattended? Hell, no, asshole! For all we know, this around-the-world junket is just part of some bullshit set-up to take me out. My uncle doesn't trust anyone, least of all my mom."

"On it, sir." Abu slips out of the car just as Hamza shouts, "*Ouch!* Yo, bitch, watch the teeth! Unless you want me to yank them out of your mouth with pliers."

A few moments later, Abu says, "SD card secured—and duplicated."

He's just about to exit the church when it happens:

The woman pleasuring the prince pulls a gun from under the front passenger seat. Hamza's guard gets a bullet to the back of the head.

Before Hamza can zip up, the gun is under his chin. His brains splatter on the limo roof.

"Abu, leave the original SD card back where you found it!" Jack hisses. "Then get the hell out of there as fast as possible—through a different exit. When you're away from the church, skip the hotel entirely. Head back to Acme's plane."

"Everyone else: out of the party—now!" Ryan commands.

He doesn't have to ask us twice.

When Hamza's date leaves the limo, it's to stroll into the church.

Something tells me she won't go back to the hotel either.

Thank goodness for that.

～

By the time Abu gets to the plane, the team has congregated in Arnie's room.

"My team has pulled up SecCam footage from the hotel to the church," Emma assures us. "We're already running the necessary analysis. And to see if we can catch the Black King in action, they've also hacked into the church's security cameras. We've got footage from the past twenty-four hours."

"Tell them to start with the most recent footage: specifically when Hamza's limo pulls up," Jack suggests.

"Why?" I ask.

"It's just a hunch I have."

"Ryan, is there any benefit for our side to have Arnie trace the path of Hamza's assassin and feed it back to the Saudis?" I ask. "I mean, sure, Hamza's extermination during this operation muddies the water between us and the Saudis. Still, we've had worse setbacks, and we've still been able to cover our tracks."

"I'll ask Marcus. Hold the line." He's gone for the next quarter hour.

During that time, no one speaks.

Why is that?

It's especially disconcerting to have Jack go radio silent. He's our team leader. He should say something, even if it's only small talk or making a joke.

Is his disgust of me so great that it's colored what he feels he can say around me, professionally and personally?

I can't let it bother me. Otherwise, I'll go to pieces.

Finally, Ryan returns: "Branham reached out to Saudi Arabia's intelligence head at the Presidency of State Security. We've been asked to pretend it didn't happen. In fact, the PSS's cleaners are already on it."

Abu guffaws. "That was quick."

"Something tells me the crown prince considered Hamza too big of a threat, or even more likely from all we've seen, a liability he didn't need," Jack reasons.

"But what about the PSS's directory?" I reply. "If it's not found on Hamza's body, they'll either assume it was stolen by us; or that he never retrieved it and come looking for it."

"I've found the answer," Emma says. "Jack was right to insist that Abu leave it in the confessional and get out of there. The assassin knew right where to go to get it."

"Who does she work for?" Dominic wonders.

"My guess: the Saudis," Jack responds. "It's why they're keen on letting sleeping dogs lie."

"Right again," Emma says. "She's already at Marco Polo. She drove onto the tarmac and walked onto a private plane headed to King Abdulaziz International Airport."

"Makes sense," Ryan declares. "They've gotten rid of their barrel's worst apple and saved their intel, too, so all's well that ends well. Take the rest of the night off, folks. You've earned it."

DOMINIC IS ON A LOWER FLOOR, SO HE'S THE FIRST TO GET OFF the elevator, leaving Jack and me alone for the rest of the trip.

He's silent. So am I.

I refuse to ask him about Dannie, but I wish he'd ask me about Lee so I can again deny his jealousy is unwarranted.

But he ignores me.

I notice only one button is pushed—

Which means our rooms are on the same floor.

When the elevator doors open, Jack waits for me to walk through first.

To my dismay, he follows me down the hall to the door next to mine.

With a tap, his opens at the same time as mine.

In unison, our doors shut with resounding clicks.

Ah…great. To make matters worse, we share an adjoining door.

I start a bubble bath to squelch the urge to go through it —to throw myself into his arms, to babble on about how much I miss him.

And lay in it until I'm shriveled.

After drying off, I grab the sheets, pillows, and blankets off the bed, making a nest by the door that separates us.

I fall asleep thinking of what I know is really keeping us apart: not this door, but Acme.

20

Attack

In chess, the best attacks occur when you move a piece to a square that will let you capture your opponent's piece with your subsequent move.

Needless to say, like you, your opponent is always contemplating ways to attack. Ergo, not only must you focus on your future offensive moves but theirs as well.

Should you find the process exhausting and anxiety-ridden, you're probably doing something wrong.

That something may be playing chess.

Solution: consider Candy Land instead.

Emma's call to discuss the Russia directory bid in Venice comes while the rest of the passengers on Lee's plane are having dinner. I excuse myself to take it in his office.

Ryan wastes no time: "The FSB is sending its highest ranking military intelligence director to bid on the intel."

Jack whistles. "You mean Igor Baronov himself?"

"The one and only," Ryan replies.

A picture appears on the monitor: a tall, barrel-chested man, perhaps in his mid-fifties, with a full head of white hair. He has a hawk nose, a smug cruel mouth, and stark blue eyes.

"What do we know about him?" I ask.

"Too much, I'm afraid. When Putin took over as head of the FSB, most of the bureaucrats were purged. Not Baronov. He'd already proven himself: not by climbing through the agency's bureaucratic ranks or in a field office but as an assassin. He's now the director of the FSB's counterintelligence division."

"Why was he given this particular assignment?" Abu asks.

"Because Putin trusts him. He's here to guarantee that nothing goes wrong," Jack reasons.

"There's more to it than that," Ryan warns us. "Keep in mind, Russia views Mason's presence in the competition as a way to thumb his nose at Putin."

"Do you think they'll try to kidnap him again?"

"It's possible," Ryan concedes. "Maybe Mason should sit this one out."

"He'll never agree to that," Jack replies.

"In fact, Mason has been coaching Jeff for this very moment. He'll want to watch him play, to be there to support him," I add. "He told me that he coached Jeff's competitor, Mikhail Sokolov, while he was in prison. He's the son of Russia's penitentiary director, Dimitri. It kept the prison guards from torturing him. Perhaps Mason thinks that his presence will lend both players confidence."

Abu shakes his head. "More than likely, he sees it as an opportunity to give a middle finger to the Russians."

"That's not Mason's style," I huff. "I'm sure he views his presence as a public show of good faith; that, despite his wrongful incarceration, he sees chess as a road to peace and unification."

Jack claps slowly as if I'd made a joke.

I squelch the urge to stick out my tongue at him.

"Jody will like that since it'll certainly garner big press," Dominic points out.

"Since our job is not to ensure the event's public relations value but instead to stop the destruction of our intelligence community, it's vital that we activate Achilles on Baronov. This will be tricky since he's elected not to stay at the hotel—the Hilton Molino Stuckey, which is on Venice's Giudecca Island—but has opted instead for a private residence."

"Do we know where yet?" I ask.

"That's the problem, we don't," Ryan admits. "He's flying in on a private jet. For the most part, his transportation will be private. No doubt his speedboat will be operated by his personal security detail."

"Perhaps we can put a tracker on him, his car, his luggage, even one of his security goons while on the tarmac?" I suggest.

Ryan nods. "It's tricky but doable. What do you think, Jack?"

"Yes, doable." Jack only addresses Ryan.

What did I expect, an 'Attagirl, Donna,' or a smile and a wink? It's not going to happen.

"We could also meet the plane and claim a paperwork delay," Abu says.

"Worth a try," Ryan concedes. "Okay, the tarmac is our Plan A. Abu and Dominic can be the greeting party. Hopefully, you can hold him on the tarmac through the twenty minutes needed for Achilles' activation. Plan B is praying he needs to make a pit stop at the airport. At that point, the rest of you are in play."

"Which brings up how we shall duplicate the directory once he gets it," Dominic points out. "This won't be easy if he's in some private palazzo."

"Ideally, we'd intercept it before he retrieves it," I suggest.

"That's a good Plan A," Ryan replies. "Who's got a Plan B?"

"Pick his pocket after the retrieval, and then plant it back on him after duplication." Jack offers.

Ryan shakes his head. "With his bodyguards around, it'll be a long shot, but slot it as Plan B." Ryan sighs. "Okay, first things first: the tarmac greeting committee by Dom and Abu. The rest of you: track him while he's walking through the airport. Good luck, folks."

I'D HAVE GUESSED THE KIDS WOULD USE THE TEN-HOUR FLIGHT between Mexico City and Venice to sleep. Instead, they watch silently but intently as Mason plays Jeff in chess.

Even more impressive is that both sides still have several pieces on the board, which leads me to wonder aloud, "Is this the same game that started right after takeoff?"

Trisha puts a finger to her lips but nods.

Incredible.

Is it too much to hope that this will replace their addiction to video games?

Better not ask. I'd rather be pleasantly surprised.

Twenty minutes later, Jeff lets loose with a triumphant

shout. "Finally! I beat Mason!" Still, he's gracious enough to offer Mason his hand.

The chess master takes it and pulls Jeff in for a hug. "Now, if you can play that way tomorrow against Russia's best opponent, Mikhail Sokolov, I'll gift you my lucky charm: my chess playbook."

Jeff's eyes grow wide. "What is that?"

"It's a diary of every winning move I've had since I started playing chess professionally. By studying it, you'll be just as good a player as me." Mason puts his hand on Jeff's shoulder. "But you only get it if you win."

"And you'll autograph it, right?"

Mason laughs. "Sure, okay."

Jeff's eyes brighten. "Can I take a peek at it now?"

"I'll grab it and be right back." A moment later, Mason is back. He holds a palm-sized leather bound notebook in his hand. "Study it between now and the game tomorrow."

"I sure will." Jeff takes off for his sleeping quarters.

The girls do the same.

And Mason heads off to Eve's cabin.

No sleep for me. I'm still not tired.

Instead, I scan a wall of shelves. Amid several years of back issues of *Foreign Affairs, The New Yorker,* and *Fortune* and heavy tomes of world history interspersed with biographies of all presidents since Washington is a dog-eared contemporary novel. In pastel tones, its illustrated cover shows a happy couple bound together by their dogs' intertwined leashes.

Perhaps it's something Eve once read. No matter. It'll be the perfect distraction, sure to get me out of my head.

It's too dark in there now.

AN HOUR LATER, I LOOK UP FROM MY BOOK—A ROMCOM chock full of witty repartee, missed opportunities for a heartfelt connection, and will-they-or-won't-they shenanigans and realize I'm crying when I should be laughing.

Would I see the humor in the characters' situation if I weren't already living my enemies-to-lovers dramedy?

Only, in my case, it's a lovers-to-enemies tragedy.

Just then, Lee walks through into the cabin. Seeing my tear-stained face, he hands me a tissue. "Is the book that bad?"

I laugh to keep from crying. "No, not at all! It's just that…" My nose blow comes out as a honk. "I thought Jack and I would have worked out our differences by now—if not for our marriage, then at least for the mission."

"Don't worry, Donna. It'll all be over soon."

Is it that obvious, even to Lee, that I've lost Jack for good? "What do you mean by that?"

"Only that Jack will come to his senses."

"I'm not so sure. If he doesn't… nothing will be the same."

He shrugs. "Sure it will! Because…well, nothing really changes in the big scheme of things. We just learn to live with the curve balls thrown at us. Sometimes we hit them over the fence. Sometimes we make it to the next base. And sometimes, we strike out. Just remember, Donna: *it's all a game.*" Leaning back, Lee shuts his eyes. His weariness is all too obvious.

He's talking about himself, about the fact that, once again, he's missed out on love.

As for me, I'm dreading a changed future: one without Jack.

I leave the book because I can guess how it ends: with a happily ever after—

Unlike my story, in which there's no happy ending in sight.

AS PLANNED, WHEN IGOR BARONOV'S PRIVATE JET LANDS, Dominic and Abu greet it on the tarmac. They hold clipboards and wear blazers with crests that call them out as San Marco Airport officials.

Although Dominic's Italian is good enough to make all the right noises about faulty paperwork on the Russians' part, Baronov glowers and blows right past him. His goon squad of three flank him on all sides to stop any counter-protest.

Ryan curses, then growls, "Plan B, folks. Hop on it!"

ARNIE MOVES QUICKLY TOWARD THE CLOSEST MEN'S LAVATORY, ducking inside. Baronov and his entourage are fifty feet away. Jack waits until they walk past him, then he's on their heels.

Baranov and one of his aides go into the lavatory while the other two stand guard. Whatever is said to the other men who are in there makes them leave in a hurry—

Including Arnie, who's walking quickly with his pants around his knees. As he jerks them to his waist and zips up, he hisses, "They pulled out their guns! When one guy insisted on staying, they put him in a choke hold until he almost passed out." He points to a man being carried out by two others.

This doesn't deter Jack, who insists on going inside.

"You cannot. International business." One of the goons shows him his gun and a badge to make his point.

Jack backs off, then walks away.

I grab Jack's arm and then Arnie's and pull them toward the entrance of the women's restroom. "When Baronov went in, what did he do?" I ask.

"He went to the last toilet stall with his aide."

"Did he make the man stand guard outside the stall?" I ask.

Arnie thinks for a moment, then shakes his head. "Um…The guard went into the stall with him now that you mention it."

"Wait here," I say to Arnie and Jack.

I go into the women's lavatory. There are only two ladies in there. "There was just a bomb scare announced over the intercom!" I tell them. "They want everyone out."

The ladies grab their bags and hurry out.

After flipping the door's FUORI SERVIZIO sign, I beckon Jack and Arnie inside. "The lavatories share a wall." I point to the ceiling, which is a grid of large tiles. "Give me a lift so that I can climb up there. I'll crawl over Baronov while he does his business. Hopefully, it'll take long enough to activate Achilles."

Jack frowns but nods. Bracing against the wall, he cups his hands low. I step into them, and he shoves me up.

I pull the tile to one side, then climb onto a wall. It's around nine inches thick. Slowly, on my hands and knees, I crawl until I'm directly over the closest stall. To balance myself, I have to put one knee and leg further out than the other. When I feel comfortable enough that I won't topple through the tile next to me, I inch another tile out of its grid to peek in.

Baronov stands behind his aide, who has his pants around his ankles. Their ecstatic groans tell me all I need to know: he's there to pleasure our target.

Better him than me.

Baronov's jacket hangs on a hook on the back of the door, putting his cell phone within range of Achilles.

I move the ceiling tile again so the opening is as wide as my mobile phone.

I say a prayer that they don't look up.

Then I count down the minutes.

I still have a minute to go when Baronov slumps over his aide, spent.

45...44...43...42...41...40....

The aide is released—

39...38...

He pulls up his pants, and leaves the stall, never looking back—

37...36...35...34...233...

While Baranov turns around to face the urinal. He is going to pee—

32...31...30...29...28...27...26...25...24...

I feel something on my back foot.

23...22...21...20...19...

It's climbing up my leg! I hold in my urge to squeal...

18...17...16....15...

Finally, Baronov's flow has stopped. He's zipping up...

14...13...12...11...

Just as the little animal climbs up my leg and onto my back. Now, Baronov is out of the stall—

10...9...8...7...6...

THE THING GOES ONTO MY NECK as Baronov washes up....

5...4...3...2...1...

AND INTO MY HAIR—

Just as Baronov walks out the door.

I slap it off my head: A RAT—

Which lands on a tile over the men's lavatory.

Shuddering, I jerk a tile loose on the women's side of the lavatory—

And jump—

Into Jack's arms.

I'm still shivering, so hard now, that he holds me tight. I look up at him and, just for a second, I see the concern in his eyes—

But then he turns away. "Is it activated?"

"Yes."

He drops me onto my feet.

"Did you see what I think you saw?" Arnie asks.

"You mean a rat? Yuck—yes! It climbed on me and into my hair—"

Jack is laughing.

Really? He thinks it's funny?

"No…I mean…*about Baronov*," Arnie prods.

"Yes, you were right. Baronov is having an affair with one of his aides. Now, if you'll excuse me, I could use a hot bath."

I still hear Jack laughing as I follow the other passengers to the exit.

I've just gotten into my tub when Ryan calls again. "Sorry, Donna. Your bath will have to wait. The Black King announces that the auction has now opened."

I sigh but open my text app to find that the rest of my mission team has joined the conference.

Why am I always the last person called?

Jack has arranged it that way.

In fact, I can hear Jack's murmur through the wall that separates us. Emma is bound and determined to make my proximity to him irresistible. Doesn't she realize that she's torturing me by putting me so near when his heart is nowhere within reach?

Ryan asks me to open the bid at one hundred million dollars.

Done.

Hamza's replacement doubles this.

China doubles it again.

Ryan tells me, "Bid six hundred million."

China makes it a flat billion.

"Make it fifty billion," Ryan commands.

I do as he says.

Saudi Arabia goes to a hundred billion.

Silence.

Then Russia bids two hundred billion.

"Donna, go to three."

I bid three hundred billion.

Silence.

Russia bids five hundred billion.

Ryan laughs. "Let them have it—since we will too."

I hope this isn't wishful thinking on his part.

Soon enough, Baronov gets these instructions:

Teatro La Fenice - Box 45C - first seat on the left

"Abu and Jack, see if you can make it there before Baronov's people and duplicate the SD card before they arrive."

"On it, Boss," Jack says.

AN HOUR LATER, AS I GET OUT OF THE TUB, MY PHONE RINGS again.

It's Emma.

"Did things go as planned?" I ask.

"Well…not exactly. Jack was shot—"

"What?" I run to our connecting door and bang hard…

Then again, but he doesn't open it. Instead, he yells, "*I'm okay*! Just…business as usual."

Yeah, right.

"Nothing to panic about." Ryan joins in. "You didn't let Emma finish. She was about to say that Jack was shot *at*—but he got away. Baronov's guards didn't go after him. They were there for the SD card, got it, and left. My guess: they assumed he was the Black King making the drop."

"Had they caught him, they probably would have tortured him to get their money back," Arnie pipes up.

"That would have served him right," I mutter. I could torture him myself, what with his rude response.

"If the Black King knows that Igor Baronov is gay—he could bargain his way out of it," I reason.

"Why is that?" Arnie asks.

"Homosexuality is illegal in Russia," I explain. "If Putin knew, Baronov would be imprisoned—or worse, murdered, since he knows too much of his fearless leader's dirty deeds."

"Yet another Russian human rights violation," Dominic mutters.

"So what's Plan B?"

"We'll need to break into Baronov's place."

My cell's screen is filled with a beautiful waterfront palace.

I hear the awe in Dominic's voice as he exclaims, "My lord! Baronov has rented the whole of Palazzi Barbaro!"

"What do you know of it?" Abu asks.

"Only that it was built in the fourteen-hundreds by Giovanni Bon and is a Baroque masterpiece. Not to mention that the wealthy American, Daniel Sargent Curtis, made it the epicenter of the British and American artistic community in the late eighteen hundreds. Its rooms are exquisite! The frescos in the ceiling were painted by Tiepelo, and the ballroom boasts a renowned depiction of *Rape of the Sabine Women* by Piazzetta—"

"We're not asking for a history lesson, just for ways to penetrate it," Jack reminds him.

"*Hmmmm.* Well, that does present a bit of a sticky wicket," Dominic admits. "You see, it's a five-story building reached only by the water: it faces the Canal Grande. Then again, you can rappel down from the roof next door..."

"Sure, piece of cake," I murmur.

NOT.

"Glad to have a volunteer," Ryan replies.

"What?...Um...Wait—"

"Godspeed, Mrs. Craig. The rest of you get busy keeping her from breaking her neck."

21

Blindfold Chess

Imagine playing chess without seeing or touching the pieces!

Imagine having to relay your moves via some sort of notation instead.

Now, imagine if this was how you learned to play the game.

Frankly, it's a great way to do so because it forces you to have a mental picture of the pieces on the board.

Word of caution: Don't try it after a boozy night because you'll only see double.

We're on the Canal Royale in two separate motorboats: Jack and I in one and Abu and Dominic in the other.

If I say so myself, I look fetching in a new summer frock: a sleeveless, belted jewel-necked Kay Unger with a midi flared skirt. The large flowers on a dark blue background look vibrant and surreal.

But am I also irresistible to Jack?

When we're two residences away from Palazzo Barbaro, Jack cuts off the engine so that we can float toward it. I realize I have my answer when he takes me in his arms and tilts me down for a lingering kiss.

Blissful.

If only we could stay this way forever…

But then he shoves me away.

Angrily, I hiss, "Hey! What was that all about?"

"I had to play to our audience. Two of Baronov's goons are smoking on one of the lower balconies."

Instinctively, I turn my head. From the light pouring out of Baronov's residence, I see what he does: Their leering sneers.

Jack pinches me—*hard.* "Jesus, Donna. Don't look up. Espionage Rule Number 1, remember?"

I stomp on his foot. "Who do you think you are, lecturing me? You…*you tease!* Why, I—"

His mouth is on mine again.

I want to fight him, but he's holding me too tightly—

At least, I think I want him to stop…

Okay, maybe I should just lean into this…

Our boat is turning…

I feel dizzy…

This time when Jack lets go, I'm almost tossed overboard, but just in time, I grab hold of the side. Looking up, I see we're no longer in the Grand Canal but in a narrow water alley. Jack tethers the boat to a pole next to the nearest steps.

"Where are we?" I ask.

"On the side of Palazzo Barbaro. There's a grass alley behind it. Arnie has rented a room on the top floor of the building that abuts it on the other side." From there, we'll climb onto the roof, rappel down through a window, and take care of business."

Sorry, but that ain't happening in *this* dress.

Not that I can say this to Jack. It'll give him another reason to diss me to Ryan and our team. Instead, I point out: "The place is huge! We have no idea which room is Baronov's."

"Considering how late it is, and with the jet lag from Mexico City, he's probably already asleep," Jack replies. "We can sneak in and out."

"But maybe his partner isn't so tired," I counter.

We'll just have to chance it; go room by room."

"What about the goons on the balcony?"

"They'll soon be asleep, too," he assures me.

"How do you know?"

"Watch Abu and Dominic."

I focus my lenses on their coordinates. Their boat is crawling by Palazzo Barbaro. When it's within fifty feet, Abu and Dominic have aimed guns at the guards.

At the same time, both men slump over the rail.

"Are they dead?" I ask.

"Nope. They were shot with tranquilizer darts."

"But…what if they'd missed?"

"It can't happen. The darts have the same heat-seeking technology used in our missile program."

"And I assume you have one of those pretty little toys?"

He holds up a gun that isn't his Sig Sauer.

"So, where's mine?"

Jack guffaws. "You're armed with your feminine wiles. Isn't that enough?"

"Not in Baronov's case." I scan Jack, top to bottom. "You, on the other hand, will be catnip to him—"

"You're right. In fact, I can do this alone. Wait here, like a good little girl." He walks toward the building from which Arnie is waving down at us.

Like hell I will.

Instead of following him, I go toward Palazzo Barbaro's courtyard.

The wrought iron gate opens.

So does the back door.

The first room I come across is a kitchen galley. Two elderly women sit in front of an old, small TV set tuned to an Italian soap opera. They must have been hired to take care of Baronov's meals. They're so engrossed in their show that they don't even look up.

I sneak beyond the kitchen until I reach a staircase. I can tell just by looking up that it rises several stories.

I start my climb.

EACH ROOM IS A HISTORIC GEM. THE MAIN FLOOR BOASTS several grand reception halls: one set up as a card room, another as a library. Some walls are covered with Rococo murals. Baroque frescos have also been painted on ceilings, moldings, and walls. Its marble floors have thick antique carpets.

Then I reach the floor where Baronov's guards are napping on the balcony. It too has several rooms, in similar furnishings and decor.

The next level has four bedrooms, bathrooms, and more fancy reception rooms, each as elaborate as the last.

The top floor is one large bedroom with its own bathroom. Someone is in there, singing a Russian pop song. He's not bad…except for his off-key super high notes.

The bed faces several paned windows overlooking the canal. A smaller room serves as a walk-in closet.

My eyes have yet to adjust to the darkness when I feel something against my neck:

A gun.

Baronov is wearing a bathrobe.

"You've come to rob me?" Baronov addresses me in Italian.

"Si," I respond.

"You choose the wrong person." After a long stare, he gloats, "Tomorrow, you'll be the prettiest body they'll fish out of the canal."

Before I can break free, he puts me in a rear choke hold.

He's not expecting me to grab him by the nuts—

And then to shove his elbow off my neck—

Then to flip him over me—

So that he ends up in the perfect position for me to twist his arm behind his back—

Oops…

What was that pop?

My bad: I yanked his arm out of its socket.

He's gasping in pain, but not for long—

Because Jack shoots him with a tranquilizer dart.

My husband holds up the SD card. "Thanks for the diversion. It's our duplicate, so let's get moving."

He doesn't have to ask twice.

As we reach the back door, the shower singer belts out *Stay the Night.*

Is it wishful thinking to hope that Jack might want to do just that?

APPARENTLY SO. JACK DOESN'T EVEN SAY GOODNIGHT WHEN we reach our hotel rooms.

I cry the whole night long.

To cover the damage the following day, I take extra care with my makeup.

I practice smiling in the mirror.

I have to bring my A-game for Jeff.

So I wear last night's dress and pray it's luckier for him than it was for me.

"WOW…MOM, YOU'RE…WELL, YOU'RE SO BEAUTIFUL!" JEFF doesn't even blush when I kiss him on the forehead.

I didn't know my smile could get any broader. But yes, my son's admiration breaks all barriers when it comes to making me happy. "It's a lucky dress, so I saved it for this match."

Spotting me, Mason's eyes open wide too. He gives me a wink and a nod.

I follow his eyes—

To Lee. His face lights up when he realizes it's me, and he makes his way over.

As does Jack, who has just walked into the room. Trisha runs up to her father for a hug and brings him over. The first thing Jack does is shake Jeff's hand. "Are you ready?"

Jeff nods. "As much as I'll ever be, thanks to Mason."

Jack shakes the chess master's hand too. "Thank you for sharing your wisdom with our children. I'll never forget the role you played in their lives."

"Just hearing you acknowledge that validates my decision at Donna's behest." He turns to me. "Such a beautiful woman! I can see why you fell in love with her."

As Jack's smile falters, my eyes haze over with tears. Time to change the subject. I look around. "Jeff, where is your opponent?"

Trisha rolls her eyes. "Apparently, Mikhail Sokolov likes to make a grand entrance."

"Is that fair?" I ask.

"It's as trivial a head game as it gets," Mason admits. "Officially, if a player arrives at the chessboard more than one hour late for the beginning of the game—or, for that matter, arrives after the expiration of the first or only time control period, whichever comes first—the player loses the game." His eyes roam the room. "Not to worry. He's just walked in."

"I assume the man behind him is his father, Pavel?" I ask. I point to a sallow, hollow-eyed tall man following Mikhail.

"Yes. So, certainly, the boy's good looks come from his mother's side. Though rumor has it, Pavel is Mikhail's father in name only." Mason leans in. "Why do you think Putin has taken such a great interest in the boy, and why Pavel's livelihood—his very life—is to be decided by a mere game?"

"Could you imagine being under Putin's thumb like that?" Jack's question, though addressed to Mason, is rhetorical.

I'm not shocked by its effect on Mason: he recoils.

"Oh… Sorry, Mason, truly I am." Jack's contrition proffered with a slight bow. "For a moment there, I forgot about your…ordeal."

Mason shrugs it off. "Understandable. It's not the usual experience, even for those in your work. At least not the ones lucky enough not to get caught by their enemies." He shrugs. "Now, if you'll excuse me, Jody is waving me over."

As he walks off, I poke Jack. "Seriously? After all he's been through, how could you be so uncaring?"

"Forgive me for being seemingly less than compassionate, dear wife. I'll figure out how to make it up to Mason and you."

Why does that sound like a threat?

I won't rise to the bait. I've got Jeff to consider.

And the rest of my life, too, if this is how he's to be from now on.

BY THE SECOND HOUR INTO THE GAME BETWEEN JEFF AND Mikhail, I've bitten off all my nail polish.

Jeff has made so many moves that might have cost him the game that I can't count. But that's just it: instead of ruffling his feathers, he flies even higher with his next one. If anyone is thinking several moves ahead, it's Jeff.

Ironically, whenever Jeff ups the ante, Mikhail does the same. Both are playing strong defense and offense—

Until Mikhail does something that has the crowd gasping.

I look down at the board to spot it.

He's taken Jeff's queen.

Jeff has a pawn close enough to the last row of the board to save her, but in doing so, he leaves his king open.

I look away because I don't want to see him make a wrong move—

Only to find myself staring into Baronov's glowering face.

He's here?

But of course, he'd be—to cheer on his home team.

And now he knows mine too.

Stupid me! My dress made it easy for him to recognize me.

I've got to get out of here.

I slip into the crowd. I almost reach the door when I feel a poke in my back: Baronov's gun. He whispers, "Shall we take a little walk?"

HE STEERS ME THROUGH THE LOBBY AND INTO AN EMPTY conference room.

I thought I recognized the infamous Donna Stone Craig! And as you're considered an international war criminal in our country, arresting or shooting you if you try to escape will be my pleasure."

"Remind me again. In what imaginary fairyland am I a criminal?"

"No matter where you are, my president wants your head on a platter, and I look forward to bringing it to him." He smirks. Unless he wishes all of you instead." He assesses me with a sideways gaze, then shudders. "Ah, well, to each their own."

At that moment, the wall-sized monitors throughout the room go live—

With the video of Baronov's liaison with his aide.

As the sounds of their bathroom stall lovemaking fill the room, his head turns from one screen to another. Horrified, he asks, How did…when…"

Arnie hoots in my ear, "Hey, Don, remind him that his

fearless leader would love to know if his generals live up to their sacred oath!"

He doesn't have to ask me twice. "You know, Igor, in democratic countries, loving whoever you want isn't a crime that gets you imprisoned—or worse, if you're a military general, shot by a firing squad. There's no better time than now to defect. But considering how you like to live dangerously, maybe you'd prefer to be a double agent—"

He collapses onto a chair and buries his head in his hands.

I pat his shoulder. It's the one I pulled out of its socket, giving him two reasons to groan. "We'll be in touch."

I GET BACK TO THE GAME ROOM IN TIME TO SEE THAT JEFF HAS now got Mikhail in check—

Make that checkmate.

The loser, shaken, stands up and walks away without shaking Jeff's hand.

His father, ashen-faced, stumbles after him.

Jeff stands proudly. Trisha puts him in a bear hug, whereas Janie does him one better and kisses him—

On the lips.

Lee looks over at me.

Jack, now at Jeff's side, is watching me too.

I ignore them, choosing to run to my son and hug him instead.

"Mom, do you know what this means? I get to keep Mason's playbook!"

He waves at his coach.

Mason looks just as stunned as me.

Amazed, he shakes his head, then walks over to shake Jeff's hand.

Throughout the room, cameras click, capturing this moment.

At some point, Jack has slipped away.

I'm no longer surprised, but it still makes me sad.

22

Desperado

A PIECE THAT WILL BE CAPTURED ANYWAY IS CALLED A "desperado."

It may not seem like it then, but this is a true act of selflessness. Think about it: the piece is paying the highest cost: sacrifice.

Not to worry! Chess pieces aren't human.

Now, if a friend or loved one is willing to do it, that's a different issue.

In that case, a desperado can only be called one thing: hero.

THE ESTONIAN SPA IN THE SMALL TOWN OF NARVA-JÕESUU has its own beach on Narva Bay, the northern-eastern finger of the Gulf of Finland.

It's not a very big resort. In fact, Lee's event has taken it over.

"Which begs the question: where will the others be located as they bid on the U.S.'s directory?" Ryan's concern is even more evident on the broadcast monitor in my suite, where my Acme team has gathered.

"Well, obviously, we're no longer tracking those who have defected or are dead, including General Jung in the former and Hamza and Philippe in the latter," Emma points out. "As for those still alive who Achilles is tracking—Lotus Blossom, the Geisha, Dannie, and Hanna—they're now in Buenos Aires, of all places!"

I cluck my tongue. "This junket has given them one thing in common—Mr. Craig. Let's hope they don't run into each other because they'll compare notes."

Jack frowns but says nothing.

He doesn't dare.

Arnie guffaws. "Imagine if Acme held an auction solely for Jack. We'd rack up!"

Jack's punch to his gut has him keeling over. As for me, I have to stop myself from giving Arnie a swift kick in the ass. Although he richly deserves it, why beat up on a stupid guy when he's down?

Feel free to applaud me for my restraint.

Ryan sighs. "I can tell the tension of this mission is getting to you, folks. Considering it's for the sale of the U.S. directory, keep your powder dry until this last auction is over."

"I don't get it," says Abu. "Why would we be here while the other bidders are halfway around the world?"

"I think I can answer that," Jack replies. "Because the Black King expects the highest bid to come from either the U.S. or Russia, which is not coincidentally right across the river. My guess: he's here too."

"It begs the question: if Baronov isn't in Buenos Aires, where is he?" I ask.

"According to Achilles, he's close by," Emma confirms.

"He's not in the hotel, but within a five-mile radius. Oddly, his coordinates put him in the river. Maybe he's on a boat?"

Arnie snickers. "He doesn't want to be near Donna, that's for sure."

"Do you blame him?" Jack's utterance is just loud enough for me to hear it.

Grrrr…

"Baronov is playing it awfully cool, considering the goods Acme has on him," Dominic declares.

"He's probably hoping that we win so that he doesn't have to be compromised," Abu reasons.

A second later, I hear a ping on my cell:

Bidding on the Ukrainian directory starts in five minutes.

I take a deep breath. "Here we go."

RUSSIA MAKES THE FIRST BID: TEN MILLION.

China either plays shill or is tweaking Russia's nose by doubling that number.

Saudi Arabia doubles it again.

Russia makes it one hundred million.

Using the Ukraine burner phone, I double that.

Russia takes it to two hundred million.

"Bid five hundred million," Ryan insists.

I accommodate.

Russia stays silent.

Finally:

Congratulations! You've proffered the winning bid! You have three minutes to wire the funds to this account, or it will go to the next highest bidder: XXXX-XXXX-XXXXX

Ryan sighs but puts through the funds. "It's the best Ukrainian aid package possible," he reasons.

A moment later, another text appears:

Funds received. Directory will be under corner table by window, cafe Ivani Juures.

"I've got it mapped," Emma declares. "It's less than a mile away, on the river."

"I'll retrieve it," Dominic offers.

"Get going—but watch your back," Ryan cautions him.

Dominic is out the door.

Just then, the U.S. burner pings:

Bidding on the U.S. directory starts in exactly one hour. Opening Minimum: $100 Million.

Ryan sighs. "Well, this certainly negates those who planned on pussy-footing around."

I look at my watch. "Jeff's rematch against Mikhail begins then."

"You can show up late." Jack's eyes avoid mine, but there's no malice in his voice.

Is it wishful thinking to take this as a concern? Because I desperately want to give him the benefit of the doubt, I reply, "Yes, you should cover for me."

"Jack will be where Acme needs him until the auction ends and we've secured the directory. In the meantime, let's plan on making this final auction also the Black King's last day as a free man," Ryan proclaims. "Arnie, I take it you've accessed Narva-Jõesuu's municipal SecCams and those of other hotels in the area?"

"Right, Chief," Arnie says.

"And Emma, despite our assumption that no operatives from other intelligence agencies other than perhaps Russia's FSB are nearby, I want you to continue to run facial recognition on all hotel personnel, guests, and anyone who sets foot within the hotel property and cross-check it with anyone who went near both retrieval sites during the last twenty-four hours."

"On it, Boss," Emma assures him.

"Abu and Jack: when Donna wins the bid, you'll shadow her to the retrieval area and back here to safety. Now that Baronov knows of her—and for that matter, you too, Jack—I wouldn't put it past him to attempt your exterminations. Even if he doesn't win the bid, he's got too much at stake to leave any loose ends, especially those who know of his secret life."

"I'll let the team know if Achilles shows Baronov anywhere near Donna," Arnie vows.

"Sounds good," Ryan says. "Should we come up with a match, Branham would prefer we apprehend, not exterminate, the Black King."

"We'll do our best," Jack promises.

He sounds tired.

Like me, he can't wait for this mission to be over.

Then we can get on with the rest of our lives—together or apart.

I hope he comes to his senses.

❧

Dominic makes it back just as the U.S. auction begins:

China opens the bid with the requisite one hundred million.

South Korea counters and doubles it.

Saudi Arabia doubles that.

Russia makes it six hundred million.

"Bid a billion," Ryan commands. I do as told.

China goes for two billion.

Then Russia takes it to five hundred billion.

Ryan lets loose with a diatribe so foul that I cover my ears. "Do you see what they're doing?" he shouts.

"Yeah, Boss. It's called payback," I remind him.

Ryan groans. "Well, then…double it!"

I text that in.

Someone is banging on the door.

Dominic goes to answer it.

Jody rushes in. "They've taken him!"

"What?… Who?" Dominic asks.

"Donna, pay attention to the bidding!" Ryan warns.

Oblivious to him, Jody screams, "The Black King! He has Mason!" She holds up her cell, where a video plays on a loop:

Mason is leaving his room. A bellman, pushing a laundry basket, is walking toward him. Just as Mason passes him, the bellman reaches over and injects him with something. As Mason slumps to the floor, the man catches him, shoves him into the cart, covers him with sheets, and rolls further down the hall to the service elevator. At that point, the man pointedly stares at the security camera:

He's wearing a mask.

When he takes off his bellman's cap, he's wearing a crown.

The elevator opens, and the Black King rolls the cart into it.

My cell pings with an incoming text:

Congratulations! You've proffered the winning bid! You have three minutes to wire the funds to this account, or it will go to the next highest bidder: XXXX-XXXX-XXXXX

"Donna, do it—now!" Ryan demands.

While Dominic and Abu take Jody into their adjoining room, I complete the transfer with shaking fingers.

Another text appears:

Funds received. You'll find the SD card with the directory right outside your door.

"What the hell? The Black King knows our room?" Jack looks through my door's peephole. "There's a cart out there. Wait here. Abu, Arnie and I will do x-ray and colorimetric scans in case it's meant to blow us sky high."

As I count down the minutes, I join Dominic in comforting Jody.

It keeps me from thinking of the hell that Mason must be going through.

A quarter-hour later, Jack walks back in. He's holding the SD card. "Arnie is going to scan it for trojans and viruses before passing it forward to Branham so that he can verify its legitimacy."

The process takes another twenty minutes. In the meantime, Emma pulls up the security camera footage showing who left the cart in front of my door:

It's the bellman who abducted Mason.

"I've got SecCam footage of the abductors leaving the premises," Emma tells us.

What we see takes away all hope of getting him back:

Two men bundle his comatose body into a cargo box, then shove it into the back of a van. They drive the few miles to the Narva-Jōsuu Piiriületuspunkt — the border crossing point at the head of the Narva River. From there, the box is loaded onto a tugboat and taken to the north side of the river.

Once again, the Russians have Mason.

23

Capture

A 'CAPTURE' OCCURS WHEN AN OPPONENT "TAKES"—THAT IS, removes—a piece from the board via a legal move.

This does not mean the piece is "killed." Other strategic moves can put it back on the board and in play.

At least, this is the rule in chess.

In real life, being off the board is a permanent reality, so do your best to stay in the game as long as possible.

EVE'S FACE IS SWOLLEN FROM ALL HER CRYING.

Lee won't leave her side. In fact, he's left Jody and her team in complete charge of the final competition.

The kids hover beside me. They, too, are anxious about Mason's disappearance.

Lee agreed with Jack and me to hold off telling the children about it until after their games. Their elation evaporated in the harsh reality of our dear friend's plight.

Mikhail never showed up for his game with Jeff. Acme

assumes that the Black King has sold Mason to Russia. And although the U.S. doesn't retaliate with kidnappings, Russia isn't taking the chance that we may change this policy.

Jeff waits until the girls have pulled Genghis into a chess game before cornering me. "Mom, will they...will they kill Mason this time?"

I don't want to remind him that Lee took in Mason to protect him from that very fate. Instead, I say, "He's too valuable as a hostage. It's why they took him in the first place."

The tension leaves Jeff's shoulders. "I'll always remember how kind he was to me. And I wouldn't have gotten this far in the competition if it hadn't been for him." He pulls Mason's small leather notebook from his backpack. "I thought I'd hold onto it forever. You know, for posterity. But if—I mean *when* he's released, I'm giving it back to him. "

I scan the pages: each number, paired with a letter, is gold to those who comprehend it.

It may be all gibberish to me, but Mason gave my son a gift he'll cherish forever.

Jeff will be devastated if Mason is murdered.

I'll make sure it won't happen.

I feel a tap on my shoulder: Lee.

His attempt at a smile is half-hearted. "You're wanted on my secure line. You can take it in my office."

Jeff looks up at me expectantly, then at Lee. Seeing Lee's face, I realize he thinks the worst has happened.

I do too.

Lee stays with Jeff as I walk away.

∾

MY ACME TEAM'S FACES ARE SEEN ON THE MONITOR, AS ARE Emma's and Ryan's.

A moment later, Marcus comes into view too. "We've just gotten a message from the Black King. He's offering Mason in exchange for Luda."

I think of how happy Eve will be to get the news—

And then I remember Luda is me.

Shite.

"When is the exchange to happen?" I ask.

Marcus replies, "This time tomorrow. Donna, as 'Luda,' accompanied by two state department officials, will arrive via yacht to a small island in the Narva River, just east of Narva-Jõesuu's border-crossing station on the Estonian side. You'll leave from a dock behind a small cafe called the Ivani Juures. The yacht is called the *Vabados.*"

"That means 'Freedom,' in Estonian," Emma informs us.

"Does anyone else see the irony in that?" Dominic mutters.

"Hopefully, other than Mason, the Black King will be alone. Whether he comes with a welcoming committee or not, you'll be armed," Ryan continues. "After Mason is safely aboard the *Vabados,* exterminate the Black King and anyone else he's brought along. Take his photo so that Acme can identify the son of a bitch after the fact. You'll then sail back to the cafe's dock. If something goes wrong and you need to escape, we'll have a second water vessel nearby: the *Lilla Pelikan.* It's a tugboat. Jack and Abu will be on it, along with its owner, Rasmus Saar, who will get you back to the Estonian side of the river."

"Sounds like I should pack my swimsuit." I'm pretending to be more chipper than I feel.

I notice Jack isn't smiling, either. When he realizes I'm staring at him, he turns to avoid my eyes.

He's still hurt.

Well, I am too.

Even this event can't bring him to my side.

THE STATE DEPARTMENT OFFICIALS—TWO YOUNG COCKY GUYS in suits and ties and dark glasses named Glen and Gary, come for 'Luda' right on time. We arrive at the cafe with fifteen minutes to spare. Even at nine at night, we're so far north that the sky is only now losing its light.

There's a chill in the air—or is that just my nerves?

The North Star, looming large, looks as if it's within reach. I'll take that as a good sign.

My Sig Sauer is holstered to the small of my back. With me between Gary and Glen, we head for the yacht.

We can see the island in the middle of the river. It takes just a few minutes to reach it. Another yacht is already there. Mason stands on its dock, his eyes widened in terror. His mouth is taped shut. His two captors flank him. They're dressed in black except for their rubber masks. The heaviest man resembles a knight in armor, and the tallest man's mask resembles a medieval king's.

Gary nudges me forward too. Taking the hint, I smile as I stroll to the yacht's side, where Glen has positioned its portable stair. He steps onto the dock, then offers his hand to help me.

As I walk toward Mason, the Black King shouts, "Walk to freedom, pawn!"

Mason winces but does as he's told.

As we pass, I hear a gunshot: Mason freezes, then falls onto me.

I feel a prick… was I shot too?

Suddenly I hear the whizz of suppressed bullets. One explodes Glen's head. The other leaves a blossom of blood on Gary's chest and propels his dead body backward through the *Vabados*.

Then darkness…

24

King versus Queen

If a queen is stupid enough to move right next to the competing king when she has no support, he may capture her.

Now, should a pawn be standing behind her and moving in that direction, it would be deadly for the king to capture her since he will yet again be in check.

In fact, he can't even capture the pawn prior to going after the queen because that would still put him within reach of her since she can move in any direction.

When beside a competing king, a queen has only got one dumb move, whereas he can blunder in so many ways.

Ladies, make that your mantra.

I wake with a splitting headache.

My arms and legs ache too.

When I open my eyes, I realize why. My appendages are bound to spread bars chained to the concrete floor and

231

ceiling. I'm dressed in a cup-less body-gasping lace-up vinyl teddy held together with a chafing G-string.

Not a good look—

Especially when you're live and in Technicolor.

In front of me, a seventy-inch video monitor is mounted on the cinder block wall. Ten feet out, I'm surrounded by three circular rails, each holding a webcam. The highest row looks down on me from a height of a few feet. The middle row has a straight-on view of me. The lower row is ankle-high and pointed upward.

The door opens. The man wearing the king's mask walks over. When he's close enough to stare down at me, I spit in his eye.

Growling, he punches me in the gut. I hold in my pain and my urge to scream. *"Send in the real Black King."* My cool taunt causes him to freeze.

Through a speaker, laughter roars through the room. A moment later, the door opens again.

Mason walks out, applauding. "Excellent! You are indeed a worthy opponent, Mrs. Craig. Tell me, what gave him away?"

"Not him, Mason. You did it—when you pricked me with the knock-out drug."

"A shame. I'd have hoped you'd bought into the charade for a few more days." He shrugs. "No matter. The rest of your friends in the intelligence community saw the incident as I'd hoped."

He takes the remote from a side table and turns on the monitor:

I watch as the Black King and his knight kill my consulate escorts.

Next, they shoot Mason and, supposedly, me. Our

captors stand over our blood-splattered supposedly dead bodies.

As the knight drags Mason's inert body offscreen, the Black King pulls me up by my hair, then peels away my prosthesis so that the camera reveals me as Donna Craig.

This leaves it up to conjecture that, all this time, I was a traitor to my country.

As the king drags away my body, the monitor goes dark.

Mason chuckles. "Wasn't it brilliant? Not just this bit of theater, but the whole thing from the start?"

"What do you want from me, a gold star?"

My impudence gets Mason's hands around my neck—

But then he backs off. "Don't want to damage the merchandise," he mutters.

"I'll credit you for having played me for so long," I concede. "Let me ask you: those welts on your back: made of peel-and-stick putty, right?"

"Not so amateurish as that, but good enough to fool you."

"And the reporters. And Eve."

"Ah, poor Eve." His sigh is heavy. "Yes, she bought my whole wounded political captive act hook, line, and sinker, albeit she almost caught me talking to Putin on a satellite phone, arranging your capture, among other things." He smirks. "Luda left a few loose ends, thanks to you."

"You're no Houdini. I take it your so-called second kidnap from the Narva-Jõesuu hotel was pre-recorded before Jody received it?"

"Excellent deduction! Tell me buckets of tears were shed."

"You had everyone fooled—even me. I'll grant you that."

"And now I've fooled them again!" he crows. "The whole world watched us die—boo-hoo!" He mimics wiping away tears. "That bit of theater was merely for the benefit of your family and the intelligence community."

"Yeah, so, about that: if I'm presumed dead, what's with the submissive sex kitten get-up and all the cameras? Is this for some cosplay snuff film?"

"Ah, if only I were satisfying some personal fetish! But no, Mrs. Craig. It's much, much worse." He pats my head. "My final auction will be *you*, Donna—*to the highest bidder*. Seeing you tarted up and chained should have the libidos rising among all those enemies who have you at the top of their hit lists. Gotta sell the merchandise, right?"

Knowing that he anticipates my horror, instead, I giggle. "Just because it's your fantasy, Mason doesn't make it everyone's."

Mason's eyes narrow. "You'd better hope I get my price. Otherwise, what I end up doing to you will be much worse. Imagine poor Jeff opening a gift box that holds your severed head! Ah, the trauma! It should throw off his game forever." He cups my face so that he doesn't miss any tell-tale sign of my reaction. "This is how you'll pay for your role in Luda's death."

"So Grigori was right. She was two-timing him with the Black King."

"She didn't want to return to Putin's snake nest any more than me." He shrugs. "Her reprieve came with her ability to please Vlad in the bedroom. Mine was to entice Russia's great leader with chess. Who doesn't want to play the world's chess master—and occasionally win against him?"

"What makes you think I had anything to do with her death?"

"Who do you think received the transmission of the intel from the Pentagon buffoon right before she died? It was me, you bitch!" He clucks his tongue in mock shame. "When I called her to confirm its receipt, she mentioned a female operative had followed her. The fact that I never heard from her again indicated she was exterminated."

"You were in love with her."

He nods. "Luda was my queen. Had she lived, we'd be far from everything that stood between us—including Putin." Mason frowns. "Before going to Los Angeles, Luda told me she'd been summoned to accompany Grigori back to Moscow. At first, she thought Putin had arranged for her to be Grigori's welcome home gift. She'd played the role before. Hated it! Grigori was a sadist, so no way in hell was she going to get onto that plane this time." Disgusted, Mason shakes his head. "Did you know she'd visited him in jail? She was his middleman with some deals that went down stateside with a few U.S. home-grown terrorists itching to move beyond AR15s to missile launchers." Mason chuckles. "But then Luda realized Putin was calling her home for good. I'd convinced her that we needed the income from that last arms deal for our getaway fund. She was afraid that Grigori had somehow found out that a few of those sales never made it into his offshore account."

"In other words, you put a target on her back," I point out.

Mason scowls and raises his hand, only to put it down again. "Then I saw her—that is, you—on the plane to take Grigori back to Moscow. We'd devised a signal she was to use on the tarmac to indicate where she'd hidden the arms to be delivered to some American patriots. I knew something was wrong when I gave it, and you didn't respond. Thankfully, while staying with Lee, I hacked Luda's secure cloud." He taps his forehead. "Note to self: I still have to salvage that deal to get paid. Later, when I met you through Lee and you asked me to be the face of Lee's competition and explained why, I realized you were the woman who had followed Luda from the bus, killed her, then taken her place to exterminate Grigori."

"And yet, you initially said no," I point out.

"Only to make you pant after me—which you did. You are *so* predictable, Mrs. Craig!" His fingers are poised over my breast, but he elects to tweak my nose instead. "You overplayed your hand by assuming no one would know you'd murdered her. I bet you nearly shit your pants when the 'Black King' sent you the note to Luda's cell phone as if he hadn't already known what you'd done to her."

He's angry enough that I think it best to change the subject: "The old guy who tried to stab you with his poison cane: was that a set-up to validate your change of heart?"

"Ha! I wish I'd thought of it! Putin was livid that Grigori's plane never made it back to Russia. The hit man he sent as retaliation was the real deal. By the way, thanks for taking care of him for me."

"Actions speak louder than words." I rattle my tethered arms as a broad hint.

Mason snickers. "Dream on."

"Worth a try." I shrug. "And now, in your guise as the Black King, you've gotten back in Putin's good graces by selling him the U.S. agent directory?"

"Brilliant, right? It was the final one I needed to acquire. And I got it, alright—thanks to my precious Luda."

"So he does have it." My heart sinks.

Mason's high-pitched giggle roils through the room. "Don't be a fool! What would be the fun of that? He'll pay dearly for it—especially after what he did to me—to my family!"

"You have Russian relatives? They, too, are being persecuted?"

"They were, yes. Sent into exile. To be condemned, never to set foot on your homeland again, to die in a country you despise. Well, now you, too, will know what that's like." His smile is cruel.

"When did you start collecting the intelligence dossiers?"

Given an opportunity to boast, Mason's eyes brighten. "My plan has been years in the making. My celebrity sends me all over the world. Like other human beings, military personnel also have routines, especially when stationed in their own countries. And those minions who meekly safe-guard their country's important secrets—especially ones highly coveted by the rest of the world—can feel taken for granted. Heaven knows they aren't compensated adequately."

"And then you come along: celebrated, brilliant, and interested in what makes them so important, so special."

"Exactly! And they lap it up with a spoon." Mason's eyes sparkle. "You'd be surprised at the pittance I've spent for my ill-gotten gains. In some cases, nothing at all. One idiot turned it over merely for the opportunity to lose to me."

"I hope that, at the very least, you allowed him to think he had a chance to win."

"But of course." He snickers. "Human nature is so predictable. Like all species, we fight to survive. But we're the only organisms that take life for granted." Mason moves so close that I inhale his hot breath. "You, for instance. You can't imagine how much I enjoyed letting you plead with me to go on the trip! And now, your mind is reeling as it takes in all the variables of your surroundings as you plot your chance to escape." He leans in. "Don't waste your time. Any moment you aren't tied up, you'll be drugged."

I smile. "You're a twisted piece of shit."

"You don't know the half of it." He shrugs. "For example, there's Jeff. I'll bet the fact he idolized me is now killing you. I enjoyed winning his loyalty. It made you fall in line too. I'll bet he was heartbroken when he heard I'd died."

"He was," I admit.

"Good. That makes up for going against my better judgment and betting him my chess playbook that he'd lose to Mikhail. He would have, too, had his last play been the one I'd trained him to make. Instead, he recognized the right move to win the game. Oh, well, you win some, you lose some." He frowns. "I tried to steal back my playbook before my supposed kidnapping, but I couldn't find where he'd hidden it. The damn thing is priceless! Not that he'd have ever figured that out." Mason shrugs. "Oh, well. Should he ever learn the truth about my role in your imminent demise, I'm sure he'll burn it. Such irony!"

I can't keep my cool any longer. "Leave my son out of this," I growl.

"I will—for now, anyway." Turning to leave, he adds, "Your auction starts soon. Enjoy these few moments of solitude without torture. Something tells me it's the last you'll ever have. I told you I'd pay you back, didn't I?"

The lights go out.

～

I take a bet that, by keeping my eyes closed, I'll fool anyone watching me via the webcam into thinking I'm sleeping.

Instead, I anticipate what I can do to free myself.

The cuffs holding my wrists aren't the sort used in titillating sex play but steel that must be opened with a key. Because they are on a spread bar attached to a taut chain secured to the ceiling, a ladder will be needed to release me, presenting a vulnerable moment for at least one of my captors.

Will both of Mason's goons be sent to do the task?

My guess is yes, and that they will be armed. Mason is no fool. He'd be sure to double his odds that at least one could contain me.

Will he be with them? If so, it will complicate matters.

As with all things in life, success is in the timing. To escape, I must make the right moves with split-second precision.

Or die trying.

The lights go on again. I'm live on the monitor. A mechanical voice—Mason's, deepened with a filter —announces:

"Ladies and gents, it's the moment we've all been waiting for: the sale of the assassin, Donna Stone Craig! Yep, that's right. The femme fatale you love to hate—and had hoped to kill—is now within one lucky bidder's reach!"

The camera wheel slowly turns around me. Their red lights correspond with the scenes that appear on the

Jumbotron. The background music crescendos with the excitement in Mason's voice:

"Let me point out that she's in excellent shape"—One of the lower cameras zooms in on my posterior— "Okay, maybe she could lose a few unsightly pounds in the caboose—"

THE NERVE OF THAT GUY!

"Still, you won't find a bruise, scratch, or welt on that soft, supple skin—"

That's more like it.

"—Because I'm leaving her ruin to you! For those who have always wanted to know how Delicious Donna would endure torture, imagine the thrill of testing those limits! Everyone wants a piece of her—*literally.* But only one of you will have her for your very own, to do with as you please—repeatedly. Priceless, right? Let's start the bidding!"

Should I be proud that Russia offers ten million?

Or that Saudi Arabia ups the ante to twenty?

And how is it that the Taliban feels I'm worth thirty mil? Let me guess: they consider me a bad role model for women and want to make an example of me.

China puts the kibosh on that with a bid of fifty million.

North Korea weighs in at seventy-five.

Russia gets back in the game by taking it up to one hundred and twenty-five million.

The bidding pauses, but then China doubles it to two hundred and fifty million.

Again, silence.

"Going once, going twice...." Mason pauses.

"Trista millionov dollarov!" I recognize the voice: Igor Baronov.

Three hundred million?…

Two minutes later, still silence.

"Sold—to Russia!" Mason exclaims.

Ah, shite…

I guess it's payback time.

A few minutes later, Mason appears. He's got my clothes folded in his arms. He drops them onto the floor.

"Let me guess: you want to undress me."

"Nope, I'm leaving that to my boys. It's an added bonus for being great henchmen! And besides, I'm on the run. Gotta be at my bank by Wednesday." Mason laughs, don't look so sad, Mrs. Craig. In your favor, you were an interesting conquest. Hey, look at it this way. Now Jack won't have to go through the drudgery of divorce because you'll already be dead—to him, anyway…"

He thinks for a moment. "Unless you want to flip for it." He pulls his pants pockets inside out. "Darn it, I don't have a coin."

"I do. In my pants." I nod toward them, on the floor.

He frowns. "Oh. Okay." Shrugging, he reaches down and pulls out Jack's coin: the one weighted to always flip to heads. "How about this? Heads, I let you go. Tails, you go to your new master, Putin."

I think back to the plane ride to Brussels when Mason showed me Eve's ring. He saw my interaction with Lee, who bet me with the heads coin. Did he also overhear our conversation?

No. There's no way he'd know that the coin is weighted. Otherwise, he'd never suggest that I take a bet where he'd have to let me go free.

"Sure, flip it." I try not to sound too cocky.

He tosses the coin. As it lands, his eyes open wide. "Well…what do you know?" He shows me:

Tails.

"But… That can't be!"

"Sure it can… Oh, wait! Let me guess: you thought I tossed *this* coin instead." He reaches into my pants pocket again and pulls out the coin I'd also taken from Jack. "Thanks to you, I've got a complete set again. You see, I given the heads coin to Janie. How lucky—*for me*—that Lee thought to gift it back to you instead."

Noting my scowl, he laughs. "Worried about my men's rough hands? Relax! Their orders are to look only, but not touch. And no need to worry as to whether your FSB escorts will get frisky either. The big guy doesn't like leftovers."

"By that, do you mean Igor Baronov?"

"Are you kidding? We both know *that* won't be the case. Sure, he'll threaten and taunt you. But not to worry: he's just the courier. You're now the property of one Vladimir Vladimirovich Putin." He strokes my face lovingly. "Sorry, Donna, but them's the breaks."

"What do you mean by that?"

Mason smirks. "I overplayed my hand. Putin found out more quickly than I'd anticipated that the Russian directory was a fake. I mean, sure, there were enough dissidents and low-end bureaucrats on it to make it plausible—even a couple of oligarchs and generals who'd rubbed me the wrong way. Silly me, I should have never included Putin's mistress in the Russian directory. He beat her senseless, then tossed her into IK-2 for the guards to have at her." He shrugs. "Until Vlad knows he's finally secured Russia's spy directory once and for all, he can take out his angst on you. Word of caution, sweet Donna: do your best to amuse him so that you prolong your inevitable final destination: IK-2. You know it's the worst penal colony Russia has, right? It has 'Welcome to Hell' written right over the door—"

My spit hits its mark: Mason's eye.

He reels back to punch me but then thinks better of it. "You're lucky I promised to deliver you in pristine condition."

At the thought of my new future, bile rises in my throat.

"Ah, sweet Donna, I know it's hard to swallow that you're just another captured pawn in the world's biggest chess game. But, hey, if you keep Putin happy, who knows? Maybe you'll get back on the board."

In other words, getting out of here is now or never.

Mason chuckles as he heads out the door.

A HALF-HOUR LATER, MASON'S TWO GOONS COME INTO THE room. They no longer wear masks, but I recognize them by their builds: one taller, the other bulkier.

They were also the chess monitors he'd assured me could be trusted.

No surprise there.

Bulkier carries a ladder. He places it beside me and climbs it to unhook my arm cuffs from the spread bar.

At the same time, Taller kneels to unlock my ankle cuffs. He's quicker than Bulkier, who's just loosened the second wrist by the time Taller rises—

With a syringe in his hand.

Despite my narrow stance, Bulkier's timing couldn't be better because he leaves me standing tall: the perfect position to let loose with a front kick that sends Taller stumbling backward, knocking down the ring of cameras.

Bulkier is too shocked to realize that my next kick takes the ladder out from under him. He falls backward and hard. A blood halo spreads behind his head. His eyes are still open, so mission accomplished.

Before Taller can get on his feet, I stomp on the hand holding the syringe. Screaming from the pain, he drops it.

I grab it—

And he grabs me from behind, around the waist.

Because he's on his knees, his neck is exposed. I jab the syringe into his jugular vein.

He gasps, loosens his grip, and falls backward.

I tap his neck for a pulse. He's still breathing…

Barely…

Until I pick up his gun and shoot him, point blank, in the heart.

I take Bulkier's gun too. Both are G47s.

Taller also has a ring of keys that includes a car fob.

I open the door slowly to verify that I'm indeed alone.

The building sits in a thicket of trees and faces a dirt road. It's surrounded by a barbed wire fence chained with a lock.

As Mason said, it sits next to a river.

A car sits in the weed-choked concrete pad in front of the building. I open the trunk. As I'd hoped, there's a case of ammo. I move it beneath the front passenger seat.

I run to the gate to unlock it. Finally, one of the smallest keys does the trick—

But I'm too late. Two vans have just crested the hill a few hundred yards from the property.

I run to the car, grab my munitions then head to the right side of the warehouse. The dumpster beside the building will give me some cover.

I duck behind it and wait.

THERE ARE TWO MEN IN EACH VAN.

I recognize one: Igor Baronov.

They don't park near the door. Instead, one van pulls to the back of the car and the other parks in front of it.

Not good.

Two men get out of their vehicle: not Baronov and his driver, but the men in the other van.

Should anything go wrong, they're the designated sitting ducks. It's why they move low and slow with weapons drawn—

And why my first shot is at Baronov instead. As the bullet shatters the glass, his head jerks back: proof I've hit my mark.

Baronov's driver—I recognize him as the general's lover—slumps low beneath the steering wheel. Instead of waiting for him to show himself, I use the other men's shock and awe at their fearless leader's death to shoot one in the heart. The other guy gets off a few shots that riddle the dumpster before he, too, hits the ground, strafed by my bullets.

Seeing the writing on the wall, Baronov's driver puts his van in reverse. I aim for the tires, but he gets away.

I take the guns, ammo, money, and IDs off the dead men. Then I hop into Taller and Bulkier's van. It's not that far to the Narva River and Estonia on its other side. If Baronov's driver calls in my escape, I'll have a dragnet on my tail, so I better haul ass out of here.

25

Sudden Death

"Sudden Death" occurs when the end of the game is decided within a certain period of time—most likely, within twenty minutes on each player's clock.

Imagine if, in real life, you knew how long you had left to live! Would it change your actions? Would you focus on the things that really matter to you and discard all your mundane petty worries?

You'd think so, right?

Well, guess what: the clock is ticking.

So, what are you waiting for?

The car's navigation system speaks Russian, but from what I can tell on its map, I'm now about eight miles from the Narva River.

The road, narrow and rough, moves in a southwesterly direction and is bordered by thick woods on both sides.

Occasionally, I pass the driveway of a small farm or cottage.

GPS announces that the Estonian Passport Control Point is straight ahead. It's now dark. Should I even attempt outrunning the guard?

Suddenly, I hear a commotion. A military police van, siren screaming, is straight ahead and coming my way, blowing past the checkpoint.

Before the van passes, I kill my headlights and pull behind the high wall of a neighboring cottage.

This 'hood may soon be swarming with police. I've got to find a place to hide.

GPS shows that there is a tributary of the Narva River nearby. It runs behind a few farms and the tavern I've just passed. I remember its billboard touting borscht, pelmeni, blinis, and seven different vodkas.

It also rents canoes.

Bingo. They won't realize one is missing until morning.

I've just walked into the tavern's car lot when I realize the police van has swung around and is heading back this way. I've got nowhere to go but inside.

ALL EYES ARE ON ME.

There are just a few folks here. Four men of varying ages sit at the bar. Two older gents in a booth pause from the joy of shoveling dumplings into their open mouths to stare at me. A younger man, wearing glasses, sits alone in another booth, a bottle of vodka in one hand and a thick book opened in front of him.

The elderly waitress freezes, as does the barkeep. But seeing that I'm not the head-cracking gun-toting goon squad that just flew past, their eyes shift back to the TV over the bar, where two Russian soccer teams are tearing up a field to the frenzied joy of a stadium filled with fans.

A moment later, the siren is back and too close for comfort.

In the parking lot, in fact.

I ignore it. Instead, I smile broadly as I saunter to the scholar's booth. He's shocked when I sit down beside him. My deep longing kiss leaves him doubly so.

The front door creaks as it opens. As I'd hoped, my scholar is too enamored with my seductive hello to do anything other than lean into the fantasy I've created for him: one in which a total stranger—a woman at that—has saved him from yet another hazy night of self-pity softened by fermented potato juice and Tolstoy's ironic rants on the human condition.

I hear three pairs of footsteps circling the room. One of my eyes is hidden by the lucky guy enjoying my tongue probing his molars. My other eye plays peek-a-boo through a scrim of my hair, allowing me to see the suited men, guns drawn, who walk slowly while scanning the faces of the silent few who seem frozen in place.

Then I feel it: the gun nuzzled against my neck. Its owner mutters: "*Dvigay zadnitsey, kukolka. Pora domoy.*"

I know enough Russian to make out the gist: something like, "Move your ass, doll. Time to go home."

It's an interesting choice of words.

So that's it: my new "home" is to be some dungeon in Putin's Black Sea-adjacent Italianate palace?

I hope the mistress accused of spying on Putin doesn't have visiting rights there. Otherwise, thanks to Mason's tomfoolery, the key to my cell may go missing forever.

My mystery date backs away. He wants no part of my new playmates.

So much for chivalry.

I'm yanked out of the booth. The other two in my captor's goon squad flank my other side and back. I'm shoved toward the front door—

And into the police van. Both of my hands are cuffed to a pole beside a bench.

Two men jump back into the van's cab, but one stays in the back with me, sitting far enough away that I couldn't kick him if I tried.

As the van peels off, I realize Jack and the kids may never know I'm alive.

I can't stop the tears from falling down my cheeks.

The man stands up and comes toward me. He's lifted his hands as if to comfort me.

We'll see about that.

When he's close enough, I lean back as if broken and fatigued. Then, using the pole as leverage, as quickly as I can and with all my might, I kick him hard—

In the groin.

He smacks into the far side of the van, then crumples onto the floor, all the while groaning in pain, eyes closed.

He's dropped the lock's key.

I slide my foot out, snag the keychain, and pull it back to me—

Only to have him grab hold of my ankle, jerking me off the bench.

I land on the floor—*hard*, on my ass. My arms feel as if they've been pulled out of their sockets. Anguished, I cry out with every curse I can think of.

My captor stumbles over. Slapping his hand over my mouth, he hisses, "Donna, for God's sake—it's *me*!"

Now I'm really crying.

And laughing.

And kissing the man who I thought held my fate in his hands.

Of course he does.

He's Jack.

26

Endgame

FRIEDRICH NIETZSCHE ONCE SAID, "IN REVENGE AND LOVE, woman is more barbarous than man."

Apparently, he played chess.

He was undoubtedly thinking of that point in every game when the king must make a move: save himself, as it were.

If he's lucky, fewer opposing pieces are on the board to make his life miserable.

However, one piece can be his worst nightmare: the opposing queen, who can move any number of spaces and in any direction.

Have no doubt: at all costs, she will save her king.

AS JACK REMOVES MY CUFFS, I ASK, "HOW DID YOU find me?"

"The night we…well, I guess we can't really call it making love—"

"Ah…right. Your demonstration of an *ops fuck.*"

Jack winces. "Yes, well, on that less-than-memorable night, I tagged you with a tracking microdot."

"But…why?"

"By then, Acme suspected Mason was the Black King."

"For how long?" I ask.

"After the first bid, it dawned on me it might be prudent for Arnie to record the comings and goings of anyone on the competition manifest: competitors, their parents or friends, spectators, and Lee's and Jody's contracted staffers. Adding facial recognition and the Paris webcam network, he could triangulate it to the bidder's retrieval spot."

"That's several hundred people!"

"Thank goodness for A.I., right? We knew it was Mason after the second bidding event: General Jung's, in Paris."

"I ran into Jody and Mason leaving the Ritz! They were going to meet some French journalists in Jardin des Tuileries, where Mason was to be interviewed."

Jack nods. "Afterward, knowing that Jody had a tight schedule, Mason suggested that she return to the hotel while he walked along the riverbank. One of the book stalls was closed for the weekend. Mason buried a tin canister deep within a fern behind it. Abu verified its location before the bid event. Once Mason texted the direction to General Jung—from a burner phone; but its GPS signal came from Mason's suite—we knew he was the Black King."

"And you didn't think it wise to let me in on this little tidbit?" I hold my hands in my lap to fight the urge to pound on him. "Or, for that matter, Lee? Let's face it: we both had much to lose: our kids, for starters. My God! Had anything happened at the hotel during the tournament—"

"As it turns out, Lee also suspected Mason by then."

"You're kidding!" I shake my head in disbelief. "Why?"

"On the flight to Singapore, Janie went looking for her dad and walked into Lee's office. Mason was at Eve's desk, trying to hack into her computer. He told Janie some cockamamie story about wanting to leave Eve a love note. But it bothered Janie enough to mention it to Lee."

"I can imagine! She may only be twelve, but still… The whole of her young life has been spent looking over her shoulder for those who wanted to harm her or her family. And besides, Eve is like a mother to her. I'm sure Janie had also been hoping Lee would finally quit pussyfooting around and appreciate the sweetness and light right before his eyes."

"Gee, had I known you were so invested in their happily ever after—"

I snort. "You knew. You just wanted to believe otherwise."

"Yeah, um…well, speaking of that…" Jack frowns. "After the conversation you and I had in Singapore—"

"You mean after you gave me the ultimatum to cut off my friendship with Lee or you'd leave me?"

"Yeah…that." He sighs. "I went down to the bar to drink away my woes and…." He hesitates. "Well, I ran into someone. I'm glad I did because I got it out of my system. You know, my jealousy. I spent the rest of the evening—"

Ah…

Here it comes…

The confession.

He wants to tell me that he picked up a strange woman to blow off steam.

Maybe it was Daniela.

This was his way of getting the vision of me with Lee out of his sight, out of his mind.

I brace myself to hear the worst: they returned to her room. And he tried hard—very, very hard—to forget me.

As for his anger fuck, the lucky gal had a night she'll never forget.

"—talking with Lee. Not just about his suspicions regarding Mason—"

"Whoa!… Say that again? You spent the night… just…*talking*?…*With Lee*?"

Jack shrugs. "Yeah. Hard to believe, right? And boy, did he set me straight on a lot of things. Including his feelings about Eve. And about you."

"So, now you believe him—and me?"

"Yes, I do. I can't blame Lee for having been infatuated with you. When you think about it, he went through the same trust issues we had: you with Carl, me with Valentina. Babette certainly did a number on his head. And then you came along and opened his eyes—about her. He'd denied the truth for the longest time. Then, when he couldn't any longer, he realized what a good friend you were to warn him that she was a Quorum operative and had been setting him up to take the fall for her." Jack takes my hand. "He does love you, Donna. But as a friend. As *a sister*. In fact, Lee divulged that before Mason arrived at Lion's Lair, he'd purchased an engagement ring for Eve."

"So, even before he got the call from POTUS asking if he'd shelter Mason, he'd planned to ask Eve to marry him?"

"On the last day of the chess events, in fact," Jack reveals. "But when he saw how Eve responded to Mason, he realized he'd waited too late."

"Heck no, he hasn't! Eve told me so! I should call her now and tell her!"

Jack raises a brow. "Despite your sisterly love for Lee, this is one time he doesn't need your advice. Trust me, he's not making the same mistake twice."

"So, just to clarify the situation, you no longer feel I should cut off contact with him?"

"No, I don't."

"Finally, you get it!" I murmur.

At that moment, I remember something Lee said to me —when?… Oh yes, on the flight to Venice: *Just remember, Donna, it's all a game…*

"Damn it, Jack! If you've been bosom buddies since Singapore, why didn't you—or Lee—let me in on your bromance? Or, for that matter, why didn't you inform me about Mason?"

"Despite how it seemed then, it wasn't my idea to keep pretending to be jealous after my heart-to-heart with Lee, or to keep you in the dark. That was Ryan's call." Jack looks me in the eye. "Mason was using different burner phones to coordinate each auction. For Acme to have eyes and ears on him throughout the mission, we needed to activate Achilles on his devices."

I ask, "Since Lee was onto Mason by then, why not just have him do it?"

Jack rolls his eyes. "Are you kidding? Even as good as Lee is at keeping secrets, he's got so many tells he would have given it away. If they're obvious to me, no doubt Mason would have picked up on them, what with all the time he spent with Lee at Lion's Lair and on the plane."

I chuckle. "You're right about that! Lee is great at many things, but he'd be lousy at covert ops."

"The best opportunity to do this was on those long

flights," Jack explains. "Acme needed it to be one of us: specifically, someone whose sudden presence on the flight wouldn't raise Mason's suspicions. When you and I had our blowup, Ryan deduced that putting you on Lee's plane gave us our best opportunity. Not only did I tell him I didn't like it, I told him in no uncertain terms how wrong it was to leave an agent out in the cold and flying blind. But he convinced me that it was the best way for you to play against someone who, for his entire life, has been a master manipulator. It's how Mason built his reputation as a chess master—not to mention every other facet of his life, professionally and personally. Ryan was right, of course. Each time Mason sidled up to you on these long flights, your proximity to him allowed us to activate Achilles on the burner he would be using next. Not to mention that your presence was catnip to him. He already knew Acme was heading up the operation to specifically track down the Black King. And, as you so painfully found out later, he knew you'd killed Luda. He was out for blood: yours."

"He was indeed. After Luda uploaded the U.S. directory she received in the handoff on the bus in Los Angeles, she told Mason she'd been followed by a female American operative," I admit. "Remember when Grigori accused 'Luda' of being the Black King's lover? He was right. During the so-called prisoner exchange, Mason realized I wasn't Luda because they had a passcode they used in each other's presence to indicate that she'd secured a deal with some American terrorists. He asked 'Luda,' 'What is your role in this gambit?' But she—that is, I— ignored him."

"Yet another reason your close proximity played into his hands," Jack reasons. "What better way to beat us at our own game than by winning you over, manipulating you, capturing you, and auctioning you off to the highest bidder? He had no doubt it would be Russia."

"Mason even used our break-up to his advantage," I reply. "He tried to convince me that you'd given up on our marriage, and that Lee would come around, now that Eve was enthralled with him. When I saw you with Daniela, I believed him."

Jack laughs, shaking his head. "Remember, Dannie was the one who tipped us off about Narva-Jõesuu. Mason was already on MI6's radar, but since he is an American citizen, they wanted the U.S. to, in her words, 'confirm nor deny.' Our hallway kiss was show and tell for Mason, who was a few steps behind you. Then I spent the next hour grousing about how upset I was for having to pretend I hated you. She called me a cad."

"That redeems her in my eyes." I sigh. "You fooled me completely. Then again, so did Mason—until he attempted to kill me." I shudder. "At least you got to me before I was shipped to IK-2." I look around at the holding cell. "Speaking of that, where did you pick up this cute little jalopy?"

"It's Russia's standard issue police van. There are a couple of them warehoused behind every station. Rasmus Saar, the owner of the *Lilla Pelikan,* is drinking buddies with the police captain of a little hamlet on the Russian side: Sarkiuly, just upriver. One night, while the guy was snoring in the bar, he made a copy of the van's key. With all the smuggling Rasmus does across the Narva River, it comes in handy. The passport guards never stop it when it flies by with the siren blaring."

"It was much better than my plan. I'd noticed the tributary behind the tavern where you found me. Had you not tracked me there, I would have canoed downstream to the Narva and into Estonia."

"You truly are a marvel," Jack declares.

"You're giving me far too much credit." I tear up. "I was exactly what Mason called me: 'the perfect pawn.'"

"Tell me: how many men did you kill to escape?"

Five," I admit.

"You've just proven my point." As Jack strokes my hair, I see the pride in his eyes. "Donna, you will always be my queen."

When he kisses me, I realize how much he's missed me.

Suddenly, I bolt away. "Oh, dear! Poor Eve! When she finds out the truth about Mason, she'll…she'll be devastated!"

Jack takes a deep breath. "If Lee is as in love with her as you say, I can't think of a better person to pick up the pieces when her world comes tumbling down."

"Do you mean that?"

"Ironically, yes. I've never seen him so gentle and loving as when Eve got word of Mason's supposed death —not even with you." Jack's smile fades. "There's something else you should know, Don. Mason is a triple agent."

I can't believe my ears. "My God! He's been working as a U.S. operative too? Let me guess. He came in on Edmonton's watch."

"No—though I'm sure Branham wishes that were the case." Jack frowns. "Three generations of Mason's family have been embedded stateside and carrying out deep-cover espionage activities for Russia."

"Wow! Talk about a long-term covert assignment!" I shake my head, awed. "How was that possible?"

"His grandparents were Russian spies. They came over before the Cold War: took a couple of names off old graves and kept on the move—until Grandpa became an administrative aide to a United States senator. They then raised their son—Mason's father, Richard—as a spy. He rose to the position of administrative aide on Capitol Hill, penetrating policy-making circles and finally hopscotching his way into the Pentagon. He even married another Russian operative who'd succeeded in doing the same. Unfortunately, while at the State Department, Branham worked under Richard Ledbetter. Ledbetter Senior was always sociable with his staff, having them over for drinks, poker, or tennis. Branham had known Mason since he was a teen. When Mason was still in college—George Washington University—Richard invited Branham to lunch. By then, Mason was already a chess prodigy. Branham thought the idea of Mason's chess career as his cover was his idea. Only after Acme proved he was also the Black King did he realize he'd been played."

"Understandably so. Still...I hope he's not considering stepping down now!"

"Sadly, yes, he's weighing the option. He was devastated when Mason was supposedly imprisoned by Putin. But then Acme proved it was all a farce. More than likely, Mason was getting further FSB training and new mandates. Branham feels he owes POTUS his resignation. And now that Mason is once again out of reach—"

"But he's not! Jack, Mason screwed over Putin, too! He didn't sell the actual operative directory but a fake one, created from names of the usual suspects: dissidents and other enemies already wanted. He gave the FSB an excuse to do so, but he overplayed his hand by putting one of Putin's mistresses on the list. When Putin realized this, she'd already been imprisoned and roughed up in the usual way. Ruined enough for him, anyway. I was to be his olive branch to Putin. As for the real directory, Mason keeps it in a safety deposit box in the same bank where the winners' fees were deposited. Putin is willing to pay him a trillion dollars to get it back. In fact, Mason is going to retrieve it on…." I leap up. "What day is today, anyway?"

"Monday."

"We've still got time. He'll be at his offshore bank on Wednesday!"

"Do you know which one?"

"No. But I know how we can find out. Mason groused that he'd given some notebook to Jeff. In his own words, one thing in it was 'the key to his success.' In fact, he attempted to steal it back but couldn't find where Jeff had hidden it from Trisha and Janie. Where are they now?"

"With Aunt Phyllis and Porter on the last leg of their honeymoon tour: Florence, Italy. She was so upset that she couldn't join us to watch the kids compete. Lee promised her he'd bring the kids there afterward. They'll all go home together sometime this weekend."

"Ha! Well, I guess it's one way for Lee to ensure Porter returns from his round-the-world honeymoon boondoggle."

Jack's laughter sparks the memory of the first time I heard it: after I kicked the wind out of him for pretending to be my husband in front of my very young and confused children. At the time, it was used derisively, to offset my distrust of him.

Since then, I've heard it numerous times. Many laughs were shared with Mary, Jeff, Trisha, and Evan while enjoying their cockeyed antics or silly jokes.

Sometimes it's an appreciative chuckle that comes after our lovemaking.

In any form, I've missed it. And I've missed Jack.

I'm glad to know he'll never doubt me again. Nor I, him.

The van picks up speed, and its siren wails again. Arnie slides open the glass panel between the van's cab and its holding pen to shout, "We're blowing through the security checkpoint again, so hold on tight, lovebirds."

Jack hugs me as if he'll never let me go.

27

The Queen's Gambit

IN CHESS, THE QUEEN IS THE MOST POWERFUL PIECE ON THE *board because she can move forward, backward, diagonally, and as many spaces as she wants, as long as there are no other pieces in the way.*

Despite this, in a move called "the Queen's Gambit"—first recognized in 1490, and a favorite since the 1873 Vienna tournament—the queen is sacrificed to a pawn.

If played by White, the goal is to exchange a wing pawn (in this case, the "c-pawn," or center pawn), allowing the player to dominate the center squares (e2 to e4).

Black can make two responses to the move: either it can accept (QGA) or decline it (QGD).

In the QGA, Black temporarily gives up the center to obtain more unrestricted movement.

In the QGD, Black usually plays to hold the center. But the odds are declining and could cramp Black's style. Still, Black aims to break free using one of two adjacent pawns (d4 and d5).

But things aren't always as they seem, are they?

In this case, Black only retains the pawn at a disadvantage. Play it, and you'll see what I mean.

As with all of life, it comes down to this:

Are you willing to sacrifice what you hold most dear to win the game?

THE FINAL STOP ON AUNT PHYLLIS AND PORTER'S honeymoon is a rooftop Florence apartment with spectacular views. On one side, it overlooks Duomo di Firenze: the city's octagonal red-domed cathedral. On another, the Arno River flows beneath colorful bridges, some flanked by tiny townhouses.

Enveloping me in a hug, my aunt declares, "You came in the nick of time."

There's no need to explain because I see just what she means. Sunset, a surreal phantasm of fuchsia, baby blue, and pink, deepens over the city's ubiquitous clay-tiled roofs.

The children are oblivious to this. They're too busy diving into the rooftop pool.

Everyone but Jeff.

"When do you think we should tell the kids the truth about Mason?" I ask Jack.

"The sooner, the better," Aunt Phyllis declares.

With Marcus' approval, Lee's security team, Porter included, has been fully briefed on Mason's duplicity. But knowing my aunt as I do, I wouldn't put it past her to listen through keyholes. And I wouldn't blame Porter for allowing it upon occasion. He understands her concern for those she knows and loves. Porter and the family Craig

tops that list, but Lee and his brood—not to mention Eve—
are second on the rung.

"We're going to take your advice," I assure her. "But
since Jeff felt especially close to Mason. Do you mind
watching the others while we talk to him?"

"Heck no! I miss their silly antics. Run along,
young'uns, and take care of business." She shoos us off.

Jack walks over to Jeff, motioning him to follow us. Jeff
seems relieved to be sidelined. Unlike the others, he's been
morose since being informed of Mason's supposed demise.

Thank goodness the children didn't see my faked
death.

Having lost my mother before adulthood, I know the
pain they'd feel.

At times, I catch my children's sidelong glances or
joyous smiles. I know they're creating a memory—

Something I will savor should the seamier part of my
life catch up to me.

"WHAT'S UP, KIDS?" LIKE HIS SMILE, JEFF'S FLIPPANCY IS
translucent enough to reveal his pain.

I start: "We have some news about Mason. First, you
need to know he's alive."

A kaleidoscope of emotions play out on Jeff's face:
shock, hope, elation. "Then…the Russians don't have
him?"

"No, they don't," Jack concedes. "Mason faked his own
death."

Stunned, Jeff sits down. "Because he's worried that
they will kill him?"

I sigh. "Jeff, Mason is known in espionage as a triple agent. He is—as were his grandparents and parents—a Russian spy. Worse yet, he was also recruited to be a U.S. operative. In other words, he was giving away our secrets to the Russians."

"You're saying he was a traitor." Jeff's voice is barely a whisper.

I nod. "Not only that, Mason kidnapped me to prove his loyalty to Russia. Luckily, I escaped. Dad was able to help me come back safely."

Jeff takes my hand. "Mom, is Mason still on the loose?"

"Yes, but he's far away from here. We know how to find him: something we want to do so that he can stand trial for his crimes. In fact, he divulged that he gave you a notebook. He wanted it back because it shows where he may have gone."

"Yes, I have it. He promised it to me if I beat Mikhail."

"He tried to steal it back before he left but couldn't find it," Jack replies.

Jeff blushes. "Knowing the girls had planned to steal it as a joke, I hid it in the last place they'd thought to look for it." He opens his suitcase. Inside is a bag labeled STINKS TO HIGH HEAVEN.

Jack stares at it. "What the heck is that?"

I'm laughing too hard to answer. Finally, I gasp, "It's Jeff's dirty underwear and socks!" I pat him on the shoulder. "Well, you're right about that! The girls wouldn't have opened it in a million years."

Jeff hands it to me. "It's got notations that are chess moves he'd made during his more famous games. But there was a page that didn't really make sense." He flips through it to the back of the book.

I see what he means. Unlike the other pages, the numbers don't reflect a chessboard's squares or pieces.

I take photos of the pages and upload them into Acme's secure cloud. Then I call Emma. "Open the file I've just created. Ask your team to decipher it. I'm especially interested in the back page. Maybe you can confirm what I think: that it's bank account numbers."

"Let's see if you're right," she replies.

In the meantime, Aunt Phyllis has a fabulous traditional dinner waiting for us, served with Chianti. We start with prosciutto, melon, and pane with an aperitif. We then move on to the primo: polenta, followed by spezzatino di maiale con piselli served with an insalata. We end with formaggio and fruit followed by gelato.

Famished, I eat everything put in front of me.

Emma rings back just as I take my last bite. Jack and I take the call in our room. When we get on the line, the rest of our team is on it too. "The numbers indicate a Monaco bank account," she informs us. "It's called Banque Fontaine. Mason also has a safety deposit box there."

"Today is Tuesday. Mason mentioned he'd be there tomorrow," I explain.

"He's got an appointment with the bank manager at 9:30 sharp," Emma tells us. "Since he's closing the account, the bank protocol is to do so in person."

That makes sense," Ryan reasons. "However, the Monacans will blow a gasket if he's arrested on the premises."

In other words, not an ounce of blood is to be shed within the heavy wooden doors of the bank.

"The moment he steps outside, anything goes, right?" Jack asks.

"That's the way I read it," Ryan replies. "It's a four-and-a-half-hour flight. You'll leave tonight."

You would think the children would be sadder about

our taking off again. Instead, they're enjoying the creature comforts of Porter and Aunt Phyllis's digs: the pool, wall-sized video game set-up, a daily visit from a chef adept at the region's cuisine, and all of Florence outside their doorstep.

Wish I could join them. But Ryan has already informed us we'll take Mason to Morocco, where some black site has been tricked out with bells and whistles specifically for him.

Seriously, it couldn't happen to a more deserving guy.

"Not to worry. We'll get the kids home safely," Aunt Phyllis promises.

I tease, "So, the honeymoon is over?"

"Since Lee is our ride, we'll be home by the weekend." She chuckles. "That's okay. Rumor has it there may be another wedding on the horizon."

"Have you been listening through keyholes again?" Jack asks.

"Not this time," Phyllis scowls at his inference. "You didn't hear him? My lord! Lee literally hollered it from the rooftop!"

She points out the window.

In the moonlight, we can make out Eve wrapped in Lee's arms as they kiss.

"About damn time," Porter mutters. "Eagle has pussy-footed around that sweet gal for too dang long."

Amen.

WE GET IN AT TWO IN THE MORNING. THE HOTEL WE'VE chosen is literally across the street from the bank. In fact, our windows overlook it.

The night shift is a two-person security detail. They sit in comfy chairs in front of a bank of monitors that switch between its classic turn-of-the-last-century marbled interiors and exteriors taken from the cameras on every corner.

Arnie wastes no time hacking into the bank's security system and has mirrored its video footage. After the cleaning crew leaves, Jack and I enter through the back door.

We open the security office door, shooting tranquilizer darts into the necks of the guards. As they snore, we pull the darts. They won't remember us since they never heard or saw us.

Remotely, Arnie unlocks the safety deposit vault. As we walk in, he informs us, "He'll still be able to enter here because he has a personal vault key. I figure he'll do that first. However, I've changed his fingerprint and eye scan for the final account closing and withdrawal."

"How did you do that?" Jack asks.

"I substituted it for my own. You're now speaking to the richest man in the world." Arnie gives two thumbs up.

We're laughing so hard that we have to hold each other.

"I've also flagged his debit and credit cards as stolen, so that will stop him from making ATM withdrawals," Arnie adds.

We go to Mason's numbered box and open it with the code jotted in the lined booklet. Inside is only one thing: a ledger filled with various codes.

We take pictures of each page. "Emma, have your team decipher these," I suggest.

"I already see a pattern based on Mason's other cipher and the amounts we know are the winning bids," she replies. "My guess: this is a list of the banks where he's deposited them."

I laugh. "Well now, these will be quite a windfall of ill-gotten gains for Uncle Sam."

I tear out an empty page. On it, I write:

Queen's Gambit! Surrender, Pawn!
     555-036-2435

The phone number relays through the Acme switchboard to my mobile and can't be traced for a GPS signal.

After pocketing the booklet, I leave my message in Mason's safety deposit box and spin the dial. "Let's get out of here."

Jack laughs. "You know he will be pissed when he calls your number."

"He'll be even angrier when he's sent to Morocco. I want to personally see him off. And I'm not leaving the tarmac until that plane flies away."

"You and me both," Jack exclaims.

THE FOLLOWING DAY AT PRECISELY 9:20 IN THE MORNING, Mason drives up to the bank in a baby blue Maserati MC20. He whistles as he walks in.

Abu parks a van in front of the sports car. Dominic and Arnie do the same behind it.

At 9:32, Mason rushes out, angry and sputtering curses. He sits in his car for a moment, fuming. Finally, he pulls out his mobile and punches the telephone number I'd left him.

Answering my phone, I purr, "Bonjour."

"Having not heard from my boys or Baronov, I'd already assumed you somehow escaped," Mason barks.

"Alas, you won't be able to do likewise." My point is made when I double-park a third van beside Mason's car.

Mason starts the Maserati anyway. Because it can do sixty miles per hour in three and a half seconds, the sports car certainly does some damage to Dominic's van when it hits it, shoving it far enough back that the sports car can jump onto the curb to get around Abu.

"Hold on tight," I tell Jack, and we're off after him.

I DON'T MAKE IT A HABIT OF TALKING ON A PHONE WHILE driving, not even in hands-free mode or when crawling in the school carpool lane. So you can imagine how I feel about zigzagging up a strange country's lush hills on narrow one-car roads in a utility van. To squelch the urge to barf, I double down on my end of witty repartee with Mason. Right now, that includes parrying the numerous ways he'd like to watch me die with my fantasies of how I'll kill him.

Halfway up this hill from hell, Jack reminds me that our endgame is to imprison Mason for the rest of his hopefully very short and aggressively tortured life. "Isn't that a better payback, sweet pea?"

That Jack would even use such a cloyingly silly term of endearment shows me just how important it is to him to make his point. I thoroughly get it. Ryan's wrath is not worth the few choice words left to be uttered to the maniac who sold me at auction to a war criminal dictator.

And besides, we're at the end of the road, quite literally.

It drops off a sharp cliff overlooking the tranquil turquoise bay. Since Mason got here faster and first, he's already flipped his roadster around so that it faces down-hill again, and he's got a gun pointed at us.

Ha! As if that means anything to a woman who's been humiliated in front of her worst enemies. Had he dressed me in designer duds instead of whore couture, perhaps I'd have more respect for his quarter-of-a-million-dollar boy toy. Instead, before he can get off a shot, I ram the Maserati as hard as I can, shoving it to the edge of the cliff.

As the car teeters, Mason scrambles onto its roof, all the while screaming that I'm crazy.

The good news for me: he's dropped his gun because he needs two hands to steady the car so that it stays on the ledge. The bad news for him: now I've got my gun out too. "Next, you may be stupid enough to infer that my ass is flabby…Oh, wait, you already did that—*on a phone call with my enemies*!"

Jack groans. "Seriously? That's what's got you all riled up?"

"Not as much as the fact that he used our son… Okay, yeah, and me."

"Bitch!… At least grab my hand and pull me to safety!" Mason leans over the car's hood, arm held out straight.

Glowering, I consider my options. I can kick the car's beautifully designed grille and watch it, and him, plunge into oblivion. Or I can do as he asks.

Now that the rest of our team is covering him, they'll vouch to Ryan that I took the high road, that we got our man. He'll never see the light of day again anyway. Instead, he'll rot in some dark-sight hellhole.

So, I hold out my hand.

Mason grabs it—

And jerks me toward him. He now holds me captive, cradling me, forward, on the car's roof. "Stupid cunt! That bodacious booty of yours is all I need for ballast. Now, tell your goons to back off."

Instead, I snap my head back, slamming it into his nose.

Cursing, he lets go. As he reels backward—

I propel myself forward—

Into Jack's arms—

Just as the car topples over the cliff.

Mason's scream can be heard echoing down the hill.

At some point, the Maserati explodes.

I hope Mason went up in flames too.

The air is filled with the wail of sirens.

Arnie monitors the activities. An hour later, he reports, "They've found a dead body in a tree further up the hill but on the same trajectory as the car. It's male, about Mason's age, and he's pretty bashed up. I can see it on the chest-cam of one of the policemen."

Appearing on our lenses is Mason's bashed up face: eyes open in horror.

Abu whistles. "Checkmate is right."

28

Checkmate

CHECKMATE IS THE TERM FOR THE WINNING MOVE THAT MAKES *capturing the king inevitable.*

Should you play chess with someone you love, remember to be gracious—both as a winner and a loser. This is especially important if you are playing your spouse. Many a fight has started over a poorly timed declaration of triumph. I mean, ask yourself: is it worth initiating divorce over a callous bellow of "In your face, sucka…"?

If your marriage is too fragile to withstand a few board game losses, you may need to stop analyzing the pieces on the board and focus on the boredom in your marriage.

There's a reason the queen and king stand side-by-side at the start of the game.

And why she always has his back.

When it comes to a marriage, the only checkmate is when both mates stay that way throughout the game of their conjoined lives.

~

For once, I love the sound of silence in an empty home.

Even more, I love the sounds Jack makes as he strips down, then does the same to me:

The clack of his belt unbuckling;

The whoosh when he pulls it from his jeans' loops;

The metallic click as his zipper moves down;

The satisfied grunts as he kicks off his pants, one leg at a time—

But then he curses when a leg gets tangled in them.

Jack curses even louder when he can't get his tee shirt off his head quickly enough.

And when his fingers fumble as he unbuttons my blouse.

I love his smile when he sees that I'm wearing his favorite bra—

Albeit not for long. Having unsnapped it with one hand, Jack gives a smug hoot.

And he groans with anticipation as he unzips my pants—

But the curses start again when he can't untangle them from my ankles.

"I've still got on my heels," I remind him.

"Well—damn it, how do you get them off?"

I smack away his hand. "I could leave them on, you know."

He finds the suggestion tantalizing enough to nod, so my pants come off—

But the heels stay on.

He gets the honor of removing my panties. Whistling at the grand reveal, he murmurs, You're right. The heels make the moment. In fact, why don't we—"

"Quit chattering. Start mattering." I shove him onto the bed and climb on top.

Afterward, Jack whispers, "I missed you."

"I missed you too." I place my hand on his face. "From now on, no matter what Ryan says, we keep each other in the know." I hold up my hand. "Pinky swear."

"Pinky swear." He curls his little finger around mine.

"Hey, I have an even better idea! Why don't we seal it with a kiss?"

Jack accommodates with a gentle one that lingers, teases, and tantalizes. "For that matter, why stop there?"

He's got a point. It's not like the kids will walk in any minute, right?

I must give credit where it's due. At least, this time, the knock on our bathroom door happens as we get out of the shower.

Trisha exclaims, "You're in there—*together?* Yuck!"

"We're just *showering!*" I yell back.

"Yeah…*together!* I don't want that vision in my head."

"You're not supposed to be here anyway," Jack retorts.

Now robed, I peek through the door. "What he said. Weren't you going to hang in Florence an extra day or two?"

"I wish!" Trisha sighs rapturously. "Italian men are…*so dreamy.*"

Jack, also robed, opens the door even wider. "Don't you mean Italian boys?"

"Anything in that part of the world with an X and a Y chromosome is fine with me," she declares. "And the way they kiss…."

Jack closes the door to mutter, "Just great. She's *boy crazy*." Then he opens it again and declares, "That better be all they've done in your presence, or I'll—"

Trisha tweaks his nose. "Dad, you're so adorable when you pontificate!"

Jack is too stunned to reply.

"Speaking of homecomings, Eve wants to talk to Mom." Trisha nods toward the hall. "When you're through, um, 'showering,' you're welcome to go up to Lion's Lair. Aunt Phyllis is there, too. And Jeff."

"He's not here?"

"Heck no. In fact, I don't think you'll see much of him anymore since Janie kissed him." She smiles brightly. "I've always wanted to be an only child."

They grow up much too fast.

As I hike up the hill, I try to think what question Eve has for me.

My guess: she'll ask me about my true feelings for Lee.

I'll tell her the truth:

That I never saw him as more than a friend.

And, honestly, there was a time I didn't even consider him that, wondering if he was Quorum. Only when, as POTUS, it was proven he'd been ensnared by the terrorist group and did his best to circumvent their missions did I see and admire his true fortitude.

We have that shared history.

Our friendship grew out of it.

I hope she can accept it.

Eve meets me at the front door of Lion's Lair.

Instead of inviting me in, she suggests we walk on the golf course. "Lee's inside working, so it'll be quiet."

We make chit-chat until we reach the third hole. It's in a wooded knoll but has a fabulous view of Hilldale and the ocean beyond.

As we take in the scenery, she comes out with it: "When we were in Florence, Lee asked me to marry him."

"Yes, Aunt Phyllis mentioned it."

"I have something to ask you, and I hope it's not too much of an imposition."

I brace myself.

"Will you be my matron of honor?"

Flabbergasted, I gasp. "I'd be…honored! I'd be delighted!"

"I'm so happy!" A jubilant smile lights up Eve's face. "I wouldn't have anyone else. You're the one person, other than me, who has always seen Lee for the kind soul he is." As we hug, she adds, "Lee hasn't come out and said anything, but I assume Mason is dead."

"Yes. Eve. I'm sorry to tell you he wasn't the person you thought." I look away. "In fact, he was—"

"Using me. Not just to get to Lee, either. Lee was just the waypoint to get to you." Eve shrugs. "I think I figured that out even before having been told why. I really wanted to believe that I could have the sort of love you have with Jack. I never knew Lee saw in me what he saw in… well, what he saw in you. I should have realized that Mason's actions were too quick and not authentic."

"In what way?"

Eve points to the tree in front of us. "Remember when I told you about seeing Mason putting a fallen bird back in its tree? This is where it happened. He told me it was a Boreal chickadee that had fallen out of a nest. Ironically, yesterday, when I'd talked to one of the groundskeepers, I learned that this particular breed is found only in Canada. That's when I remembered I never saw the chick or the nest. I was just so anxious to believe Mason that I fell for his lie. He'd already recognized my yearning for love, and played into it."

"Why do you think he lied?"

"Your guess is as good as mine. There is one thing that stood out about that day: it was as if his charm was turned on with a switch. I refused to admit this to myself until after I knew the truth about him."

Curious now, I climb up.

A satellite phone, wrapped in a waterproof bag, is hidden in the arm of the tree's split trunk.

I check the last phone numbers called. One is a Russian area code. Seeing that another was made to Idaho, I remember Mason mentioned an arms deal with some domestic terrorists.

Further back in the month—on the same day Luda died and around the same time—there's a call from Los Angeles to Russia. Mason had received her call about securing the U.S. directory.

I call Jack and ask him to grab the car and pick me up so we can take Mason's phone to Acme headquarters.

"WE NOW HAVE VERIFICATION THAT MASON WAS RUNNING Luda," Ryan declares. "And we've forwarded the domestic terrorist's cell number to the FBI so that they can run a sting. As for the calls to Russia, the phone allows us to locate Mason's handler. If it's Putin, even better. Great find, Donna."

"Thank you, Chief." I pause. "With Mason dead, I hope Marcus has reconsidered any thought of offering President Kentfield his resignation."

Ryan shrugs. "Too late, he's done so."

I sigh. "That's a shame."

"I didn't say she accepted it. In fact, she reminded him how he's saved this country in too many ways to count."

"I'll second that," I declare. "Speaking of which, here's an idea that Marcus may get behind: Russia thinks the Black King is still in play. Besides giving back its spy directory, Mason also promised to hand over Ukraine's as well. Do you want to ask Kostyantyn if he'd like to dummy up one that works to his country's advantage?"

He laughs. "I'm sure he'll appreciate the opportunity. By the way, he passed along his thanks for saving his life and that of his country's other intelligence operatives. " Ryan waves me away. "Now, get going. The clock is ticking on your vacation."

"Our what?" *Oops! Maybe I should keep my mouth shut in case he's lost his mind…*

Ryan's eyes move from mine to Jack's. "I've granted Mr. Craig's request for a two-week leave for you both." Ryan looks at the clock on the wall. "Starting now, in fact."

I turn to Jack. "Really?"

"Sure. Mary and Evan got home from their getaway about an hour ago. Now it's our turn. I'm whisking you away, just the two of us, to a tropical island." I love seeing his ear-to-ear grin.

"Then I'll need to pack—"

"I've already done it for you." He holds up a hot pink velvet bag from Penelope's boutique, CUM & GET IT.

I flinch. "I'm afraid to ask what's inside."

"Trust me."

Because I do, I open it to find a sheer white silk peignoir with strategically placed lace insets. "I'll admit I am pleasantly surprised. Still, I don't think the airline allows this as travel attire."

Jack laughs. "Not to worry since we're going private: Air Chiffray. It's Lee's way of thanking us in advance for participating in his wedding party."

My eyes open wide. "Eve asked me to be her matron of honor. What role do you have?"

"Best man, of course."

"But of course. You've proven it yet again." I hold up the peignoir. "So, just the two of us? No mission, no other people, no interruptions?"

"Scout's honor." Jack crosses his heart.

"I'm holding you to that promise, Mr. Craig."

"Always and forever," he replies as he takes me in his arms.

THE END

Other Books by Josie Brown

The Extracurricular Series

Books 1, 2, and 3

The Totlandia Series

The Onesies - Book 1 (Fall)

The Onesies - Book 2 (Winter)

The Onesies - Book 3 (Spring)

The Onesies - Book 4 (Summer)

The Twosies - Book 5 (Fall)

The Twosies – Book 6 (Winter)

The Twosies - Book 7 (Spring)

The Twosies - Book 8 (Summer)

The True Hollywood Lies Series

Hollywood Hunk

Hollywood Whore

More Josie Brown Novels

The Candidate

Secret Lives of Husbands and Wives

The Baby Planner

How to Reach Josie

To write Josie, go to:
mailfromjosie@gmail.com

To find out more about Josie, or to get on her eLetter list
for book launch announcements, go to her website:
www.JosieBrown.com

You can also find her at:

www.AuthorProvocateur.com

twitter.com/JosieBrownCA

facebook.com/josiebrownauthor

pinterest.com/josiebrownca

instagram.com/josiebrownnovels